THE SPIDER'S TOUCH

The Spider's Touch

by

VALENTINE WILLIAMS

The spider's touch, how exquisitely fine,
Feels at each thread, and lives along the line.
POPE, *An Essay on Man*

Secret Service Series

WILDSIDE PRESS

www.wildsidepress.com

CONTENTS

THE SPIDER'S TOUCH

CHAPTER I

Soldier of Fortune

THE evening activity at Schulte's had not yet begun when Ned Hartigan, as though propelled by the force of the storm, burst in. There was snow on the front of his threadbare overcoat and snow on his sodden and shabby shoes, and the March wind, razor-edged and wild, battered at the door as he closed it. Behind him New York was a vista of whitened roofs and pavements, and the lights of Third Avenue seemed to weep through the dancing curtain of snowflakes whirled aloft by the gale.

The modest saloon was warm and bright after the weather outside. Wolf was the only customer. His peaked cap was pushed back on his grizzled head and he wore his overcoat and scarf as he stood at the bar, a gaunt figure, absorbed in his thoughts as usual, a schooner of beer before him. In his grave German way he nodded to the new arrival and said gravely, 'So, Ned? You want a beer?'

'Beer, nothing!' cried the other and hammered on the bar. 'Schulte, you misbegotten Aryan,' he roared at the fat and placid Teuton who sidled up, 'whisky, and step on it! The firm's in funds. And turn on the radio, damn it, and let's have some music!' He slapped Wolf on the back. 'The colonel and I are going to celebrate tonight.'

The rattle and stamp of a rumba filled the saloon with noise. Schulte brought a measure, a glass, the whisky bottle, and the water jug and slapped them down. 'So, Major!' he announced gutturally.

Wolf was burbling gently at Hartigan's announce‑
ment — he had a peculiarly silent laugh. 'Celebrate, is
it?' he rumbled. '*Ach, du lieber Gott*, what with?'

Hartigan looked mysterious. 'I had a break today.
The two o'clock at Hialeah...'

The other grunted. 'So? You play the ponies now?'

'Not as a rule. But wait till you hear the gee's name!
"Soldier of Fortune" — what I mean, a guy simply had
to have a bit on a horse with a name like that!'

His companion hoisted square shoulders in a con‑
temptuous shrug. 'Such a stupid expression I always
thought it! Soldier, yes; but fortune? No. Plenty of
kicks and no money — you and I found that out, old
friend!'

'There you go, grousing again!' Hartigan laughed.
'At twenty to one it was a gift. I had a buck on, but,
like a perfect gentleman, I split with the dame that gave
me the tip.' He winked and, pouring himself a tot of
neat whisky, tossed it off. Then he smacked a note down
on the bar. 'There you are, you old death's head, a
tenspot!'

Wolf grunted. 'I thought there'd be a skirt in it
somewhere,' he observed darkly.

Hartigan chuckled. 'It's one of the girls over at our
place. Her sister works for a bookie in the Bronx —
she's brought me tips before, though I've never followed
them. But "Soldier of Fortune," I ask you!' With a
wag of the head he took another drink. 'She's a nice
kid,' he said, refilling his glass. 'I'd quite a job to make
her take a share.'

He was thinking about Ruth as meditatively he con‑
sidered himself in the mirror behind the bar. When he
had thrust the ten dollars into her hand, there on the
dark stairway behind the timekeeper's box, with a little
cry she had flung her arms about his neck. When he'd

kissed her back, she had timidly put out her hand and stroked his obstreperous curls. It was funny, but women were always that way about him. He was broke, sure, and, with snow about, his shoulder was giving him hell. But what the heck! There'd always be a girl somewhere who'd want to run her fingers through his hair.

He surveyed it now in the glass, thick and crisp and black — not bad for an old buffer of forty-eight. He was the type of man, loosely built and deep-chested, who contrives to look untidy in whatever he wears. On top of this, his gray suit was on its last legs, his blue shirt clean but frayed at the collar, his tie hanging out, his hat old and greasy. But he wore it with an air. Something of this manner of his was reflected in the face that confronted him in the mirror — a bold face, the face of a fighter, with an impudent button nose and broadly humorous mouth.

The music on the radio had given way to the news hour. The commentator's voice boomed breezily through the room: 'But the League of Nations writ don't run beyond the Andes. On the Gran Chaco, folks, they're at it again. According to the latest reports, heavy fighting was resumed this morning. The Bolivian forces, said to number some fifty thousand ...'

The Gran Chaco! At the words Hartigan's eyes dropped away from the mirror. That strident voice, the dull rumble of traffic in the street, had suddenly become transmuted into the sounds of battle reverberating in and out of a rocky defile all speckled with shell-bursts. As he stood at the bar, his head bowed over his glass, he seemed to breathe once more the sparkling mountain air, the sun blisteringly hot on his face, the reek of the camp incinerators acrid in his nostrils. High above the gorge a lone buzzard wheeled ...

Wolf was trying to make himself heard above the din.

Hartigan lifted his head sharply. 'Stop that bloody row, can't you?' he bade the proprietor.

The radio fell silent. 'What's that you say?' Hartigan remarked to his friend.

'I said I thought, maybe, you'd found yourself a better job!'

The other shook his head. 'I'm still clocking 'em in and out at the old box factory. And lucky to be in work!'

Wolf looked for the cuspidor, found it, and deposited his tribute. 'Such a job!' he growled.

Hartigan laughed. 'The pay's not so hot. But it's more than I got with the Princess Pats, more even than Uncle Sam paid me, after America came in ...'

'Sure! Perhaps you'll tell me also it's more than we earned with the Spanish Legion. We'd have done better to join up with Abd el Krim and his Riffs, Ned — those sons of guns still owe me eighty-four pesetas back pay!'

His friend grinned. 'I didn't get any pay at all. But then, of course, I lit out. But what's the use of bellyaching? How's hacking, *Herr Oberst*?'

Wolf shrugged. 'Tough. A fellow scarcely gets a living any more. It's the heck of a town, Ned. When they're not standing you up, they're shaking you down. Pancho Villa should have driven a cab in New York. He'd have done well. He had the right mentality!'

The other guffawed and slapped him on the shoulder. 'What a laugh the old brigand would get to see you, a staff colonel, driving a New York taxi, and me, in command of the guns, working from seven to four as timekeeper in a box factory!'

His companion grunted. 'I take life as it comes. One of our German poets wrote, "*Du glaubst zu schieben und du wirst geschoben*," which means that Fate'll kick you around, no matter what you plan. But it's tough on you, Ned. You were a good soldier, *verdammt*, and I should know who say it. Five campaigns, only two less than mine, then a lousy Paraguayan bullet and *fertig! Sapristi*, it's hard!'

'Aw, nuts! It might have been the old bean instead of the shoulder, and that would have been harder still!' Hartigan emptied another dram, then put down his glass suddenly. 'Why, hullo, Ruthie!'

A girl in a shabby coat with a rubbed fur collar had come in out of the snow. She carried a newspaper in her hand. 'Ned,' she said very earnestly, 'I've got to talk to you privately.'

'Why, sure!' He turned to Wolf. 'Excuse me, Colonel — another rendezvous!' He winked and followed the girl to a table at the far end of the saloon.

'Eddy said you were coming here,' she explained nervously. 'I only saw it after you'd gone . . .'

'Saw what?'

'This.' She produced her newspaper, folded back to display the personal advertisement column. 'The *Times*?' remarked Hartigan in his casual way. 'The *Mirror's* more my mark, I'm afraid . . .'

She pointed with her finger and read:

TWO HUNDRED AND FIFTY DOLLARS REWARD

The above reward will be paid to anyone communicating the present whereabouts of Major Edward Hartigan, formerly of the Bolivian Army, at present believed to be living in New York. As the matter is pressing, kindly telephone immediately Hastings, care of Brace, Hastings & Close, 40A Wall Street, New York City. HANover 2–9999.

Hartigan wagged his black head. 'Well, well, well; here's a surprise! Looks like someone up and left me a fortune!'

'It's one of the biggest law firms in New York, the superintendent was telling me,' said the girl.

'You bet. Everybody knows William Cadwallader Hastings!' He caught her arm. 'Glory be to God, child, you didn't show that ugly Mick this newspaper? If you did, he'll surely have beaten you to the 'phone and claimed the reward!'

'I didn't tell anyone anything — I just asked who Hastings was. And I didn't come here after you on account of the reward — don't think that, Ned!'

He laughed and patted her shoulder. 'I know it, kiddo.' He pointed towards the telephone cabinet. 'You go straight to that 'phone and call this Hastings guy. You tell him to come here pronto and you'll produce the missing heir. But he'd better bring the cash with him, see? Go ahead! What are you waiting for?'

While she went slowly to the booth, he picked up the newspaper and took it to Wolf at the bar.

Wolf read the announcement and handed back the newspaper without comment.

D'you know what I think?' declared the other. 'It's that little widow at La Paz I told you about, who took such a shine to me. She's died and made me her heir, that's what!' He sighed. 'Gosh, she certainly did reek of garlic!'

Wolf drank composedly. 'It'd have to be a woman, sure,' he retorted, wiping his mouth. 'Maybe it's the German countess who used to send you candy when you were on the Rhine with the Army, or that fat Moroccan Jewess who hid you from the M.P.'s at Tetuan the night you deserted from the Legion!'

Hartigan sighed. 'Dear little Zorra! She wasn't fat and I didn't desert...'

His friend grunted. 'So? Then why did you beat it out of the Spanish zone, hidden under a rug in the English officer's car?'

'I meant, the fighting was over, and you'll admit the chow was terrible. Hullo, here's Ruthie coming back!'

'He'd left the office,' the girl reported. 'They told me to ring him uptown — he's calling on a client on Park Avenue. I spoke to him. He's coming right over.'

'Did you tell him to bring the cash?'

She nodded impressively. 'I guess I'll scram now, Ned.'

'Scram, my foot! You stick around, baby — you're going out of this joint with two hundred and fifty smackers. In the meantime, you and I are going to have a little snifter together.' He spoke a whispered word to Schulte, then, nursing the whisky bottle and two glasses, propelled the girl across the saloon to a table, screened by a pillar from the view of anyone entering by the swing doors.

The major was pressing his companion to her second drink when Schulte, rather flurried, stood before him. 'Dere's a gent asking for your friend, Major,' he was saying when, from behind the pillar, a large man appeared.

He was sleek and gray-haired and had a portfolio tucked under his arm. He gazed severely at Ruth and remarked: 'I'm Mr. Hastings. Someone rang me from this place. Are you Ruth Green?'

Hartigan and the girl had stood up. He nudged her with his elbow.

'That's me!' she faltered.

The gray-haired man was staring at the major. 'Are you Major Hartigan?'

'Did you bring the money?' was the blunt reply.

Hastings drew an envelope from his portfolio, showed a fold of bills.

'I'm Hartigan,' the major announced. He thrust a sheaf of somewhat grimy papers in the lawyer's hand. 'These will identify me.'

Holding them under the light, Hastings examined the papers, then silently returned them.

Hartigan jerked his thumb at Ruth. 'Give her the dough!' he ordered, and the attorney put the envelope in her hand.

She pulled out the bills, gazing at them blankly. 'But, Ned,' she said tremulously, 'I can't take all this money!'

The major laughed and, putting up finger and thumb, squeezed her chin. 'Beat it, honey! This gentleman and I want to talk business!'

He swung about, for a voice behind him — a woman's voice — said, 'Are you really Major Hartigan?'

A tall girl, very elegant in furs, stood there. The major's approving glance enveloped her.

'That's my name, my dear,' he rejoined briskly.

She gave a little sigh. 'Thank God, we've found you at last!' she cried.

CHAPTER II

The Major Goes to the Telephone

SHE was quite young — not more than twenty-three or twenty-four, Hartigan judged — and beautifully dressed. Her hat, tall of crown and rakish like a Napoleonic hussar's, was modish, and she was slim and well-groomed and generally alluring. A very faint breath of perfume clung to her furs, all glistening with a fine powdering of snow. The major paid little heed to her looks — his attention was rivetted on her mink coat. A year with the Hudson's Bay Company was included among the numerous occupations he had followed in the intervals of soldiering, and he knew something of fur values. Eyeing the skins, small and dark and glossy, 'Labrador,' he murmured. 'Twelve thousand dollars or I'm a Dutchman!' and let his glance stray to the pearls that clasped her throat — a short string, but every pearl large and rounded and as milkily white as the neck they encircled. He stared unashamedly.

Ruth had disappeared. By this time the saloon was filling, and from the bar a line of heads was craned in the direction of the girl in the mink coat. But she seemed disdainfully unaware of her surroundings, or of anyone, indeed, except the ugly, shabby man who stared so hard at her.

Sinking into a chair she gazed up at him and said, 'Where's Robin Dallas?'

'Now, Patricia,' the lawyer broke in testily, 'you promised if I'd let you come...'

'Be quiet, Willie!' she bade imperiously, and spoke to Hartigan again. 'This Englishman's a friend of yours, isn't he? Where's he to be reached?'

The brusqueness of her tone seemed to nettle the major. 'Supposing he is,' was the blunt retort, 'What do you want with him?'

'My brother,' she answered in the same hurried tone she had used before. 'He's vanished. In Germany. Your friend Dallas has got to find him.'

The major said nothing, but only stared.

'One moment, my dear ' Hastings broke in smoothly. 'This is Miss Patricia Fane,' he told Hartigan, 'and I'm her lawyer. I'm also one of the trustees under her late father's will. And now let's sit down, shall we?'

He pronounced the girl's name as though the other should know it, as, indeed, what newspaper reader did not? So this was the much-advertised Patricia Fane, Hartigan reflected in bewilderment. Headlines from the tabloid he was wont to read, swaying from a strap in the crowded subway on his way to work, swam into his mind: *'Fane Heiress Off to Europe': 'Nobleman to Wed Fane Millions, Rumor': 'Patricia Still Heartwhole, Tells Press'*; and the spasmodic record of her innumerable activities set forth in blurred half-tones — Patricia Fane in overalls landing her Lockheed at Roosevelt Field, Patricia Fane in ermine at the Noel Coward opening, walking on Park Avenue, lunching at the Colony. His perplexity deepened, and he continued to stare, but in a forbidding, mistrustful way.

They took chairs, and Hastings said: 'Major, may I speak in confidence? Major Okewood, of London, gave me your name. He said that, as far as he knew, you were the only person on this side of the Atlantic who was likely to be in touch with Robin Dallas...'

Hartigan spoke. 'Is this a secret service job?' he demanded curtly.

The attorney spread his hands. 'The matter's so delicate that, for the moment...' As the other shrugged and turned away, he added quickly: 'All I'm willing to say at present is that James Fane, who's temporarily attached to the American diplomatic service, disappeared a month ago while engaged on a highly confidential mission to Germany. Certain allegations have been made...'

'Oh, for goodness' sake, stop beating about the bush, Willie,' the girl struck in. 'They're trying to tell us that Jimmy's a traitor,' she said to Hartigan. 'As if my brother would betray his country! This man Dallas is a friend of yours, Major Okewood says; he told us that Dallas once rendered you a great service...'

The major nodded. 'That's right!'

'What sort of service?' demanded the lawyer suspiciously.

'It was in the Riff war,' said the major simply. 'I'd put in eight months with the Spanish Foreign Legion, and when the fighting was over, I was fed up. So I cleared out. I ran into this Englishman, who was touring Morocco in a car, and he smuggled me down to Casablanca and on board a boat for Bordeaux. If it hadn't been for him the military police would have got me and I'd certainly have been shot.'

'Major Okewood says that Dallas is the one man in the world who can find young Fane,' Hastings explained, 'and we want you to put us in touch with him...'

Hartigan shook his head. 'Take it from me, Robin Dallas will have nothing to do with it.' He paused. 'I suppose you know that Francis Okewood was a celebrated British secret service man in Germany during the war. Why don't you hire him?' His tone was gruff.

The girl answered: 'Didn't we both talk to him until we were tired? He was over from London on business and I met him at dinner — they were telling me about his marvellous exploits in the war. But he declares that nothing will induce him to go back to secret service work. He's married, he says he's too old — I don't know: anyway, he turned us down flat and he sailed home in the *Majestic* last night...'

'But he did say that Dallas...' the attorney began.

'Forget it!' the major interrupted him. 'Okewood was just passing the buck. He knows, as well as I do, that Robin Dallas won't touch it. And what's more, I'm not going to ask him!'

Miss Fane gazed at him frigidly. 'Why ever not?'

'There are reasons...' He broke off.

'You're every bit as aggravating as Major Okewood,' she declared pettishly. 'Every time I questioned him about this man's background, he shied off. He says he can vouch for him in every way, but we'll have to take him on trust!'

'He was kidding you. Wild horses won't drag Dallas back to Europe and Okewood knows it. And why Dallas, anyway? He's a magnificent linguist, of course, and speaks French and German like a native...'

The attorney struck in. 'He possesses another indispensable qualification...' He paused, fingering his lip and considering the major dubiously. 'You see, he knows the man we believe to be back of James Fane's mysterious disappearance. Or so Major Okewood asserts.'

Hartigan was suddenly on the alert.

'You've knocked around a bit in your time, I gather, Major,' Hastings proceeded. 'Tell me, did you ever hear of a former German secret service man called Grundt — Doctor Adolf Grundt?'

The major made no answer, but only gazed at the speaker with a blank, incredulous air.

'At one time this man is said to have been head of the Kaiser's personal secret service,' the lawyer continued. 'But since the war he's drifted into international espionage on a grand scale, Okewood says. He has a deformed foot and walks with a limp — "Clubfoot," Okewood calls him. It appears that Dallas knows Grundt well and has had dealings with him in recent years.'

'That's right,' Hartigan agreed.

'Okewood believes that young Fane was deliberately trapped by this man. The point is that Grundt is a highly elusive personage. Since Nazi Germany is barred to him, as Okewood tells us, although apparently it did not prevent him from putting in an appearance at Hamburg, no one knows where he makes his headquarters and, as he operates mainly through secondary agents, very few people have ever seen him. Moreover, he never forgets a face. This was one of the grounds on which, apart from everything else, Okewood declined the job...'

The major nodded. 'They met in the war, didn't they?'

'It is also one of the reasons why Okewood recommended your friend Dallas,' Hastings pursued. 'It appears that Dallas has seen Grundt, but that Grundt has never seen him, or so Major Okewood assures me...'

Hartigan nodded again. 'And what's the other reason?' he asked bluntly.

'Okewood declares that, once Dallas knows that Grundt is at the back of this business, he'll jump at the chance!'

'Okewood didn't say why?'

'He refused to commit himself further.'

The major was silent for a spell. 'I don't want to scare you,' he remarked at last, his eyes on the girl. 'But I know something of this clubfooted man — suppose James Fane's dead?'

Hastings shook his head. 'On the contrary, we have evidence that he's very much alive — hence these very disturbing allegations...'

'What's the job worth if Dallas takes it on?'

'I'm willing to pay a hundred thousand dollars to have my brother's name cleared,' said Miss Fane in a brisk, businesslike voice, 'and all expenses, in addition.'

The major gasped. 'But — it's a fortune!'

The lawyer cleared his throat. 'Miss Fane fixed the price herself. James Fane is the only relative she has in the world. He's also her twin.' He doffed his rimless glasses and, breathing on them carefully, began to polish them. 'You'll understand, Major, that if your friend undertakes the mission we shall have to know a little more about him. For example, from something Major Okewood let drop, I infer that Dallas isn't his real name...'

'If he accepts the job, you've got to take him on trust, as Okewood warned you,' was the uncompromising reply. 'You'll not find a better man, but he'll answer no questions about his past...'

'You know his story?'

The major nodded.

'His real name, too?' asked the girl.

Hartigan nodded once more. 'You can take it from me,' he said, 'he has the strongest possible motive for giving you a square deal.'

Hastings laughed — he seemed a trifle nettled. 'Obviously. Because he'll be paid by results, and results only — I'll see to that!'

Hartigan shook his head gravely. 'He has a motive stronger than money, Mr. Hastings...'

'Stronger than money? What do you mean?' Miss Fane demanded.

'I mean that his honour's in this man's hands, and he'll pursue him to the ends of the earth to recover it!'

'Then find him!' she ordered quickly. 'When can you have him at my apartment?'

'The last I heard of him he was in Canada, selling goods on commission,' the major told her. 'But that was six months ago. I'll have to put in some long-distance calls — I may have to ring London . . .'

'Go ahead! I'm paying the charges!'

With his rather swaggering gait the major went to the telephone.

CHAPTER III

Dallas

THE boudoir had an intimate air in the lamplight — a blazing log fire, plain pine panelling, a baby grand, the latest books, a backgammon board as the players had left it, with the men strewn about, pink roses in shining crystal. As soon as Mr. Hastings arrived, he was to announce them, the elderly butler informed the two visitors, drawing jade-green curtains upon snowy glimpses of the terrace through the windows and the lights of New York forty floors below. He retired on noiseless feet, leaving Major Hartigan and the young man with him to listen to the wind whistling around the penthouse.

With a grunt of content Ned Hartigan threw himself into a chair. His companion remained standing, gazing about him with a dour expression.

'I thought I'd put all this behind me,' he murmured. 'I wish to God I'd never listened to you, Ned. Why couldn't you have let me be?'

The major laughed. 'I give you the chance, apart from everything else, to split four ways in a hundred grand proposition, and you've done nothing but grouse ever since you landed in New York. Robin, you give me a pain in the neck!'

He frowned. 'I'm not ungrateful, really. You and Francis Okewood are the best pals a man ever had...'

Hartigan sighed. 'Okewood spoke up for you at the trial, at least. I did nothing. If I could have quit my gallant Bolivians...'

'You sent that long cable to the president of the court-martial which I know damn well you couldn't afford — I don't forget that, Ned. But when I went to Canada I made a clean cut with the past and ...'

Hartigan grinned indulgently. 'Is the life of a drummer in the wilds of Ontario really such a cinch? What's the name again of this forgotten dorp where I ran you to earth at last?'

The other's smile was evanescent. 'It was pretty ghastly to start off with. But after six months of it I was getting hardened. At least, I led my own life out of business hours — for instance, when you rang through to me at Hartsburg, two nights ago, I was lying on my bed at the hotel reading Hamley's *Military Operations*.'

The major's ugly face softened. 'Still hankering after the Army, then?'

'It's the only trade I know ...'

'Handle this job right and maybe you'll be able to go back to it!'

'Pipe dreams!' was the bitter answer. 'So many times they've come to me as I've lain in bed in these ghastly little hotels — the outfit on parade and the adjutant reading out the order restoring my commission. But I don't kid myself, old man. When a fellow's out in England, he's out: if His Majesty the King has no further use for your services and says so in print, you're through for good!'

'Bunk! There was that battalion commander at Mons you told me about ...'

'He didn't go to jail, Ned: he wasn't branded as a traitor to his country. Hell, don't let's talk about it!'

'At least, you'll be sensible and let me tell the little Fane your story?'

He shook himself unwillingly. 'No! And that's final. I'll have no rich American patronizing me! "*So this is Robin Dallas, who was discharged from an English prison last summer and is trying to turn over a new leaf. A de-*

serving case, you say? Parker, my lorgnette!" No, by God!'

His friend sighed. 'Still as proud as Lucifer, aren't you?'

'What about you? You could have let a fellow know you were down to ——'

The other coloured. 'I don't care to sponge on my pals!'

'But, Ned, this job of yours — it's an outrage!'

The major laughed. 'It's over now, thanks to you. I walked out on them this morning, and did I give that pork-fed, yaller-bellied, big-mouthed slob of a sup a piece of my mind, or did I?' He chuckled. 'Listen, son! As soon as I've turned you over to la Fane, I'll slide and meet you at Schulte's — you have the address. And by the by, Cant will be there!'

'No! He's still in New York, then?'

'Yep — a nice hunt I had for him. His job went flat on him soon after you were through here last fall and I haven't set eyes on him for months...'

'Do you think he'll go with us?'

'You bet your sweet life he will. He's been waiting in a French restaurant in Greenwich Village, poor devil!'

'Dear old Cant! I remember him so well when we were on harka together in the Atlas against the Ait-el-Tanouin. It was the first time I was ever under fire; but he was as cool as be damned. How about Wolf?'

'He'll be at Schulte's, too. He's crazy at the idea that he might be going back to the Fatherland after all these years...'

'He never actually set eyes on Grundt, even all that time ago, did he?'

'No — you have the edge of us there, old man...'

He jumped up. The door had opened. Patricia Fane appeared with Hastings.

The major said, 'This is Robin Dallas, Miss Fane!'

CHAPTER IV

The Connecting Link

Her flowing black velvet, with its train and drooping sleeves, its sombreness lightened only by the diamond buckle at her belt, stressed her grace of line as she extended her hand. 'I'm so glad you were able to come,' she said, faintly condescending, as her glance took in with interest the man before her.

Her first impression was rather favourable. Above medium height, broad of chest, and narrow-hipped, he had the build of a runner, the fine-drawn air of a whippet. It was a lean face, clean-shaven and blue-shadowed about lips and cheeks, with a very straight nose and determined mouth and chin — the sort of face that would look well under a Roman helmet, she decided. His guarded manner, which might be merely shyness, gave off a sense of strength that appealed to her, and she liked his hands, well-kept, with long, strong fingers. By contrast with the major in his wrinkled suit, the stubble glistening where his chin caught the light, he was quite well-groomed, his dark hair close-cropped and smoothly brushed, his tweeds hard-worn but still presentable.

The major was going. 'See you at Schulte's!' he whispered to his friend as he strutted out.

Hastings was wasting no time. 'Mr. Dallas,' he said in his direct fashion, 'I understand from Major Hartigan that you're willing to accept this mission and that the terms are satisfactory . . .'

Holding himself very erect, the Englishman bowed.

'And you know this man Grundt?'

He nodded, his face inscrutable. 'That's right!'

The attorney cleared his throat. 'You wouldn't care to

tell Miss Fane — in strict confidence, of course — the
circumstances of your acquaintanceship with this individual?'

He frowned. 'I understood from Ned Hartigan that
Major Okewood's guaranty...'

'Oh, quite!' The lawyer was a little flustered. 'I
merely thought — however, just as you like. Let's get
down to business, shall we? for I positively must be back
at my office by six for a consultation...'

Patricia Fane had perched herself on the leather fire-
rail under the large portrait of a grave little girl, hugging
a cocker spaniel, that hung above the mantelpiece.
Dallas sat down on the chesterfield facing her and Hastings took a chair.

'To start with,' the lawyer began importantly, crossing
one leg over the other, 'let me impress upon you the fact
that the whole affair is highly confidential. For obvious
reasons, neither we nor the State Department are anxious
for any publicity: one breath of this in the newspapers...'

'I understand,' said the Englishman.

'Before we go any farther and between ourselves —
James Fane has always given a lot of trouble. For
instance, I managed to land him with this job as honorary
attaché at our London Embassy, simply to extricate him
from the clutches of a young woman who was threatening
to sue him for breach.'

'My brother's wild and headstrong and crazy — anything you like,' the girl struck in with feeling. 'But he'd
never have done what they accuse him of — no, not in a
million years!'

'Four weeks ago — on the eighteenth of February, to
be precise,' the attorney inexorably proceeded, 'young
Fane left London on a confidential mission. His instructions were simple enough. He was to go to Hamburg, and
at the Hotel Astoria there await the arrival of a certain

person who would hand him a packet which he was to
bring straight back to London . . .'

'They chose Jimmy,' the girl interposed, 'because he'd
only been two months at the Embassy and I suppose
they thought he was less likely to be spotted than one of
the regular secretaries. Besides, no one would ever dream
of taking Jimmy for a diplomat: I mean, he's young and
kind of cheerful-looking . . .'

'What was this packet?' Dallas demanded.

Hastings's air was mysterious. 'Plans. Of considerable interest to our Navy Department. I understand
they refer to the fortifications of a group of Pacific
islands' — he cleared his throat — 'er, not in American
hands. Well, young Fane never came back from Hamburg . . .'

'And the man he went to meet?'

'Likewise vanished!'

'An American?'

'A Japanese. At least, his name's Akawa . . .'

Dallas looked dubious. 'A Chinese or a Filipino posing
as a Jap, more like. I don't see a Jap taking on a job like
that . . .'

'With considerable difficulty,' the lawyer continued,
'our consul at Hamburg, instructed by the State Department to make a discreet investigation, has established
young Jimmy's movements from the moment of his arrival at Hamburg. Fortunately, the consul went to the
Hotel Astoria first, for after he'd appealed to the police,
the hotel people refused all further information . . .'

'Awkward, but not unexpected,' the Englishman commented dryly.

'Fane didn't move out all day and made but one
telephone call — to the port office, to enquire for news of
the *Selma Blomquist*, the cargo boat by which Akawa was
travelling. He was told she had been delayed and

wouldn't dock until after dark. Around six o'clock someone telephoned him from outside, and soon after eight a
woman arrived and asked for him. They dined alone together in the grill.'

'Do they know who she was?'

'We've reason to believe it was a woman Fane had
been associating with in London; but I'm coming to that.
The *maître d'hôtel* had never seen her before — he
describes her as an attractive blonde.'

'Ah!' said Dallas.

'She was wearing day clothes. She left around ten and
Fane went to his suite. About an hour later he received a
telephone call and, after paying his bill, immediately
checked out. He was never seen again.'

'Who telephoned him? The woman, was it?'

'The hotel professes to have no information. I think it
was Akawa, or someone speaking for him. The *Selma
Blomquist* docked soon after ten, and half an hour later
Akawa went ashore — the consul got that from the passport people. A note was waiting for him on the dock...'

'From Fane?'

'I suspect so, changing the rendezvous. At any rate,
there's no record of any Japanese having called on Fane
at the Astoria that night...'

'And Akawa telephoned on landing to acknowledge the
change of plan, is that it?'

'So I should surmise.'

'What about Fane's luggage?'

'He had only a travelling-bag and he took it away with
him — the point has its importance, as you'll see. The
outside porter at the Astoria goes off duty at eleven, and
we haven't been able to discover, even, whether the boy
took a taxi...'

'The police could find out quick enough...'

'The police will do nothing: as soon as the consul

started asking questions, they shut up. Fane was due
back on the night of March 2. He'd left his manservant
in London, and owing to the fellow being in a motor
smash, it wasn't ascertained until nearly a week later
that, on the afternoon of March 2, in response to a wire
from Fane at Hamburg, he despatched two suitcases of
clothing to him, care of Thomas Cook, Paris . . .'

Dallas nodded. 'You said he had only a travelling-
bag with him, didn't you?'

'On March 3,' the attorney went on, 'acting on a letter
from Fane mailed in Paris, Cook's forwarded the suitcases to the baggage room at the Gare de l'Est, sub-
sequently handing the vouchers over to a lady who,
Fane said in his letter, would be calling for them. That's
the last trace we have; but it shows at least that the boy
was alive and in Paris three days after he disappeared . . .'

Dallas remaining silent, Hastings proceeded: 'Meanwhile, the Embassy was investigating the young man's
life in London. Some highly disturbing facts were disclosed . . .'

The girl struck in hotly: 'Jimmy never had any money
sense — you know that, Willie. My brother's a gambler,
Mr. Dallas — even at Harvard he was playing for high
stakes. That's why Father altered his will, leaving the
bulk of his money to me and putting Jimmy on an allowance until he should marry . . .'

'At my suggestion,' the attorney explained icily.

'He's always exceeded his allowance — I've paid his
debts over and over. But just because he's in a jam
again, to say he sold those plans . . .' She was tremulous
with indignation.

'*Sold* them?' The Englishman's tone was politely incredulous.

'That's what the State Department told Willie . . .'

Hastings wore a haggard air. 'Those plans were offered

to one of our agents over there, more than a fortnight
ago — for seventy-five thousand dollars...'

'Ah!' said the other enigmatically.

'They're very reluctant to speak of it at Washington,'
the lawyer went on, 'but I understand they've been
stalling on the deal until they get some light on young
Fane's part in the business. The intermediary was a
Belgian called Bartels, Guido Bartels...'

Dallas nodded darkly. 'I know the rat. One of Clubfoot's men. He was out here in the war, working for the
German espionage service.'

'Meanwhile, they've suspended Jimmy,' Miss Fane
broke in, 'and the Secret Service are trailing him. Before we know it, he'll be arrested as a spy against his own
country!' With a shaky hand she crushed her cigarette
out on the tray beside her.

'It looks bad for the boy,' said Hastings. 'Examination of his affairs in London showed that he was badly in
debt — although that's nothing out of the ordinary.' He
paused. 'Have you ever heard of a woman calling herself Arlette Lassagne?'

For a second the Englishman hesitated. 'No. At
least, not under that name. Who is she?'

'French, I think — that's to say, she comes from
Paris. She had been living in London for about a month
with a furnished flat off Park Lane — Fane used to visit
her there. They've ascertained that she left for Hamburg
the day after he did, taking the morning plane...'

'The lady who dined with him that night, eh?'

'So it would seem.'

'And where does Grundt come into this?'

'He fetched her after dinner that night with a car. He
did not enter the hotel but remained outside. The door-
man describes him as "a great ape of a man" with a clubfoot. Major Okewood recognized him immediately from
the description '

Dallas nodded briefly. 'It's he!' was all he said.

The March gale raved and tore at the windows. The Englishman sat like a statue, nursing his knee and staring at the fire.

Patricia Fane spoke suddenly: 'I don't care if Jimmy was running around with this creature. He never sold those plans — I'd sooner think him dead!'

With panther swiftness Dallas swung to Hastings. 'He might be — haven't you thought of that?'

The attorney was taken aback. 'The consul enquired at the morgue — there was no trace of him — of Akawa, either...'

'If Jimmy were dead, I'd know it,' the girl declared with spirit. 'It's because we're twins, I suppose, but all our lives, although we've often been separated, we've remained close to one another in mind. Whenever Jimmy's in trouble — bad trouble, I mean — I've a curious feeling of unrest. For the past month I've had it: in fact, it was so strong that I cabled him, and when he didn't answer I got his London apartment on the telephone and then the Embassy — that's how we first knew he was missing. I'm terribly worried about him, of course, but if he were dead...' She broke off.

The lawyer was consulting his watch. 'I'll have to run.' He handed the visitor an envelope. 'There's a thousand dollars in cash on account of expenses: we can complete our financial arrangements tomorrow — I want you to come downtown to my office and sign a short form of agreement I shall draw up. At the same time you can study the material I've gathered on the case, though I've given you the gist of it. Your passport's in order, is it?'

'Yes.'

'When can you leave for Germany?'

'The *Bremen* sails tomorrow night...'

Hastings beamed approval. 'Excellent. And you're at

the Roosevelt until then? Now is there anything else?'

Dallas made a pause. 'Mr. Hastings,' he said at last, 'there are three men in New York who have scores to settle with Grundt. I propose to take them with me.'

The lawyer was on his guard at once. 'This is a highly confidential matter, my dear sir,' he said, frowning. He began to speak of his 'quite exceptional sources of information at Washington' and 'a regular conspiracy of silence at the State Department.' 'You realize,' he added darkly, 'that if young Fane's alive, as I am very sure he is, you'll be pitting yourself against the best brains in our secret service? Have you thought of that?'

'Absolutely. It's a race between us and them. But, as I see it, the main trail we have to follow is Grundt's. I know Grundt — he's elusive and resourceful and the chase may easily take us through half a dozen countries. Since speed is the essence of success, four will be better than one...'

'Who are these men?'

'Major Hartigan; Captain Roger de Cantigny, late of the French Army; a certain Colonel Wolfgang von König. I can vouch personally for all three.'

'And they're all here in New York, you say?'

'Yes. They can leave with me tomorrow night.'

Patricia Fane spoke up. 'And they all have scores to settle with this man Grundt?'

'Yes, Miss Fane. In 1917, Hartigan's closest friend, George Ross, at that time in the American Intelligence Service in Holland, was trapped and secretly murdered at Grundt's instigation, and de Cantigny lost his only brother Alain, a staff officer with the French on the Rhine, who was ambushed and stabbed to death in 1922 by this ruffian's orders. As for Colonel von König, who's an ex-Prussian officer, he has an old quarrel with Grundt going back to pre-war days.'

'What you'd call the long arm of coincidence, isn't it?' remarked Hastings dryly. 'Three fellows, all with a grievance against this man, being on hand just when they're wanted!'

'Say, rather, the long arm of destiny!'

'I don't follow ...'

'It was written in the stars that we four should undertake this mission together. This grievance, as you call it, has been the tie uniting these three for years. And now it's brought me back into their circle ...'

'I wish you'd be more explicit!'

'It's like a chain, built up link by link. Ross died in '17. Two years later, in a Coblenz café, Hartigan, at that time a doughboy on the Rhine, hears two French officers speaking of Grundt. One is Roger de Cantigny. Hartigan gets into conversation with him and learns of Alain de Cantigny's death. That conversation sealed their friendship. Link number one!'

'And where does the other fellow come in?'

'Wolf and Ned Hartigan were comrades in Mexico in '13. Years later they met again in the Spanish Legion in Morocco. Hartigan happened to tell von König the stories of Ross and de Cantigny's brother and discovered that von König, too, had a score to settle with Grundt. They've been close friends ever since. Link number two!'

'Hartigan's a New-Yorker, he told me. But how are the other two here?'

'Von König has made New York his headquarters between wars for years. De Cantigny, who speaks English well, came out to take a job in Wall Street when he retired from the Army and has been here ever since.'

'And link number three?' the girl enquired.

Dallas shrugged. 'I'd met Hartigan in Morocco ...'

She smiled. 'He told us.'

'De Cantigny, also.'

'Did you smuggle Captain de Cantigny down to Casablanca as well?'

He laughed. 'No. I was attached to the French Army for a while during the Riff campaign. He was on the staff.'

'And he told you about his brother, I suppose?' Hastings suggested.

The Englishman shook his head. 'I'd never heard of Clubfoot then — that was to come later...' He made a longish pause, and when he spoke the phrases seemed to emerge piecemeal. 'Three years ago I had an experience with Grundt. It was pretty disastrous for me. I don't want to say more except that Francis Okewood and Ned Hartigan were the only fellows that stood by me. When I arrived in New York last year, it was only natural I should look Hartigan up.' His embarrassment seemed to increase. 'The story I had to tell — well, it sort of automatically brought the four of us together...'

'You mean because you, too, had a grudge against Grundt?' the girl prompted.

'Because I, too, have a grudge,' he replied gravely, and added, 'You see, it was fated.'

The attorney glanced towards Miss Fane. 'As far as I'm concerned...'

'What does it matter who goes with him, Willie?' she broke in impatiently. 'The important thing is to have Jimmy found.'

'The terms remain the same, that's understood?' Hastings cannily reminded the Englishman.

'Of course!'

On that the interview ended. But when Dallas would have followed the lawyer out, the girl stopped him.

'Don't go!' she said. 'I want to talk to you!'

She took Hastings into the hall.

CHAPTER V

The Barrier

THE visitor was gazing at the portrait over the fireplace when she came back.

'Harrington Mann,' she proffered, standing beside him. 'I was only eight when he painted it. It's rather cute, don't you think? Though my friends find it hard to believe I ever looked quite as angelic as all that!'

'It's charming,' he said in his grave way, 'and very like you still!'

She laughed. 'Willie wouldn't agree with you, I'm afraid. He's always telling me I look discontented.'

'I should have said you were the last person in the world to be that.'

'Because I have a lot of money?' she said, polishing her nails on her palm with a listless air. 'I daresay it's my own fault, but life bores me. It gives me nothing.'

'Isn't it supposed to give you back what you put in it?'

'It doesn't to me. I'm always looking for adventure. I pilot my own plane, I ride to hounds, I travel all the time, and yet I seem to get no kick out of anything. How do you account for it?'

His eyes rested thoughtfully on hers. 'Might I ask how old you are?'

'Twenty-five...'

'Perhaps it's because you don't find what you're looking for!'

She was puzzled. 'How do you mean?'

He jerked his head towards the portrait. 'You and that little girl have the same expression — the artist was clever enough to catch it. As though you were looking for something...'

'Looking for what?'

'I don't know. Something under the surface. Wondering what life's all about...'

With a reflective air she helped herself to a cigarette. 'It's true,' she admitted slowly, 'though nobody else ever guessed it before.' She stooped to the lighter he held to her cigarette and sat down on the fire-rail. 'Tell me some more about me!' she bade him.

He had a curious, oblique way of regarding a person, she noticed — he would look her straight in the face, but almost at once his glance would drop away. The eyes were the bluest she had ever seen, frank and fearless when they gazed at one, but hard to hold.

'Go on!' she encouraged him. 'I never hear the truth from anyone except Willie, and he regards me as a sort of scarlet woman. I'm sure you're more broadminded.'

He shrugged and looked about him, as though he were mindful of escape.

'Tupper's bringing us a cocktail,' she said. 'Come on, speak up! I should adore to know a stranger's opinion of me.'

He smiled — his smile was wistful and fugitive. 'I've no business to form any opinion about my employer!'

'Don't be tiresome! You know you've been summing me up ever since you set eyes on me. I've no doubt you think me a vain, spoiled, conceited sort of person!'

He shook his head. 'On the contrary, I'm struck by your extraordinary humbleness of mind...'

She gave a little squeak of laughter. 'Oh, my goodness! I must tell Willie that. He says I'm the most bumptious person he knows.'

'If you appear to be, it's because of this inferiority complex of yours. Underneath, you're still as shy as that little girl in the picture. And frightfully jealous of other people's happiness. I shouldn't be surprised if you envy your maid every time her young man takes her dancing.'

She giggled. 'She's British and over fifty, with the moral outlook of Queen Victoria.' She grew serious. 'But you're right. So you think I'm unhappy, do you?'

He gave her his fleeting glance. 'Not very happy. But it's your fault, I'd say. You always want your own way, and often it's the wrong way!'

Her eyes danced. 'I know,' she confessed penitently. 'But it's fun. In my blackest moods of depression I often console myself by thinking that I'm free, free as the wind, and that there's no one in the whole wide world, not even Willie, who can make me do what I don't like!'

He pursed his lips, and she was aware of bitter lines about his mouth. 'You're right to prize your freedom,' he said with his dourest air. 'It's the greatest thing in the world!'

The white-haired butler appeared with a tray of cocktails and appetizers. The visitor let the man give him a dry Martini.

When the butler had withdrawn, the girl, nibbling at a caviar square, said casually: 'You know, you interest me. I wish you'd tell me about yourself. Were you a soldier of fortune like the others?'

He had resumed his seat on the couch, facing her. 'No,' he answered curtly, staring down at his glass.

'You're the same type as Major Okewood, only much younger,' she persisted. 'You've been a British officer, haven't you?'

He sipped his drink and placed the glass on the table beside him. 'Does it matter?'

She bristled a little. 'Doesn't it? I'm going to employ you — surely I'm entitled to know something about you.'

He shook his head. 'I've no references. As Major Hartigan told you...'

There was a touch of hauteur in his voice and she shifted her ground. 'You can trust me, you know,' she said cajolingly. 'I'm not being merely inquisitive. You said you'd had a disastrous experience with this man Grundt — I'm naturally interested, on account of Jimmy. I don't let on to Willie because I'm sure that, in his heart of hearts, he believes Jimmy guilty, but I'm desperately worried about this sweet, crackpot brother of mine, Mr. Dallas. Jimmy's such a lamb, but he's always doing the craziest things and I'm so afraid for him. You know, I like you — you know what you want, don't you? And I adore people who know what they want. Can't we get together on this?'

Her eyes, starry and trustful, like the eyes of the child in the portrait above her head, were fastened eagerly on his. He turned his head aside.

'What I was, or am, has really no bearing on the case,' he replied. With an air of finality he picked up his glass and drained it.

'You mean, you're still resolved to answer no questions about yourself?'

He shrugged. 'I'm sorry...'

She was clearly chagrined. To hide the pique in her face she swung half round to retrieve her cocktail from the mantelpiece at her back.

'Of course, if you feel that way about it —' she observed distantly. 'I merely thought, as I shall probably be seeing a good deal of you...'

He stared, 'You weren't thinking of going to Germany with us, by any chance?'

'Why not?'

He shook his head. 'Oh, no, Miss Fane!'

'I can settle down quietly at some Hamburg hotel while you're investigating!'

'Out of the question, I tell you! You keep out of this!'
His brusqueness brought a spot of colour to her cheeks.
'I'm paying for this expedition, I believe?'

He nodded. 'Absolutely — it's the second time you've
reminded me. But I'm in charge, and I shouldn't dream
of letting you run into danger.' His voice was friendly
but firm.

'Danger? What danger?' she cried contemptuously.
'Jimmy's probably careering about the South of France
with this female — the worst you're likely to discover is
that she's blackmailing him!'

'I know what I'm talking about,' he answered quietly,
'and you're not coming!'

Her charming face set obstinately. 'I was going to
Europe this month, anyway. Can't you understand that
I'm worried to death about Jimmy? I must be over there
with you when he's found!'

Her eyes glistened, her tone was plaintive. The
Englishman took alarm. 'You're entitled to know how
we're progressing, I suppose,' he conceded grudgingly.
'You'll be going to Paris, I imagine — where do you
stop?'

'At the Ritz.'

He reflected. 'This is the twenty-ninth of March. I'll
report to you at the Ritz in Paris this day month, that's
the twenty-ninth of April. How's that?'

Her shrug was sulky, but, as if the matter were disposed
of, he went on: 'Tell me about this brother of yours —
how shall I recognize him?'

By way of reply she fetched a photograph framed in
silver from the desk.

'He's the dead image of you,' said Dallas, 'but then, of
course, you're twins.' He raised his eyes to her as she
stood over him. 'What's he like, otherwise?' he questioned.

'He's long-legged and scrawny, like me, rather fair-complexioned, and he has a lot of funny freckles across his nose. One way you'll know him is by his hair — it's exactly the same carrotty shade as mine.'

Back to the fire she faced him provocatively. My nose is too short, she was thinking, my chin too round, but my hair's lovely — men always admire my hair. She glanced into the mirror behind her — how well the fire-light brought out the red-brown tones! He looked her over coolly — 'as though I were a filly,' she was to tell Hastings next day.

'Sort of red,' was his casual comment. 'It's an unusual shade.' His eyes returned to the photograph. 'How tall?'

'Just under six feet!' Her manner was rather short.

Dallas disregarded it. 'Any distinguishing marks?' he enquired imperturbably.

'He has a butterfly tattooed on his right forearm. And that reminds me — he's left-handed.'

'Has he ever spoken to you about this woman, Arlette Lassagne?'

She shook her head. 'No. But I bet she's stunning — Jimmy's taste in blondes is excellent.'

He held up the photograph. 'Could I show this to the others?'

'Of course. I've plenty more.' She slipped it from its frame and gave it to him.

He had stood up. 'Do we meet tomorrow?'

'I'll be at Willie's.' She pressed a button in the wall beside the fireplace.

Carrying the photograph, he turned to go, then hesitated. 'Don't think me a boor for not answering your questions!' he said, and paused. 'It's not worth while looking beneath the surface as far as I'm concerned, Miss Fane — there's nothing there.'

Her polite smile froze him. 'That's quite all right — I shan't give it another thought!'

Then the butler appeared, and he was shown out.

When the visitor had gone, the girl called the butler back into the room. 'Tupper, isn't there a place called Pinkerton's that finds out about people?'

'I believe so, Miss Fane!'

'Get them on the telephone and put them through in here, please!'

With a pensive air, she took a cigarette.

CHAPTER VI
Council of War

In HIS suite on board the *Bremen*, Robin Dallas faced his friend Captain de Cantigny across the table. They had sailed on the stroke of midnight and it was getting on for two o'clock; the glare of New York had faded from the sky and the ship was beginning to lift to the roll of the open Atlantic.

'*Voilà!*' said the Frenchman apologetically. 'It's not much of a plan, my old Robin, but it's the best I can produce at short notice!'

Except for a tendency to roll his *r*'s, his English was almost accentless. He was a slightly built man who seemed to be in his early forties, with face and hands so finely moulded that he suggested a porcelain figure. An olive skin, dark eyes, and a fine, black moustache lent him a somewhat romantic appearance. His bearing was lackadaisical, his manner faintly derisive.

'It's good,' Dallas pronounced, cramming his pipe. 'We'll see what the others think of it. I wonder what's keeping them.'

'They were going to stop for a drink at the bar on the way down,' said the other. 'You know what Ned is when he has any money in his pocket?' He shrugged expressively.

Dallas sighed. 'I hope he's going to lay off the whisky on this trip. I had a word with him and he promised he would. All the same, I'm a bit worried ...'

The cabin door opened: Hartigan and Wolf came in, the former brandishing a large cigar, Wolf smoking his pipe. At the sight of Dallas the major held up his hand.

'No reproaches, old man! Two little snorts, no more, no less, as Wolf will tell you. I know what you're think-

ing, you old son of a gun, but no one's going to see Ned
Hartigan pie-eyed, pickled, or plastered, so help me, till
Jimmy Fane's restored to the arms of his lovely sister and
old Grundt has toed the line, clubfoot and all. As witness
my hand and seal. Signed Edward Hartigan!' And he
dropped into a chair.

Dallas laughed. 'All right, Ned. Find yourself a pew,
Wolf, and let's get down to business. Here's the plan,' he
went on, when they were all seated. 'We have three lines
of enquiry: one, the hotel at Hamburg; two, Grundt; and
three, the woman, whose trail begins in Paris, if those
suitcases of Fane's are any guide. The Hamburg end I
propose to take on myself in company with Cant here:
Wolf, to start off with, will make for Berlin, to try and
discover Grundt's present whereabouts; while you, Ned,
as you speak French well, you'll cover Paris!'

'Why not Cant?' the major wanted to know, arranging
a conspicuously new handkerchief in the outside pocket
of a no less conspicuously new suit. 'Surely, Paris is his
territory?'

'I'm thinking of the lady,' Dallas answered. 'She'll
want handling, if ever we catch up with her, and that's
your specialty, I believe, Ned!'

Wolf removed his pipe to emit his almost noiseless
chuckle. 'And how?' he rumbled. 'Flat as a row of
Kegel he bowls 'em over — never was there such a man!'

Hartigan grinned; but he was not satisfied. Looking
enquiringly at Dallas, he said, 'The only thing is, old man,
supposing it's the same old decoy, supposing it's your
Liselotte lady, wouldn't it be better if you yourself...'

The Englishman frowned. 'Time enough for that!' he
retorted, between clenched teeth. 'Our first business is
to find out, if we can, what became of Fane that night.
For that, Hamburg's the natural jumping-off place. Besides, apart from the fact that we both speak German

well, Cant has made a pretty good suggestion.' He
glanced across the table. 'Tell them, Cant!'

The Frenchman's pale face lit up. 'All these big hotels,'
he explained, 'have a certain proportion of French, or
at least French-speaking, personnel — chefs, *maîtres
d'hôtel*, waiters, *quoi*? The staff at the Astoria have their
orders from the police, it appears: they button their
mouths before the guests about the *affaire* Fane; but who
ever prevented servants from gossiping among themselves? This, then, is my plan. We go boldly to the
Astoria, Robin and I. He takes the best suite in the
house and I figure as his *valet de chambre*. Since he has a
Canadian passport he can present himself as a wealthy
Canadian and I shall be his French-Canadian servant.
Is it an idea, no?'

'It's good,' said the major approvingly.

'It'd better be good,' was Wolf's morose comment.
'You don't know Nazi Germany. No freedom of speech,
no freedom of thought — the country's a vacuum, *sum
Donnerwetter*, and there are no leaks in a vacuum, *mein
lieber!*'

'Bah!' cried de Cantigny. 'If there's a single French
employee in the hotel, I'll have the full story of this poor
Fane's movements that night within ⁺twenty-four hours,
you'll see! Do not forget, my friends, that already I am
of them a little. For the past six months, as head waiter
of Madame Ernestine's Petit Savoyard Restaurant down
in the Village, I have learned to conduct myself like these
people!' He laughed gaily.

'It's the best plan we can think of for the moment, anyway,' said Dallas. 'Wolf, you'll go to Berlin. You'll find
your Prussian Guards vanished into the *Ewigkeit*, I'm
afraid, and what with recent changes, I doubt whether
you'll recognize the place. However, notwithstanding the
fact that our clubfooted friend has bobbed up at Ham-

burg, I'm very sure that, as a former staunch supporter of the monarchy, his very name stinks in the nostrils of the Nazis, and I'm counting on this to help you in our search for him. As an ex-Prussian officer, at any rate, you'll know exactly the right tone to take with the officials — am I right?'

'It's already twenty-seven years since I went away,' was the placid answer. 'But I shall manage.'

'You leave the ship at Southampton,' Dallas continued, 'and travel to Berlin by way of London and Ostend. Ned will get off at Cherbourg, while Cant and I will land at Hamburg. In this way we shall be mixed up a bit — it's safer. We must keep in touch with each other so that the four of us can concentrate on the first real clue that any one of us strikes. We've got to work fast — sooner or later, we're bound to catch up with the Department of Justice people who're already hot on young Fane's trail; besides, I promised Miss Fane to report progress to her in Paris on April 29.'

Cant ruffled his eyebrows. 'It's only four weeks away — hardly more than three from the day we land.'

Dallas shrugged his shoulders. 'The alternative was having her with us ...'

'And why not?' demanded the major. 'It's her brother, ain't it? She might fall in love with you, old man — there's a grand match!'

'God forbid!' Dallas exclaimed with feeling, and glanced at the clock above the door. 'One last word before we turn in. Conditions in Europe have changed enormously since most of us were over there, even during the two years that have elapsed since I was last on the Continent. International espionage is rampant and we're headed for its darkest spots. As you three know, I've had some experience of Grundt. He's as clever as a wagonload of monkeys — and as mischievous. I still believe that Nazi Germany's too hot for him and that he's over the hills and far away by this; but, mark my words! once we get on his trail, it won't be long before the old man finds it out. We've got to keep our mouths shut — do you hear me, Ned? — and our eyes skinned. That's all now, I think!' He stood up, and the others followed suit.

An envelope protruded from under the door. Hartigan picked it up. 'A radio — for you!' He handed the message to Dallas.

The Englishman indulged in one of his rare smiles as he read it. 'From Miss Fane!' he announced. The others crowded about him. The message was dated New York and ran:

GOOD LUCK TO YOU AND THE THREE MUSKETEERS

PATRICIA FANE

The Frenchman's eyes sparkled. '*Tiens!* She has a pretty wit, *la petite!*' He put his arms affectionately about Hartigan and Wolf. 'Well, here we are, veterans like Athos, Porthos, and Aramis. And you, my old Robin,' he said to Dallas, 'you are d'Artagnan, the cadet!' And, drawing an imaginary sword, he cried, 'All for one, and one for all!'

'All for one, and one for all!' boomed the major, and Wolf chimed in; but Dallas remained silent.

'Listen, you fellows,' he said very earnestly; 'once we solve the mystery of young Fane's disappearance, that lets us out as far as Miss Fane's concerned. But Grundt remains. Each of us has an account to settle with him — let's swear that, whatever the result of our mission, we'll stick together until the reckoning has been paid in full!'

'I'll swear to that!' cried de Cantigny, his face aflame. 'I, also!' said Wolf in his guttural voice. 'Count me in, old man!' the major declared.

They clasped hands on it.

CHAPTER VII

The Limping Foot

GEORGE BREWER, plump and bald-headed, a Shriner's emblem in his coat lapel, leaned back in his chair. 'Another round, Mr. Dallas?'

His friend Clarence Wilson was scooping up the cards. 'You betcher,' he answered for the other spryly.

Dallas glanced at his watch. The hands pointed to eleven o'clock. 'I'm for bed,' he remarked. 'This sight-seeing racket's the very devil!'

'Aw, shoot!' said Wilson, shuffling the pack. 'Stick around, brother, and I'll buy you a drink!'

'I don't believe I will,' was the smiling rejoinder. 'I told that Canuck of mine to pack my things tonight and I want to see how he's making out.'

Brewer was totalling up the score. 'That's eight marks you owe me, Mr. Dallas, and, Clarence, I get five marks eighty from you. Pulling out so soon?' he remarked to Dallas.

'I guess so,' replied the other, counting the money over. 'Where do you go from here?'

Dallas smothered a yawn. 'Excuse me. Oh, Paris or somewhere. I might stop off and take a look at Berlin.'

The lounge waiter approached. 'There's a gentleman asking for you, Herr Dallas!'

Dallas glanced up, then, for a fleeting second, seemed to stiffen. Wolf's bony form was visible between the palms at the entrance to the lounge.

For the moment he was so elated he could hardly speak. If Wolf had sought him out, it meant there was news. It was four days since Robin Dallas, of Montreal, accompanied by his manservant, had registered at the Hotel Astoria, and to Dallas they had been four days of almost unbearable inaction. It had rained incessantly ever since their arrival in Hamburg: the whole city seemed inert and lifeless in the Nazi grip, the foreign tourist traffic virtually at a standstill. As prearranged, he had left the hotel staff to Cant and spent most of the day in vague prowlings about the streets and docks in his guise of wealthy tourist, visiting the Alster cafés, gossiping with waiters and taxi-drivers, in a vain attempt to pick up a trail which appeared to be hopelessly effaced.

Cant had failed him. In his Gallic way, the other was forever bubbling with hope. Now it was a Swiss chambermaid, now a French kitchen helper, with whom he had scraped acquaintance below-stairs — each evening he was out somewhere, to a dance-hall or a pool-room, with some member of the Astoria staff. But to date these contacts had led nowhere: meanwhile, there was nothing from Wolf, no word from Ned in Paris — Dallas felt as if he was up against an iron curtain.

The hotel was half empty, and out of half a dozen transient Americans and English, the only two he ever spoke with were Brewer and the latter's friend Wilson, whom he had met in the bar. They bored him, but their company helped to pass the time while he was waiting to hear the result of Cant's evening activities. They had invited him to play rummy with them, and he accepted because the game checked Brewer's interminable dissertations on economics — he explained that he was investigating financial conditions in Germany for a group of Illinois banks — and the interminable stories of his friend, who appeared to be a salesman representing an American harvester concern.

Now Wolf had come — Dallas was thrilled. The rain drummed on the glass roof as he strode through the lounge, but he scarce heard it, so sure was he that Wolf's arrival signified action, liberation. In the ugly yellow overcoat he sported, with his hair clipped close to his head and wearing the gold spectacles he usually donned only for reading, the ex-taxi-driver had a decidedly Teuton air, melting imperceptibly into the German background: it even appeared to Dallas that he exaggerated his German accent as, from a good three paces, he hailed his friend: 'Hello, there, Mr. Dallas!'

At the formal nature of the greeting the Englishman turned his head and saw that Wilson had come out behind him. Wolf was saying in a jovial, paternal voice: 'I had to run ofer from Berlin for the day on business so I thought I'd yoost see were you still here. And how's eferything in Canada?'

Wilson had drifted off, but Wolf went on playing his part. 'I haf to catch the night train back to Berlin,' he rumbled. 'I'd like to vash up a leetle, no?'

'Come to my room!' said Dallas, and led the way to the elevators.

No sooner were they in the suite with the door shut when Wolf swung to his friend. 'Listen,' he said, 'do you know a man called Brewer stopping in this hotel?' His tone was grave.

'Why, yes,' said Dallas. 'I've just been playing cards with him.'

'He's a Fed!'

The Englishman frowned. 'A Department of Justice man, you mean — looking for Fane?'

'That's it. He's been in Berlin, conferring with the secret police — what they call the *Gestapo!*'

'You're sure of this?'

'Listen, I find a former brother officer of mine who's in the Ministry for Home Affairs. The authorities would like to get their hands on Grundt: they think he's still in

Hamburg. This man Brewer is working in with them. Does he suspect you?'

'I doubt it. We're merely bar acquaintances, and they've displayed no undue curiosity in my movements so far. That man who came out of the lounge behind me just now, Wilson — he's a friend of Brewer's. He's probably a Fed, too.'

'I wouldn't risk the telephone or wiring — I caught the first train out,' said Wolf, and looked at his watch. 'I mustn't miss that train back, Robin. My friend von Siepen takes breakfast with me in the morning. At seven — can you imagine it? — so that he may be at the Ministry at eight. You've no idea how hard these Brown Shirts work!'

'What have you told him — about yourself, I mean?'

Wolf indulged in one of his muted chuckles. 'Didn't you tell me that Bartels, Grundt's man who's handling the sale of these plans, was connected with the German espionage service in America during the war?'

'Yes.'

'I've told Siepen that I'm a New York lawyer since many years and that I'm looking for Bartels, because someone in America has died and left him money, see? Siepen don't give a damn for me or Bartels, either: all he knows is that I want to find Bartels. He's willing to help me because he thinks, maybe, that through Bartels I shall lead him to Clubfoot.'

Dallas nodded approvingly. 'Very ingenious!'

'At one time Bartels had a villa somewhere on the outskirts of Salzburg...'

'Salzburg? In Austria?'

'Sure! The Salzkammergut, they tell me, is full of refugees from Nazi Germany — of Nazi spies, as well: I was wondering whether perhaps Grundt may not have his headquarters in those parts. Anyhow, Siepen is en-

quiring in the region and I hope to have some news from
him at breakfast tomorrow. In the meantime, I don't go
hunting wild goose until I have something definite. If I
decide to go to Salzburg, I wire you, yes? Anything from
Ned?'

'Not a word.' Disgustedly.

'And you — how are you and Cant making out?'

Dallas shrugged. 'We're up against a brick wall so far.
Cant's away tonight with one of the waiters who works on
the sixth floor where Fane had his suite; but I'm not hope-
ful. He said he'd be back by eleven. If you stay awhile,
you'll see him.'

Wolf shook his head. 'I must go now if I'm to make
the train. Keep your eye on Brewer, Robin!' He clapped
on his hat, a green felt with a badger brush behind. '*Na,*
what do you think of the ensemble? The Yorkville sheik,
was?'

Dallas chuckled and took him to the door.

It was half an hour before de Cantigny appeared. He
burst in suddenly and, motioning to the other to close the
door, said tensely, '*Eh bien, ça y est!*'

Dallas sprang up from the table. 'You have something?'

'Something — or nothing!'

'Damn it, man, out with it!'

The Frenchman's manner was mysterious. 'Jules, this
waiter I went out with tonight, he's from Luxemburg, he
speaks French, *quoi?* He's scared because it appears that,
after the American consul came investigating the first
time, the staff was warned it was the prison camp for anyone who should know anything about Fane. But tonight,
when he was full of red wine, Jules talked . . .'

'Well?'

'The night Fane disappeared, Jules was on duty on
Fane's floor. Fane rings for a whisky soda. Jules brings

It. It is past eleven o'clock and Fane is at the telephone. Jules hears him say, "I'll come right away!" and then he repeats the name of the street, "Lotsen-Kai"...'

'Lotsen-Kai?'

'Wait! Fane says then, "Hold on! I'll write it down!" and signs to Jules to give him his pencil, and he writes on the menu which is beside the telephone. Jules is curious because he knows that the Lotsen-Kai is a street in Saint Pauli, down by the old port, a very low quarter, and he wonders what a rich young American like Fane should want there in the middle of the night. So he looks over Fane's shoulder and sees he has written, "Café Helga." The next moment Fane has torn off the piece of paper, has seized his coat and hat, his bag, and dashes from the room!'

'What is this place?'

'Jules didn't know and he didn't have the curiosity to enquire. But I can tell you.' De Cantigny laughed excitedly. 'I asked about among the women at this dance-hall we went to at Altona tonight. None of them seemed to have heard of it until one, an old one, speaks up, a terrible ogress, oh, là, là, with mostachios like a sergeant-major — Irma, they call her. "The Café Helga?" she says, hoarse like a crow. "Many's the bright sailor boy I've met there in the old days. If it's still standing, you'll find it down on the waterfront in Saint Pauli, the corner of the Lotsen-Kai and the Teer-Gasse — Ole Jansen's place, they used to call it!"'

'A sailor's dive, eh?' Dallas commented meditatively. 'Well, we'd better investigate!' He disappeared into the bedroom and returned with an automatic, which, after a glance at the magazine, he slid into his pocket. A rain-coat lay across a chair and he slipped it on, then from a drawer took a cap and an electric torch. He paused and looked at de Cantigny. 'Wolf was here,' he said.

'Wolf?' said the Frenchman in surprise. 'What brought *him*?'

'He came to warn us. Those two Americans I've been sitting with, they're Feds! You haven't noticed anything fishy about them, have you?'

The other laughed. 'Only that they seem to do most of their investigating in the bar.'

Dallas shook his head dubiously. 'Don't fool yourself. Brewer looks simple, but he's shrewd. From now on we must be on our guard. We'd better not be seen leaving the hotel together, to start with.'

Cant nodded. 'I'll go first. Meet me at the corner of the Jungfernsteg in five minutes. I'll have a cab . . .'

'What about your gun?'

The other tapped his pocket significantly and crept out.

The rain was relentless. In a thousand dancing knives it beat down upon the worn cobbles of the quay. The bracket lamp at the corner, illuminating the sign 'Lotsen-Kai,' guttered in its ring of haze to the savage buffetings of the wind. Deserted derricks made geometrical patterns against the sky and shrouded barges bulked blackly against spars and smokestacks dimly clustered. Above the noises of the gale ropes creaked and water lapped invisibly without even a ship's lantern to challenge the gloom — it was as though all those craft, weary of river and sea, had crept to this forgotten cranny of the docks to die. In the whole vista of warehouses and go-downs curving about that remote basin, no light showed, not a soul stirred.

They had dismissed the cab amid the brightness and bustle of the Spielbuden-Platz at Saint Pauli and, with the help of a directory map consulted in a café, found themselves, at the end of a ten-minute tramp through the rain, at the Lotsen-Kai. There were houses, squat and

sordid, in the Teer-Gasse, but never a window glowed.
In the flickering light of the corner lamp they read the
sign over the ramshackle building that made the angle of
the quay: 'Café Helga, Inhaber Ole Jansen.'

The café was one-storied, with a single dormer window
above, and it was dark. The time was twenty minutes to
one, and at first they thought the place had closed for the
night. But as soon as they entered the street, they were
aware of its abandoned air, with every window shuttered
and the board covering the door placarded with tattered,
weather-beaten posters flapping in the wet. They tried
the door. It was fast, and all was still as death inside.

A narrow lane, running behind, detached the café from
the rest of the street. Round the angle of the house a
wooden fence loomed up beside them with a gate and a
yard beyond. Across an expanse of grass-grown flags,
they could make out a door with a window beside it.

Dallas explored the door with his torch, tested the
latch: the door held. His companion was trying the window. 'Stand back!' he ordered, and lifted his elbow.
Dallas thrust him aside and, with a knife he drew from
his pocket, began to fumble at the fastening. In a moment he noiselessly lowered the upper half of the window.
'Shut it behind you!' he whispered and disappeared inside the house.

A fetid kitchen brought them to a long, low-pitched
room, with an opening in the farther wall and a line of
recesses curtained with festoons of artificial vines —
from the small platform with music-stands, it seemed to
be a dance-room. The door they had remarked revealed
a short passage, a stair mounting at the side, another
room at the end. This was the café proper, low-ceilinged
like the other, with oil lamps hanging from blackened
beams and liquor advertisements on the leprous walls.
Here was the main entrance and a line of shuttered win-

dows, giving on the street. The air was dank and evil-smelling: out of the inky blackness beyond the range of their flashlights the squeak and scamper of rats came to their ears. But, though the establishment had clearly been shut up for some considerable time, it was not disordered — the bar, beside the passage leading to the dance-floor, was clear, the small tables, covered with cheerful, red-chequered cloths, neatly aligned.

'There's nothing here,' said Dallas. 'Keep your ears open, Cant — I'm going upstairs!'

The narrow flight led straight up to a bedroom under the eaves, so tiny that Dallas's flashlight revealed the details in a single sweep — a camp bed with a table beside it, a wash-hand stand, a row of empty hooks against the wall. The bed had not been slept in, but there was a depression on the pillow as though someone had rested there.

A newspaper lay on the brown blanket that served as a quilt. As the beam fell upon it, with a muttered exclamation Dallas snatched it up, scrutinized it, then thrust it under his coat. Torch in hand, he investigated further. The brim of a hat protruded from under the bed — a man's brown felt: with a set face he examined it, inside and out, in the ray of the flashlight and thoughtfully laid it aside. There were cigarette ends in a saucer beside the bed and these he pored over, then turned his attention to the wash-hand stand, and after that, to the uncarpeted floor. Now it was a woman's handkerchief, soiled and bedraggled, he came across. He was studying it, when a sharp 'P-st!' rang out from the bottom of the stairs.

Crushing the handkerchief in his hand, he switched off his torch. As he did so his ear caught a sound from the room below. It was an undefinable noise, but it rang like an explosion through the quiet, a single, dull crash, followed by silence. At the same time he was aware of an icy draught mounting through the warped planking under his feet. There was no doubt about it — someone had opened the door or one of the windows in the café.

Two stealthy strides brought him to the staircase. Cant was at the foot, a dim shadow in the darkness, facing the closed door leading to the café. For a moment all was still, then a rim of light showed under the door and in the deathly hush both heard the rhythmic tap of a stick, the clump of a limping foot, on the bare boards within.

His lips set close to his companion's ear, Dallas breathed a single word. 'Clubfoot!' he said. The whisper was as soft as a sigh, yet his voice was almost exultant. Grasping Cant's wrist, he drew him noiselessly back along the passage to the dance-room. There he pointed silently to one of the curtained recesses that commanded a view of the passage and the closed door, edged in light, at the end, and they slipped inside.

CHAPTER VIII

Interlude in the Dark

THE door gaped. In the café, out of their range of vision, a steady light now burned: in its dispersed glow a fantastic shadow leaped across walls and ceiling to merge into a black shape that loomed up in the opening. With the light behind it, the face was invisible: all that Dallas and his companion, lurking behind their curtain, could distinguish was that it was a man of huge proportions who stood there. He was enveloped in some dark, voluminous ulster and carried his hat: the massive head, set on the bull neck and shorn to the scalp, showed a triangle of bristles, iron-gray and wiry, that glistened in the dim radiance. For a breathless moment the figure lingered, shaven poll cocked at a watchful angle; then it slowly veered about and, with tapping stick, hobbled laboriously back into the café. The misshapen boot encasing the right foot was plainly visible: its hollow thump echoed through the silence after he was out of sight.

The thump ceased and a voice, deep and guttural, speaking German, rolled along the passage. 'It's as cold as the tomb in here, *verflucht!*' it rumbled. '*Herr Je*, what a night! See if there's any schnapps, will you? I'm chilled to the bone.'

A shadow crossed the light; bottles clinked.

'There's nothing here, *Herr Doktor*,' came the deferential answer in German. 'But there's rum in my flask.'

'Give here!'

A long, gurgling sound, a contented grunt. A throat was cleared raspingly.

'Gr-r, how the cold strikes home!' the first voice said.

'You haven't brought me here on a fool's errand, have you, you dog?'

In a servile tone the other replied: 'I obeyed the *Herr Doktor* to the letter. I was over at Blumberg's within a little quarter of an hour of old Irma calling you, and I never lost sight of him all the way back to the Astoria ...'

Cant's hand groped for his companion's in the dark and gripped it tensely.

'I was close behind him,' the voice went on, 'in the shadow of the newspaper kiosk at the corner of the Jungfernsteg, when he was asking the taxi-driver if he knew the Lotsen-Kai. I came across to you at the Wein-Stube at once ...'

'And let their cab get away, *sapristi!*'

'We weren't five minutes behind them. We're here first, that's all!'

'How did they get on to the Café Helga in the first place? — that's what I want to know.'

A nervous laugh. 'I don't have to tell the *Herr Doktor* — the American secret service is very efficient!'

Back in the stuffy darkness of their recess, the Frenchman was aware that the figure at his side had gone suddenly rigid.

'How do we know they're not here already?' the harsh voice boomed from the café challengingly.

'As the *Herr Doktor* saw, the door was locked: the windows are fast, too ...'

'There's a back door, isn't there, *Schafskopf?*'

In their hiding-place the two men were taut with suspense as a flashlight shone down the passage. They flattened themselves against the wall behind the dusty curtain. The light vanished: a step creaked up the stair to the bedroom and, after an interval, creaked down again. Now they could see one another's faces, strained and watchful, as the rays of the torch, sweeping the dance-room, struck between the looped-back hangings of their retreat to rest in a bright white disk upon the wall at their side. They caught their breath again only when the beam swung away and the step passed on. Now it changed its key as it rang on the flags of the kitchen, now it was returning, a firm tread that shook the curtains. An instant of palpitating foreboding, and they were in the dark again, the step reverberating away from them along the passage.

'There's no one in the place,' they heard the emissary report.

A bass growl responded. 'Then shut that door!' it grumbled. 'Do you want me to catch my death, Sis Kamel?' The door closed, the passage went black, silence fell once more.

De Cantigny was swearing under his breath. 'Ah, *bon Dieu de bon Dieu*, that old hag at the dance-hall, she was a spy! They followed me back from Altona, did you hear that, Robin? Ah, *nom d'un chien!*'

There was a faint chuckle beside him in the darkness: a rattling sound, as though a skeleton had laughed. 'He takes us for the Feds, Cant,' came the other's derisive whisper. The Frenchman's arm was gripped. 'Don't budge from there! I'll be right back!'

'Robin! Where are you going?'

But Dallas had slipped away. The minutes dragged on to five before he was back. 'Quiet now, and follow me!' he whispered. On tiptoe he led the way through the kitchen to the back door. The window, which de Cantigny had scrupulously closed and bolted behind them, now stood wide. 'Out with you!' said Dallas. 'I've had a look round outside — the coast's clear!'

The Frenchman drew back suspiciously. 'Do we run away and leave that ruffian here? Ah, *non, mon cher!*' he cried in a wrathful undertone.

A faint lightness from the night sky, falling upon his companion's face, showed that Dallas was smiling. 'Out and don't argue!' his good-humoured whisper bade the other.

De Cantigny glared. 'I have a word to say to this person,' he declared between clenched teeth. 'It seems to me, also, that he holds in his hands the key to this young man's disappearance. Clear out, you, if you like — I stay. I'm going in to Grundt!' He drew his pistol.

Dallas caught his arm. 'Idiot! Do you want to ruin everything? We're both going in — but openly, by the front door! And no guns — do you hear?'

His companion stared at him. 'Have you gone crazy?'

With a backward glance across his shoulder, the Englishman laughed — his laugh was eager, mischievous — and shook his head. 'He's expecting visitors, isn't he?'

De Cantigny had all the quick-wittedness of his race. On the instant a delighted smile broke over his face and he put the automatic away. 'Ah, ça,' he murmured ecstatically, 'ça, c'est rigolo! Pardon my stupidness, old friend! You are the prince of diplomats!'

Dallas laughed light-heartedly. 'That remains to be seen. The important thing to remember — but only if we're asked — is that your name's Clarence Wilson and mine, George Brewer!'

The Frenchman still vacillated. 'But why must we go outside?'

'Because he mustn't suspect we've been here already. I can't stop to explain now. Are you going through that window of your own accord, or do I boot you out?'

His friend chuckled. 'After you, Mr. Brewer!' They clambered out and Dallas carefully raised the sash behind them.

A funereal silence reigned outside. It had stopped raining, but the night was sombre and without moon or stars. The lane was deserted, the Teer-Gasse the same.

At the corner of the house Cant halted. 'I see no car — how did he get here?' he said suspiciously.

Dallas shrugged. 'Maybe he walked, as we did. Or came by boat. Come on!'

But the Frenchman stood his ground. 'But how did he enter the house, *nom d'un chien?*'

'By the front door, of course. Why?'

Cant shook his head. 'I must have heard the latch — I was only in the passage, not a dozen yards away. The first I knew there were voices, inside the house but rather faint, and I shut the door quickly. After that, there was a sort of thud; but I heard no door open, I tell you.'

'What does it matter? Come on, or we'll miss him!'

'Wait!' The sensitive face wore an anxious look in the rays of the distant lamp. 'You're sure he's never seen you, Robin?'

'Never. He doesn't know me from Adam!'

'There are two of them in there — what about the other man?'

The Englishman shrugged.

'It isn't Bartels, is it?' Cant persisted.

Dallas shook his head. 'I don't think so, by his voice.' He paused. 'Listen, Cant, and remember what I say — in a job like this a fellow can't hang about, waiting for a lucky break. He has to command fate by leaving nothing to chance. You went after this clue and found it, and now Destiny has repaid us by giving us this heaven-sent opportunity for getting the truth out of Grundt. If he or the other bloke recognizes me, it can't be helped — at any rate, we're evenly matched. Keep your eyes skinned and leave the talking to me. We'll walk straight in. Chin up!'

He led the way to the front. No light was visible

through the closed shutters. He laid his hand on the latch: this time the door yielded, swung inward.

A rumbling voice said in English, 'Good-evening, gentlemen!'

CHAPTER IX

The Battle is Engaged

ONE of the hanging lamps had been lit. It shed a smoky radiance upon a figure hunched below it in a chair opposite the door. It was a man so massively built that the chair, drawn out from the nearest table, all but disappeared beneath the spread of that gigantic body. Paunched and flabby, but with the hint of tremendous power in the muscular development of the barrel chest and the disproportionately long arms, he sat silently regarding the intruders from under extravagantly tufted eyebrows, his hands, large and hairy, folded on the crutch-handle of his stick, the right foot, shod in its monstrous boot, slightly drawn back.

It was a forbidding face, apelike in structure, the forehead with its shaggy eyebrows jutting like a crag overhung with whins, the nose flat and broad with cavernous nostrils, the mouth a gash parting coarse and cruel lips; while the eyes burned with an uncertain fire that spoke of accesses of rage, sudden and uncontrollable. He was fantastically hirsute, with hands and cheek-bones darkly thatched and little tendrils of hair sprouting at the nostrils and the ungainly, protruding ears. The grizzled toothbrush moustache was so stiff in growth and so closely clipped that the bristles stood out like spines. The man's whole personality seemed to exude a sort of elemental savagery that suggested a giant ape.

Yet his greeting was spoken in a friendly tone. Now, with a smile that bared a glimpse of blackened teeth alternating with gold stoppings, he said ingratiatingly

in excellent English: 'Might I ask you to have the goodness to come inside? At my time of life I find myself
singularly susceptible to the inclemencies of our North
German climate. Hans, shut the door!'

Something rustled in the shadows and a thick-set
individual emerged from behind the bar. He glanced
sullenly at the two visitors and, motioning de Cantigny,
who was staring at him intently, out of the way, laid
his hand on the latch and drew the door to without a
sound.

'Would you leave our guests standing? Chairs, *Esel!*'
the command rang out harshly.

With the same unwilling air the subordinate obeyed.
Dallas's glance sought his companion uneasily. The
Frenchman seemed unable to take his eyes off the man
in the chair, his regard sombre, his olive face paler than
ever.

They sat down, and silently the big man jerked his
head towards the passage as a sign to his underling to
withdraw.

'And now, my friends,' he said in a fluty voice, as
Hans went out, 'perhaps you'll tell me what you're
doing here?'

His tone was even, but his manner was guarded:
he kept darting swift, suspicious glances from one to the
other of the two visitors.

Leaning back in his chair, his arms crossed, Dallas
shrugged his shoulders. 'I guess we might ask you the
same question,' he retorted challengingly, purposely
giving his voice a nasal ring.

The other gave a strident laugh. 'You may,' he rejoined suavely, 'and I'll answer it. You'll see, gentlemen,
I shall be frank with you — that's my policy, absolute
candour!' He tittered and screwed up his eyes. 'Word
reached me that you two gentlemen were on your way

here and it occurred to me that the occasion and the surroundings alike were propitious for a little chat. But you'll permit me to doubt' — he chuckled once more — 'that you had the same idea.' And when neither spoke: 'Come, gentlemen, be frank in your turn! You'll scarcely pretend that you came all the way out here, on such a night, for the purpose of sampling Ole Jansen's abominable schnapps? You may speak freely. There's no one here but ourselves. My old friend Jansen is at present enjoying the hospitality of a prison camp, for the hardening of his body and the purging of his political ideas.' He emitted his cackling laugh. 'Well, shall I give you a lead? You're American secret service men, are you not? You see, I know all about you!'

The words streamed from him in a swift gabble, the heavy face, malleable as rubber, reflecting every change of thought and mood. The eyes, sharply vigilant, were never still, now raking the faces of the men before him, now ranging round the peeling walls of the café, as though ever on the alert to pluck from the shadows beyond the circle of light any shape that lurked there. While he talked, he seemed to be listening, too — the large head was cocked at an angle suggesting that he was continually straining his ear for any sound outside. Squatted in his chair, his chin sunk on his mighty chest above the ample paunch, he was like some giant spider waiting for its prey.

'And if we are?' said Dallas.

The other showed his teeth in a smile. 'Am I to take it, *lieber Herr*,' he enquired softly, 'that my fame, such as it is, has penetrated as far afield as Washington? For I perceive that your comrade can hardly lift his eyes from my unfortunate disfigurement.' De Cantigny started, flushed. 'Do not be embarrassed, *junger Mann*,' the man in the chair told him easily. 'Yes, I am Doctor

Grundt, old Clubfoot, as they call me, no longer, perhaps, the power I used to be in the land of my birth, but still a factor to be reckoned with!'

His jaw set solid as a rock and his fingers seemed to tighten their grip on the handle of his stick.

Bending his brows at Dallas, he said: 'You've been to the Hamburg police about Fane, *nicht wahr?* To the *Gestapo* in Berlin, too, I hear?' He snapped his fingers airily. 'Let's see, how was your name again?'

Dallas evaded the trap. With a glance at de Cantigny, he countered: 'What does it matter? It'd be an alias, anyway!'

A shadow seemed to darken the rugged features, but it passed at once. Then Grundt said, while his eyes searched the Englishman's face, 'Haven't I seen you somewhere before?'

A second's pause, taut with suspense. Dallas shrugged his shoulders indifferently. 'It's improbable, unless it was on the other side,' he answered.

The German grunted: he continued to stare. Out of the tail of his eye Dallas saw de Cantigny stir uneasily in his chair.

'It wasn't in America,' said Grundt, frowning and pursing his lips. 'Odd, your face seems strangely familiar.' He broke off. 'No matter. You're wise to be on your guard in dealing with this gutter riff-raff, these scourings of the jails, the g-great General Goering's famous secret police. *Pfui Deibel!*' He hawked resonantly and spat on the floor. 'Ah, my dear colleagues,' he resumed in honeyed tones, 'you made a mistake in going to these people — you should have put yourselves in touch with me from the start, since it's evident that my connection with this affair is not unknown to you.' He licked his lips with a gloating air. '*Ei, ei*, what fellows you are, you Yankees! Not a detail escapes you! *Mein*

Kompliment, junger Herr!' He rolled his eye in de Cantigny's direction. 'Your comrade is American, too?' he questioned innocently.

Once more Dallas was quick to perceive the pitfall. 'Sure,' he answered easily, 'but of French-Canadian extraction. He's often taken for a Frenchman.'

Grundt indulged in a long stare. Then he nodded slowly. 'So they tell me, *ja!*' he remarked. Then, rubbing his spadelike hands together, he went on. 'But come, my friends, let's put our cards on the table, as is fitting between colleagues. You've come here in search of a certain packet, *nicht wahr?* Well, you'll not find it at the Café Helga — no, not within five hundred miles of it!'

'So I gather,' was the imperturbable reply. 'Our people in Brussels are negotiating with your man, Bartels, about it, aren't they?'

An indignant snort broke from the cavernous chest. '*Ja*, and what has happened? What always happens when Government departments come poking their noses in? Delay, discussion, and every kind of chicane! Would you believe it, your State Department has had the effrontery to suggest that the plans we offered might be fakes?'

'Why not?' said Dallas casually. 'It strikes me as being a whale of a good suggestion!'

The *Herr Doktor* did not take this pleasantry amiss. 'Pardon me, I have my reputation to consider,' he pointed out with dignity. 'With every Power in the world busily increasing its armaments, military information is today a commodity like anything else and I'm the largest wholesaler in the field. I'm prepared to supply any Government on demand with information on any feature of the national defence of any Power, from submarines to tanks, from poison gas to the latest thing in rays — my list of clients would astonish you!'

'I bet it would,' said the Englishman and winked at Cant. The Frenchman looked startled: his companion was like a man transformed — he seemed to be in the highest spirits.

Grundt was warming to his theme. Pressing his finger-tips together, he went on sententiously:

'For the first time in history I think I may claim to have organized international espionage on business lines. With me, gentlemen, it is no longer a matter of hush-hush and hugger-mugger — I have raised it to the level of an industry. I pay the best prices, I bring the experience of a lifetime to the job, and since the abdication of my old master, I am a man without a country and therefore above suspicion of being corrupted — if you'll pardon the expression — by any patriotic considerations whatever. My only aim is to furnish my clients with prompt and reliable information. But in this, as in every other industry, the labourer is worthy of his hire, and I must say I'm amazed and not a little mortified to find your State Department treating the excellent Bartels, who's the ablest salesman in my organization, as though he were the commonest double-cross.' His voice grew stern. 'At seventy-five thousand dollars those plans are dirt cheap, and your people know it. At this very moment I could name another Government which is prepared to pay handsomely for them.'

Dallas brushed a hair from his coat. 'Then why not sell to them?'

Grundt's mouth closed with a snap. 'Because those plans are worth more to yours — I admit it. The other party would merely be buying back its own property, which is not the same thing at all.' One elbow propped on his thigh, he leaned forward. 'You strike me as being a couple of bright young fellows,' he said engagingly. 'Why not get authority from Washington to handle the matter? We shan't quarrel about terms. And listen' — his eyes were mere slits — 'I'll take care of you two in the way of commission.' He prodded the Englishman's leg with his stick. 'What do you say?'

'Not interested,' was the curt answer. 'We want Fane. Where is he?'

The tufted eyebrows came down swiftly. 'Fane?' Grundt echoed suspiciously. 'What do you want with Fane?'

'He's a Government servant who's been guilty of a breach of trust,' Dallas snapped back in a hard, metallic voice. 'Our job is to turn him over to the folks back home for trial.'

'*Ach, so?*' Grundt seemed relieved. 'But why bother about Fane?' he demanded, all blandness. 'Those plans are of far more importance, surely...'

'Orders are orders, that's why! If you want to do business with us, Doctor, we must have the facts. Now, we know you got the plans from Fane — the question is, how? Did he sell 'em to you, or what?'

De Cantigny shot an admiring glance at his friend. Dallas's manner was brusque and staccato, his English manner of speaking replaced by a careful but not exaggerated American intonation. It occurred to him that Dallas was probably basing himself upon Brewer: it was a plausible performance, he felt. At any rate, it seemed to satisfy Grundt.

The German took time to answer the question. 'Say, rather,' he observed at last, 'that he bartered them for a pair of rosy lips!' He smiled seraphically.

'Meaning the Lassagne dame, I take it?'

The hot eyes were mocking. '*Ei, ei, junger Herr,* you know all my little secrets!' he murmured approvingly.

'What happened? You know whom the young man

came to Hamburg to meet, I guess? You don't deny
that Fane was here at the café that night, do you?'
'No.'
'How did you lure him to this joint?'
Grundt simmered gently. 'You'd better ask the lady '
'It's you I'm asking. Did he meet his Jap here?'
'I surmise as much, since the plans were forthcoming.'
'Surmise, hell! Don't you know?'
The German frowned. 'As it happens, I was delayed
on my way here. The police were displaying inconvenient
curiosity as to my movements that night, and when I
arrived, the gentleman in question had already taken
his departure.' His manner was precise and dignified.
'What gentleman? The Jap, is it? Where did he go?'
Grundt shook his head. 'I can't tell you. Jansen
could, I daresay, but he was nabbed in the raid. Hence
the inhospitable appearance of the café — it has been
closed ever since.'
'Raid? What raid?'
'The police. Looking for me.' His tone was mild.
'Scarcely had I arrived when they descended upon the
place...'
'What became of Fane and the woman?'
'They got away, thanks to me...'
'And where did they go?'
He shrugged. 'Where do lovers go? Cannes, Capri,
Villa d'Este...'
Dallas looked at him hard — the German's eyes were
polite and friendly.
'We've only your word for it,' Dallas remarked.
'You claim a woman wheedled the plans away from
him; but a tap on the head would have done as well!'
The other smiled. 'You wouldn't say that if you'd
ever seen her. *Entzückend!*' He kissed the tips of his
fingers gaily. 'But very expensive.' He chuckled. 'It

may be because she spends so much of her time in Paris, but she certainly seems to have absorbed all the acquisitive qualities of the French.'

His gibe seemed to strike de Cantigny on the raw. At any rate, he was moved for the first time to speak. 'As to that,' he said rather coldly, 'money meant nothing to Fane.'

'*So?*' was the somewhat bored reply. 'On principle I interfere as little as possible with my agents and I know very little about the young man. But my information is that he consistently lived above his means...'

'Nevertheless, his family is one of the richest in the United States!'

The roguish eyes narrowed suddenly. Now they ferreted in de Cantigny's face, now in his companion's. '*So, so?*' The big head was dandled gently; a hairy hand pawed the chin. 'Wait!' he murmured. 'In the old days, when I used to go to Kiel for the Regatta in attendance upon His Majesty, an American was sometimes there with his yacht. Cyrus M. Fane — they said he was a multi-millionaire. Any relation?'

'Only his father,' said de Cantigny dryly, and added. 'He's dead now.'

'Then the young lady called, I think, Patricia — am I right? — of whom I sometimes read in the Paris *Herald*...?'

'His sister!'

'*Donnerwetter!*' He seemed impressed, frowning to himself, his forehead furrowed in thought. After a pause he said, addressing de Cantigny in his oiliest manner:

'In effect, like you, my dear colleague, I'm at a loss to account for the young man's motive. A bad business, indeed! What,' he went on dithyrambically, rolling his eyes from one to the other of them, 'what must be the feelings of that respectable and highly placed family, of this so charming and no doubt fashionable young lady, at finding Cyrus M. Fane's son branded as a traitor? For I take it,' he added with some eagerness, 'since you two gentlemen have your orders to apprehend the young man, that the State Department is convinced of his guilt!'

'Absolutely,' Dallas declared with much conviction, 'and we're relying on your help to find him. If, in return, we can be of service to you in the matter of disposing of the plans...'

'Tchah!' said the big man airily. 'The matter is not so simple as you think. I have long since dismissed the young man and his inamorata from my mind; and, to tell you the truth, since they neither informed me, nor did I question them, about their intentions, at the present moment I haven't the least idea where they may be!'

'Come, come, Doctor,' Dallas encouraged him, 'you may have lost sight of them for the time, but I'm very sure you can put your hands on them if you want to.'

'*Ja*, it's not so easy!' He spoke absently, his eyes glinting between his half-closed lids as he gazed moodily at the two men before him while he nervously prodded the floor with his stick. 'I must look into the matter: maybe, a little later...'

The words died on his lips. Then he was out of his chair, kicking it out of the way with his crippled foot and stepping backward, at the same time whipping out an automatic — as it seemed, in one motion, so swiftly was it done. Dallas veered about. Noiselessly, inch by inch, the street door was opening. Now, at the clatter of the chair on the bare boards, it was flung violently back. A figure clad from head to foot in black leather gleaming with the wet stood on the threshold.

Without a moment's hesitation Grundt fired. With a sharp exclamation the man in the doorway toppled

backwards. Before their ears had finished singing from
the roar of the explosion under the low-pitched roof, a
clamour of whistles and running feet broke out in the
street. The door was banging in the wind: Dallas
jumped for it, shot the bolt. At the same instant Hans
came whirling from the passage. '*Gestapo!*' he grasped,
eyes wide with terror, and sped for the bar, Grundt
hobbling after.

From front and rear heavy blows thundering on doors
and shutters reverberated through the house. Beside a
flap that lifted in the counter, Hans, stooping to the
floor, pulled up a trapdoor. A flight of stairs led down-
ward and, without paying further heed to the visitors,
Grundt went scrambling down. Dallas and de Cantigny
dashed forward, but Hans stepped in front of the Frenchman who was leading. '*Zurück!*' he barked and, thrust-
ing at his chest, sent him reeling back.

But Dallas was close behind. His left shot out, and
catching the assailant on the point of the jaw, stretched
him on the floor. Cant had picked himself up and was
already halfway down the stair. Dallas was about to
follow when angry voices, the trampling of feet, came
rolling along the passage.

He turned back, and with the flat of his hand sent the
hanging lamp, the only light in the café, swinging upward against the rafters. To the jangle of breaking glass
darkness fell, but the next instant a jagged tongue of
flame ran flaring along a beam. He was down the trap
and was lowering the heavy door into place behind him
when a stentorian voice went trumpeting through the
café, '*Staats-Polizei! Halt da!*' At the same moment a
spurt of orange flamed in the dark above his head.

But the sound of the shot was muffled by the closing
of the trap. He paused only to shoot a well-greased
bolt noiselessly into its slot, then, switching on his torch,
hurried down the wooden stair.

CHAPTER X

What the Upper Room Revealed

DALLAS had drawn his pistol. At the bottom of the steps he stopped to look about him. But also to decide upon his next move. He was temporarily nonplussed. His flashlight disclosed a cavernous chamber with vaulted roof, a row of wine-barrels along one wall, billets for firing stacked along the other. The air was tomblike and so was the silence.

The silence intrigued him. He had expected to catch up with Grundt here — with Cant, at least. The Frenchman must have been hard on Grundt's heels; both Cant and Grundt, however, had mysteriously vanished. A confused medley of sounds was faintly audible from above; but the rain of blows he was momentarily expecting to hear upon the trap he had closed behind him was unaccountably delayed. Underground the stillness was absolute.

Then, as his light traversed the far wall of the cellar, he made out the mouth of a passage. He smiled grimly. Trust Clubfoot not to go blundering into a blind alley! Here was certainly an egress — to a waiting car, a boat. One might have guessed that a sailors' dive of that order would have some such secluded means of communication with outside, handy for smuggling or crimping operations.

He was halfway across the greasy floor when a slight sound brought him up short. The next instant a figure staggered out of the passage — in the swathe of light eyeballs glinted whitely in a face as black as a Negro's.

'Halt!' cried Dallas tensely: then, with a laugh, he lowered the automatic. A torrent of French came to him out of the dark.

It was Cant, smeared from head to foot with coaldust and muttering curses upon himself.

'Ah, idiot! Ah, pig! Ah, camel that I am!' he fulminated. 'I see it now: he let me go dashing past him in the dark, then slipped out by some hidden exit. But he'll not escape us. Quick, Robin, there must be a way out here: there's none back there!' He jerked his head towards the opening from which he had emerged. 'Quick, I say, we've got to find it!'

'You bet,' was the desultory reply. 'The sooner we're out of this ourselves, the better I shall be pleased. Those were secret police up there: I can't imagine why they haven't come after us, especially as one of the bonny lads took a shot at me. What happened to you, old man? You look as if you'd taken a header into the coal bin!' He was prowling with his torch behind the barrels.

The Frenchman gritted his teeth. '*Et comment!*' he declared bitterly. 'There's a three-foot drop through that hole and I landed full length among the coal — I don't know how I didn't break my neck. Ah, *zut!* Ah, *par exemple!* Not alone are my eyes, my mouth, my hair full of their filthy coal-dust, but this monster of a man, this triple brute, this orang-utang, has given us the slip! Did you see him shoot that policeman? *Bon Dieu*, what a savage!'

An ejaculation from Dallas, out of sight behind the wine-vats, cut short his flow of objurgative.

'Here we are!' Dallas called softly.

The other darted behind the barrels to find Dallas exploring with his flashlight an aperture, no more than four feet high and brick-lined.

'It must have been a tight fit for the old man,' the

Englishman remarked. 'But here goes!' He crept into
the hole.

They were in a sort of gallery with roof and walls
of brick that gleamed wetly in the rays of their torches.
The floor was of earth, and Dallas, shining his light down-
ward, showed enormous footprints, the round marks of a
stick's ferule, in the mud.

'At least, the scent's fresh!' he commented.

'After him!' his companion exclaimed.

With several twists the passage ran for perhaps two
hundred paces, then a turn brought them unexpectedly
face to face with an iron door that stood ajar. Beyond
was a bare cellar, clean and dry, which seemed, from
the shelves all round, to be a storage place. A stair
mounted to a trap at the far end. Guns in hand they
pushed cautiously at the trap. It opened, and they
found themselves staring across a warehouse or shed,
dusty and long abandoned, double doors beyond, drawn
together and padlocked. But the timbers had rotted
and they discovered where a couple of planks had been
pulled out, leaving an opening through which they
could squeeze.

They emerged upon the basin, but on the lower level,
where a row of sheds faced the water across a timber
staging. A flight of steps against the stone embankment
led to the quay above.

Dallas caught de Cantigny's arm. 'Listen!' he said.

The beat of a propeller, rapidly growing fainter, came
out of the dark.

'Clubfoot!' said Dallas. 'He must have had a boat
tied up at the landing — he probably has a yacht or
something of the kind out there!'

'Then we've lost him,' the Frenchman growled. 'You
were too gentle with him, Robin. I'd have put a gun
to his head and given the great ape ten seconds to tell
us where to find Fane!'

His friend laughed softly. 'We didn't do too badly. But let's get out of here. This uncanny quiet puts the wind up me. In five minutes every plain-clothes man in Hamburg will be combing the neighbourhood...'

'But where are we?' Cant demanded.

'At the lower end of the Lotsen-Kai, I imagine. If we cross it and take the first street in, we ought to get back into town. We've got to find a café where you can clean up — you can't go back to the hotel like that!'

The street at the top of the steps was deserted. 'Lotsen-Kai' was the name on the lamps. They took at random the first turning that presented itself, uneasily aware, as they hurried along, of a faint stir that seemed afoot within the dark and shuttered houses they passed. Now a window was thrown up: farther on, in a doorway two men stood in their night-shirts talking. They paid no heed to the two scurrying figures: they were staring up at the sky.

Somewhere in the distance a child seemed to be blowing on a toy trumpet. De Cantigny stopped short. 'That's the fire call!' he said. He pointed aloft. 'Look!'

There was a glare close at hand behind the houses. Suddenly, with clanging bell, a fire-engine thundered past the top of the street. 'Lord!' exclaimed Dallas, but without undue excitement, 'I believe it's the Café Helga.' He gripped the other's arm. 'Old man, we've got to step on it if we don't want our heads chopped off like the bird they accused of firing the Reichstag!'

They started off once more. The cross-street where the fire-engine had gone by was the Teer-Gasse — with surprise they came upon the name on the corner. At the far end they could discern the lurid reflection of flames, a reddened sky, smoke. People were running towards the fire in the wake of the engine.

'It's the Helga, all right,' said Cant, slowing down. 'Look, you can see those derricks on the quay in front!'

'There goes the evidence,' muttered Dallas. 'Odd to think that it was I who started it!'

'You, Robin?'

'The lamp — I smashed it, or I shouldn't have got away!'

'But what evidence are you talking of?'

'I'll tell you later. We'll save our breath now — we're going to need it!'

With clamorous gong a second engine roared by, and they ran on.

As they left the scene of the fire behind, the excitement died down. It was past two o'clock in the morning, but they were approaching a region of shops and tram-lines, and there were still a number of people about. Nevertheless, though they slowed down to a walk, the passers-by, and even an occasional policeman, seemed to display no particular interest in Cant's deplorable appearance. 'In a seamen's quarter like this,' said Dallas gaily, in the new and almost reckless mood which had been his all the evening, 'gents with grimy faces and hands are practically part of the landscape.' Nor, when at last they had chosen as suited to their purpose a humble coffee bar behind a square still ablaze with the lights of dance-halls and cafés, did Cant's entry appear to excite suspicion; he retired unmolested to the wash-room to remove the traces of his mishap.

When he returned to the little bar, he found Dallas eating liver sausage and drinking beer.

'Bock!' he announced, indicating the foaming tank-ard. 'It's good. Have some!'

But Cant, with a brooding air, ordered coffee and lit a cigarette. 'I don't know how you can take things so easily,' he said sulkily. 'And why that grin on your face? I don't see anything to grin about!'

'I do,' was the cheerful retort. 'Action always stimulates me. And things are moving at last!'

'I don't see how you make that out. We had Grundt there in our power and, instead of forcing the truth out of him, you let him waste our time with a pack of lies until it's too late. Even if you're not interested in Fane, I should have thought you'd at least have tried to identify the woman. After all, the only reason you took this job on was, to try and rehabilitate yourself, wasn't it?'

'That can wait,' was the firm rejoinder. 'I know our job's to find Fane, and because I know it, I purposely refrained from questioning Grundt about the girl. If it's Liselotte, he'd have been on his guard at once — as it was he damned nearly recognized me ...'

'I thought you said he didn't know you?'

'He may have seen my picture in the newspapers — it was all over the press at the time ...'

'And knowing this, you took a chance?'

He nodded. 'I explained that to you already.'

De Cantigny moved hands and shoulders in a resigned gesture. 'You take a risk like that — it's magnificent, *mon vieux*. But are we any wiser than we were before? We don't even know for certain that Fane ever reached the Café Helag that night!'

'Oh, yes, we do,' said Dallas promptly.

'Because Grundt says so?'

He shook his head and drew a newspaper from under his coat. 'Look at this!'

It was a copy of the London *Evening News*—the final edition, as the red lozenge beside the title proclaimed.

'It was in the bedroom upstairs,' Dallas explained

and pointed to the date. 'February twenty-eight,' he precised, 'the night the boy left London. He bought this newspaper at the railway station, I should imagine. How should a copy of a London newspaper come to be in this obscure Hamburg café if Fane didn't bring it?' He paused. 'Then there's this!'

His forefinger and thumb dipped into his waistcoat pocket and dropped a small handkerchief into the Frenchman's palm.

De Cantigny looked up sharply. 'A woman's handkerchief?'

Dallas nodded. 'You'll find an initial — "L."'

'Lassagne, eh?'

The Englishman shrugged, his lean face a mask. 'Or Liselotte!'

Cant gave a low cry — he was turning the handkerchief. 'These are bloodstains, Robin!' He showed brownish marks on the small square of cambric. Dallas nodded.

'Then Clubfoot told only half the truth. She brought Fane there, but Fane never left — they killed him.'

The other glanced cautiously about him, then shook his head. 'I think that Grundt told us the whole truth — about Fane!'

'Then what do these bloodstains signify?'

His voice sank to a whisper. 'Akawa!' he said.

The Frenchman's dark eyes widened. 'Are you sure?'

'There was a man's hat up there, the lining soaked with blood. It was half-hidden under the bed. It was bought in Sydney — the maker's name is inside! Akawa's ship called at Sydney.'

'*Dieu!*'

'If they killed him, they don't seem to have done it outright. I found a bloodstained towel on the washstand and the basin still contains some dregs of reddish water.

And there were wads of cotton wool, also bloodstained, on the floor. It was a head wound, evidently — I suppose they slugged him from behind. Apparently, they laid him on the bed, for there's the mark of a head on the pillow.'

'And where was Fane, while this was going on?'

He shrugged. 'At some time or other that night he was in that upper room ...'

'Anyone could have carried that newspaper up there.'

'I'm not thinking of the newspaper.' He fished in his pocket and, opening his fingers, showed a couple of cigarette stubs lying on his palm. 'Those are American cigarettes, Cant.' He pointed at part of the lettering which appeared on one. 'They were in a saucer beside the bed ...'

The Frenchman shrugged. 'Many Europeans smoke American brands. How do you know it wasn't the girl? Or it might have been Akawa. It's scarcely conclusive, Robin.'

'This is,' was the curt answer. From another pocket he drew a match-folder, elegantly got up in blue and gold and bearing the advertisement of a London hotel. 'The name is almost sufficient corroboration in itself,' he pointed out, 'but look inside!' Cant obeyed. About half of the matches, white with blue heads, had been torn from the strip. 'He's left-handed — his sister told me,' Dallas explained. His little finger touched the strip: on the right it was still intact — the matches had been torn away from the left.

De Cantigny gazed at him in dismay. 'But surely you don't think that young Fane had anything to do with this crime?'

'Directly, no!'

'Isn't it more probable that they killed him, too?'

He sighed. 'I'd like to think so — if only for his sister's

sake. But Fane's alive, I feel sure: and Grundt knows
where he is.'

'What makes you think that?'

'At first he was concerned only with getting his price
for those plans — I believe he was perfectly genuine
when he told us that Fane didn't interest him. But as
soon as he discovered that Fane had money — I don't
think you should have let that out, old son — his tone
changed. There was no more talk of the plans, and it
was going to be very difficult to get in touch with the
girl. Which is sheer moonshine, as she's obviously his
agent, and on the regular payroll, whoever she is.'

'Then what's his game?'

The keen face darkened. 'I don't know — yet. It's
unfortunate that Grundt got away, but at least we know
that whenever we pick up his trial again, it'll lead us
straight to the girl. But I'm not waiting for that. We're
moving to Paris. That's where Fane's trail ended and
that's where we've got to pick it up. I can't think why
we haven't heard from Ned...' He tapped the table
with a coin. '*Herr Ober, zahlen!*'

'And when do we leave?' asked Cant when the waiter
had been paid.

'At once, as soon as there's a train. We'll stop off
in Berlin for a word with Wolf and go on to Paris by the
afternoon plane. One of us will have to go back to the
hotel in case there's a message from Ned — I'm afraid
it'll have to be you, Cant, because, if all's clear, you, as
my servant, can collect my traps; but unfortunately
in the circumstances I can scarcely do as much for you.
There's no risk, really: those fellows were looking for
Clubfoot, not us, and I'm pretty sure that the bird who
fired didn't see me — at any rate, the shot seemed to
go wild. But mind yourself, and if they ask any questions, tell them I had to take the night train to Bremen —

or anywhere you like, as long as it isn't Berlin; you'll
send on a forwarding address.'

'And if Ned wires after we've left?'

'We must chance that — we'll be in Paris by this
evening, anyway. Now, are you all set? I'll be waiting
for you in the buffet at the main station — if you're
not there by five, say, I'll hop the first train out...'

'I'll be there,' his friend promised quietly.

From the threshold de Cantigny surveyed the
brightly lit restaurant. At that hour the main station
was strangely quiet, the buffet almost deserted. A Brown
Shirt snored full length on a bench: an old woman,
clasping a basket, dozed in a corner; behind the bar a
waiter nodded. Dallas, reclining uncomfortably on two
chairs, was asleep. The Frenchman went over and, with
a hand pressed on his, roused him.

'Step on it!' he said curtly. 'We've got to get out of
this!'

The other rubbed sleepy eyes. 'But the first train
doesn't leave till five-forty-five. What time is it?'

'Past four. We're not waiting for any train. They've
pinched Brewer and Wilson!'

On that the Englishman was suddenly wide awake.
He swung his legs to the ground and laughed softly.

'Oh, dear,' he remarked, 'I'm afraid Wilson won't
like that — he's a peppery bloke. That'll be Hans's
doing, of course — I forgot about Hans. Well, I'm
glad the poor devil wasn't burnt alive. He was rather
on my conscience, was Hans. Did you have any trouble
in getting away?'

Knowingly Cant shook his head. 'The plain-clothes
men were just bringing them out when I reached the
hotel. Wilson was like a madman, shouting and waving
his arms...'

Dallas chuckled. 'I said he'd be annoyed...'

'I'd paid off my taxi at the corner, and I kept out of sight until all the fuss was over. Fortunately, neither of them speaks a word of German and the night clerk was much too scared to try and help them out.'

'That ought to delay things a bit. Did he try and detain you?'

'Bah! You know how terrified of the *Gestapo* they are in this country. He didn't breathe a word about the arrests, and as for the manager and the rest of the staff, they took good care to remain quietly in their beds. But we can't risk hanging about for the train. I stopped at the first garage I found open and rented a car and driver to take us to Berlin. It's outside now with the bags...'

'Good boy!'

'The Paris plane doesn't leave until eleven-thirty-five, and we shall get to Berlin in plenty of time to breakfast with Wolf and make it. That is, if you still want to go to Paris.' He drew a telegram from his pocket. 'From Ned...'

'Ah!' Dallas snatched the telegram and read:

TRAIL LEADS TO BADEN-BADEN STOP GOING
THERE TOMORROW EVENING MEANWHILE CON-
TINUING ENQUIRIES HERE STOP ADDRESS
LATER   NED

He scowled. 'Confound the fellow, why can't he be more explicit? Still, he's on to something, evidently — it looks to me as though he'd traced those suitcases to Baden-Baden. I think we'll go to Paris just the same, Cant, if only to get out of this country while the going's good. Ned says he's not leaving until tomorrow evening, and our plane's due in when?'

'Half-past three!'

'That'll give us plenty of time to see Ned and decide on our next move. Now, where's that car?'

The pale April sun was glittering on the Berlin house-tops as they rolled through the Brandenburg Gate. The clocks were striking nine. At the Adlon a surprise awaited them. Wolf had already left. He had returned to the hotel early in the morning, the desk clerk said, and, after breakfasting with a gentleman in the restaurant, had called for his bill and checked out. They had only just missed him — he was not gone more than a little half-hour.

'Did he leave any address?' Dallas asked.

The clerk consulted a book. 'Salzburg — the Hotel Erzherzog,' he replied.

Dallas drew de Cantigny aside. 'Bartels has a villa outside Salzburg. But Wolf said he wouldn't go down there unless he got something definite to work on.' For once in a way he was excited. 'By Jove, Cant, it looks like business!'

'Then it's Salzburg for us, not Paris?'

'Ultimately, yes. But we'll go to Paris first and see what Ned has to tell us. Wolf can hold the fort in the meantime. We'll wire him to Salzburg and tell him what's happened. But not until we're clear of Germany.' He glanced cautiously round the busy hotel lobby. 'We won't hang about Berlin, either. We'll drive straight out to the airport and breakfast there.' He frowned. 'I shan't be happy until we're up in the air.'

At Tempelhof they dismissed their car and settled up with the driver. Outwardly, Dallas was as calm as ever, but the Frenchman noticed, as they sat over their ham and eggs and coffee in the bright, clean café, that his companion's eyes shifted to the door every time it opened. Breakfast done, they lit their pipes and strolled out upon the flying-field.

Out of a blue sky the sun shone over the flat plain. Dallas pointed towards it. 'What an age we live in!' he murmured. 'There's the whole map of Europe unrolling before us to the south. We shall see it on a not much larger scale than did Napoleon on his large-scale maps; but he was earthbound, and we're free!' He glanced at his wrist. 'Half an hour to go! If only no word comes through from Hamburg about us before we're off the ground! Come on! We'll get our seats!'

In the booking-office they were weighed, together with their bags, bought their tickets, presented their passports. 'Our luck holds!' Dallas whispered. At last, with a group of fellow passengers, they went out to the plane. The door was slammed, the propellers roared as they taxied across the field, and all the time Dallas was looking backward at the group of buildings on the edge of the field. Now the propellers sounded another note, the ground fled away. Robin Dallas turned from the window and glanced across the aisle at de Cantigny. He had doffed his cap and Cant saw the perspiration beaded upon his forehead. 'Ouf!' said Robin, and winked.

That afternoon they were in Paris.

CHAPTER XI

The Major Relaxes

THE first stirrings of spring were making themselves apparent in Paris. Already the horse-chestnuts along the Champs Élysées showed a lacy pattern of green, and there were bundles of forget-me-nots, tightly packed and blue as newborn babies' eyes, at the flower kiosks on the Grands Boulevards. Under the influence of the mild April afternoon, Ned Hartigan, on his way to the post-office in the rue des Capucines, to send off his telegram to Dallas at Hamburg, stopped outside the Grand Hotel and bought himself a bunch of violets. He had resolved, whatever happened, to leave for Baden-Baden the following evening. But in the interim he was free and, after the strenuous five days he had spent in Paris, he felt in the mood for relaxation.

The bearded beldame who presided at the kiosk tucked the violets into the lapel of his new gray overcoat, and, with an approving glance at his buttonhole, he crossed the boulevard, headed for the rue des Capucines. But as he reached the corner, a klaxon squawked piercingly on a double note and the largest and most rakish-looking coupé he had ever seen slid to the opposite kerb. A little brown hat protruded from the driving-seat, a white-gloved hand waved.

He went over to the car. It was Patricia Fane. Save for a very clean Sealyham, who was bounding up and down beside her on the seat, she was alone.

'My, my!' she exclaimed mischievously, 'how smart we look, Major! You haven't forgotten me, have you?'

The amusing little hat stressed the vital eagerness of

her face: the russet and jade scarf knotted loosely at
her neck was most becoming.

The major took off his hat with a flourish. 'I should
say not! But, my gracious, I could hardly believe my
eyes. Where do you spring from?'

'New York,' she answered casually. 'I landed only
three days ago. I brought the plane with me and flew
up from Hâvre.' She shifted into neutral and slipped
her arm about the dog, which was leaping up and down
in a frenzy of excitement. 'Phil and I came all on our
own with only Mrs. Evans to look after us, didn't we,
my beautiful?' The Sealyham whined ecstatically and
tried to thrust his black nose in her face. 'His name's
Phil, because he's so fidgety,' she explained, clasping the
dog tight. 'If you remember your *Struwelpeter*, Major:
"Fidgety Phil, could never keep still!" How would
you like to give me a cocktail?'

'I'm all for it!'

'Hop in, then, and we'll go and see if the tulips are
out in the Bois. The big places will be closed still, but
we'll find something open. I've been shopping all day —
if anybody calls me "Moddom" again, I shall scream!'
She opened the door for him. 'Mind Phil! Quiet now,
darling! Dear me,' she observed as, the major having
clambered in beside her, they moved off, 'there seems
to be a lot of excitement going on. I'd forgotten what a
noisy place Paris is. Did you ever hear such a row?'

A perfect bedlam of horns and klaxons was arising
about them. 'I fancy we're travelling in the wrong
direction,' observed the major mildly. 'That disc,
"*Sens Interdit*"'— he pointed at a lamp-post — 'means
it's a one-way street against us!'

'Why, so it does!' she answered calmly. 'I thought
it seemed familiar. I haven't driven in Paris for a year.
Funny, how one forgets!' She stopped, reversed: there

was a crash in rear, a barrage of explosive French. They went forward and scraped a fender, backed and banged once more. From the sidewalk, well out of the way of the traffic, a policeman yelled and brandished his white bâton. Miss Fane was superbly unmoved. 'These long chassis are the devil to turn,' she observed confidingly as at last they swung clear. 'Give me a plane every time. No one-way streets in the air, Major —— No, Toni — no chestnuts today!'

This last remark was addressed to a taxi-driver whose crimson, infuriated face bobbed unexpectedly at the window. They shot smoothly away along the Boulevard des Capucines.

Hartigan sniffed his violets with great contentment. He had suddenly made up his mind to enjoy himself. Ever since his arrival in Paris, it seemed to him, he had been consorting with scrubby people, interviewing baggage clerks, concierges, small tradesfolk; pumping the unsavoury night guides who hang about the travel agencies; hobnobbing with blue-bloused porters in bars behind the Gare de l'Est; haunting the dreary corridors of the Police Prefecture and the Ministry of War. He felt that this elegant and entertaining young woman and her beautiful car were a fitting background for his smart new clothes, his bunch of violets, his buckskin gloves, his spats. The car moved like the wind. Sitting back, he prepared to relax.

The girl was speaking to him. 'You know, I've been looking for you,' she said, as they headed west. 'I even went so far as to give Willie Hastings a buzz on the telephone from here, but he couldn't tell me your address. Where are you staying?'

'At the Grand,' the major replied. 'But there are a dozen places where you could have had news of me. All my life I've been dodging in and out of Paris between campaigns, it seems to me. When I appear on the Place de l'Opéra armament shares jump five points and all the pacifist societies go into mourning. But you're here ahead of time, surely? I thought Dallas wasn't going to report to you until the end of the month.'

She made a little face. 'That was his arrangement, not mine. I couldn't sit around in New York doing nothing, so I followed on the next boat after yours. I'm distracted about Jimmy, Major. Is there any news of him? What's Dallas up to?'

'He and de Cantigny are still at Hamburg, as far as I know. And Wolf's in Berlin. I haven't heard from any of them since I arrived in Paris.'

'And you — what have you found out?'

'Me? Oh, I've been following up certain lines. Nothing very definite as yet!'

She slowed down at a pedestrian crossing. 'The four of you have been on this side for nearly a week and there's still nothing to show for it, is that it?' Her tone was crisp.

He shrugged. 'I can't speak for the others — as I told you, I haven't heard from them. But it's not the fact as far as I'm concerned.'

She took her eyes away from the road long enough to fling him an eagerly enquiring glance. 'You were to follow up the woman, weren't you? You haven't found her, have you?'

He shook his head. 'Not yet. But I believe I'm on her track.'

She gave a little excited gurgle. 'Truly? I knew you wouldn't fail me, Major. You gave me a feeling of confidence the first time I met you, that evening in that funny old saloon over on Third Avenue — I wish I'd put you in charge from the start. Tell me, they're not in Paris, by any chance, this woman and Jimmy, are they?'

'Not so far as I know, Miss Fane!'

She flashed another glance at him. 'Don't be provoking! Just what do you know?'

He paused. 'Well,' he said slowly, 'I've discovered where those suitcases of your brother's went to...'

'No! Where?'

'I'd rather not say for the present — I don't want to raise false hopes. I expect to know more in a day or two — between ourselves, I'm leaving Paris tomorrow to investigate.'

She turned and stared at him with a crestfallen air. 'You're leaving Paris? And I was just thinking we might do a little sleuthing together.'

He smiled indulgently and shook his head. 'I'm afraid that'd hardly do, Miss Fane!'

Her glance challenged him. 'Because your friend Dallas wouldn't approve, perhaps?'

Hartigan looked rather sheepish. 'I know, of course, that you're paying for this expedition...' he began.

'I want to talk to you about Dallas,' she said severely. She fell silent then and they spoke no more until they found themselves seated opposite each other on the terrace of a small café near the Lac Inférieur.

She waited until the waiter had brought their dry Martinis, then said evenly, her elbows propped on the table, her eyes searching the ugly, honest face before her, 'Why didn't you tell me that Dallas had been in prison?'

The major sighed. 'So you found out about that, did you?' he said sadly.

Her expression was severe. 'His real name's Robert Merrall and he was an officer in the British Royal Air Force. He was sentenced to three years' penal servitude in England for espionage and was released from jail only last summer after serving two years and five months of his sentence. When I heard the particulars, I remembered the case — I read about it in the American newspapers at the time.'

'It wasn't espionage,' Hartigan broke in firmly. 'The charge was selling military information to a foreign Power, which isn't the same thing at all.'

'I know all about the charge,' she retorted. 'He was a staff officer or something in connection with the air defences of London and he sold a secret cipher for five thousand pounds to a woman who was spoken of all through the trial simply as Liselotte. The court-martial was held in secret, but Pinkertons say...'

The major, who was staring miserably into his glass, looked up sharply. '*Pinkertons?*' he echoed. His tone was horrified and he frowned heavily.

With colour rising she met his indignant glance. 'Why not?' she said defiantly. 'I like to know whom I'm dealing with.'

Hartigan shook his head gravely. 'You shouldn't have done that, my dear.'

'Then why couldn't he have told me himself? I was employing him on a highly confidential mission, a mission of trust, yet he refused to answer a single question! I'd every right to make enquiries.'

Her companion shrugged despondently. 'I wanted him to let me drop you a hint, but he wouldn't have it. His standpoint is that, since the world at large believes him guilty and his career's ruined, it's no use going on proclaiming his innocence.'

She took a gold case from her bag. 'You're his friend, I know,' she said. 'But let's be reasonable about it. The English don't make mistakes like that!' She sprung her lighter and touched the flame to her cigarette.

'Robin was innocent, nevertheless,' Hartigan replied simply. 'The evidence against him was purely circumstantial. As you're presumably aware, the cipher

was in his keeping and one day it was discovered that
messages in this code concerning some very secret air
manoeuvres on the English coast were being deciphered
by a foreign Power. There was an investigation. Robin
swore . . .'

'That the code had never been out of his possession. I
know. But he had it at his apartment, and it was supposed never to leave the office!'

The major nodded unhappily. 'That's right. He was
working on it at home. Technically, it was a breach of
the regulations . . .'

'And this cheque for five thousand pounds which they
traced to his bank, drawn in his favour by this woman
Liselotte, who was proved to be a notorious secret agent,
that was a technical breach of the regulations, too, I suppose?' Her tone was scathing.

'He was in love with this woman and wanted to marry
her, but she was married already. That cheque was in re-
payment of sums he advanced her to enable her to get a
divorce. He had no evidence of this, however, and so he
wasn't believed. Yet there's not a shadow of doubt in my
mind that this woman stole the code from his rooms, had
it photographed, and then replaced it. And what's more
our friend Doctor Grundt was at the back of the whole
thing.'

'How do you know that?' Her manner was less hostile.

'Robin often used to go across to Germany — he was
studying the German air service. He first met Liselotte
at Munich. She used to go about with Grundt — she
called him her guardian; but she would never let the two
men meet. For all we know, she's identical with this
Arlette Lassagne who vamped young Jimmy. After all,
the procedure in either case was very similar.'

She nodded gravely. 'Yes. I thought of that.'

'Then don't you see that Robin's the ideal man to find

your brother? I don't say this because he's my friend, but
he's a grand guy, brave as a bull terrier and loyal up to
the hilt. If you knew him as I do, you wouldn't doubt his
innocence in all this wretched business for a single minute.
But, putting that aside, why dredge up this old scandal
which has nothing to do with the job in hand, except in
so far as it may prove that the interests of both of you are
the same?'

She puffed reflectively at her cigarette. With a sigh she
said: 'You're a good pleader, Major Ned — he's lucky to
have a friend like you. Shall I tell you something? When
I met you this afternoon, I'd almost made up my mind to
get rid of Dallas and put you in charge.'

With a dogged air Hartigan shook his head. 'Oh, no!'
he rejoined quickly. 'Oh, no!'

'I don't say I won't do it yet,' she answered, her mouth
mutinous. 'You're a human person — at least I can talk
to you.' Veiling her eyes, she expelled a long plume of
smoke. 'What was she like, this Liselotte of his?'

'Very beautiful, I believe.'

'Fair or dark?'

'Very fair and *petite.*'

'Was she his mistress?'

He moved his head cannily. 'One doesn't ask a man
like Robin a question like that. Speaking for myself, I'd
say no. He has rather definite ideas on that subject.'

'Was he very much in love with her?'

The major sighed. 'I guess so. She could have cleared
him at the trial, but she stayed away.' He shrugged.
'He's been kind of cagey about women ever since.'

She nodded dreamily. 'I know. He's like a man with a
wall around him. I never saw such haunted eyes. Yet
I'm sure he's human underneath. I believe I could like
him, if he'd give me the chance. Of course, if he really was
innocent...'

'He was innocent, all right. He behaved like a crazy man; but then, so did your brother.'

She heaved a little sigh. 'He said such a tragic thing to me — I can't get it out of my mind since I found out about him. He spoke of freedom as being "the greatest thing in the world." Prison must have been slow torture to a man like him, especially if ...' She broke off. 'I did all I knew to make him talk, that first day you brought him to the house, but he only snubbed me. And you expect me to trust him? How can you trust someone who doesn't tell you anything?'

The major cocked his head cannily. 'Can you wonder if he's a bit girl-shy? I mean, to be suddenly yanked out of this hopeless backwater of his, selling pencils or something round the kerosene circuit in Canada, and confronted with someone like you. You're rather a breath-taking person, you know, Miss Patricia!'

Her grave mood melted. 'And you're a very clever one, Major Ned,' she retorted with a mischievous smile. 'That nice Colonel Wolf told Willie that you have women sighing for you all over the globe. And no wonder. You know how to handle us!'

'That dumb Dutchman has a fixed idea that I'm a combination of Casanova and Clark Gable,' was the affable reply. 'The only man who knew how to handle women was Henry the Eighth and he ran out of headsmen or something ...'

She laughed and cocked a merry eye at him. 'Just a wife-beater, eh?'

'I repeat,' he declared sturdily, 'you're a breath-taking person, but also' — he laid his hand briefly on hers — 'a darn good sort. So let's have no more crabbing of the man at the wheel and, above all, no more nonsense about my replacing him! You know as well as I do that you can have that guy eating out of your hand, any time you want!'

She knit her brow prettily. 'I'm not so sure...' She seemed to change her mind. 'I'm not sure that I want to.' She flaked the ash from her cigarette. 'By the way, when are you going to see him?' she enquired casually.

'Wirra!' the major cried, clapping his hand to his pocket. 'When I met you this afternoon I was on my way to send him a wire — I forgot all about it.' He drew forth the telegram. 'Would you mind if we went back now? It's rather important!'

She extended her hand. 'Show me, please!'

He hesitated. 'Honestly, I don't know whether I...'

'It's on my business, isn't it? Very well, then!' Her fingers closed about the message — he let her take it. 'Baden-Baden, eh?' she commented and raised her eyes to his. 'And you think they're there?'

'It's where those suitcases went to.' He paused, gazing at her dubiously. 'If you promise to be tactful about it and won't let on to Dallas that I told you...'

'Tact,' she said sweetly, 'is what I've nothing else but!' She signalled to the waiter. '*Encore deux martinis et la carte!*' she ordered.

'It's nice here,' she told the major before he could speak, 'and, barring a very stuffy dinner-party at Alice de Kérouaille's, which I meant to cut, anyway, I'm at a loose end. We'll dine here quietly together and take in a revue or a movie. You're not leaving Paris until tomorrow evening, are you? So I'm quite sure it doesn't matter whether you send off that telegram before dinner or after.' She gave him the menu which the waiter had brought. 'Order us something nice!' she bade him.

'Well, I'm sure I don't know,' said the major uncertainly; but he ran his eye down the card. 'In a place like this the only way to get a decent meal is to go into the kitchen and interview the chef!'

Patricia jumped up. 'Come on — I'd adore it!'

It was great fun in the kitchen. They were some time getting under way because the major discovered that the chef, beaming greasily from under his white cap, had fought against the Riffs, and the visitors had first to be shown, with the aid of the salt-box, a sauce-boat, and a couple of wooden spoons, the exact disposition of the engagement in which the cook had received a Berber slug — 'mes exuses à vot' dame, mon commandant!' — in the lower and fleshy part of the back. A sole marguéry was finally chosen, followed by a sweetbread *en casserole* and a cheese soufflé — the last was the major's selection; hand on heart, Monsieur Armand promised it would send them into ecstasies. Patricia wanted to drink champagne; but Monsieur Armand placed a fat finger on a certain Vouvray in the list of wines which the waiter laid before them and whispered hoarsely, 'Drink that and you will give me news of it!' — which, as the major explained to his companion afterwards, is a French way of saying 'It's the top!'

'And now about those suitcases,' said the girl when they were in front of their second Martini at the table.

'Well,' the major replied, 'a woman, described as blonde and "*très chic*," collected them up at the Gare de l'Est on March 4 and gave orders for them to be forwarded by train to Baden-Baden, where she said they would be collected...'

'March 4? That's more than a month ago.'

'I picked up the trail only this morning — I've been working on it ever since I landed in Paris. I realized that after all these weeks all trace of them might be lost, so I had a friend wire to Baden-Baden to try and find out who collected the suitcases there and where they were taken. I expect to get the answer tomorrow afternoon.'

'What have you found out about the woman?'

'Not much. She has an apartment at Neuilly in the

name of Lassagne, but she hasn't been there in two
months — she's often away for long periods, the concierge told me. She lived quietly and paid her bills
regularly. The secret police have nothing against her —
but then, they've nothing against Liselotte, either, beyond her record in poor old Robin's case. In the neighbourhood she was believed to be a foreigner, although
opinions differ on this point. The concierge thinks she's
Russian, while the daily woman who takes care of the
flat when she's in Paris is quite sure she's an American,
because she's heard her talking English on the telephone
and because she's so lavish with her stockings. Actually
she's an Austrian, Robin says.'

Patricia Fane sipped her cocktail. 'I've never been to
Baden-Baden,' she remarked reflectively. 'I hear it's
charming. And there's a famous reducing cure there.'
She glanced over her impeccable line, then lifted her eyes
to her companion. 'Do you know I believe I'm putting
on weight?'

The major took fright at once. 'Now, look here, young
lady . . .'

She put a small, warm hand on his. 'Why don't you
let me fly you down? The ship can be ready at two hours'
notice, even less, and I'll send the car by train. There's
your transport for every imaginable sort of emergency.
What do you say?'

He shook his head dubiously. 'I'd have to ask Robin . . .'

'Oh, the heck with your Robin! We could start first
thing in the morning and be there in time for breakfast.
If there's nothing doing we could be back in Paris next
day and your blessed Robin needn't know a thing about
it.' Her eyes sparkled. 'Have a heart, Major Ned —
this is going to be fun. It's a four-seater plane — you can
sit in the back with Phil and Mrs. Evans.'

'Is Mrs. Evans another Sealyham?'

She laughed. 'Good gracious, no. She's my maid. She's the most air-minded person in the whole of the United States — she'd have to be, travelling with me. She'll simply adore having you flirt with her.'

He shook his head dubiously. 'You go altogether too fast for me, Miss Patricia. I'll have to think about it. In any case, I can't leave Paris until I've had the reply from Baden-Baden, and that won't be before tomorrow afternoon.'

But she was already on her feet. 'I've got to ring the Kérouailles to tell them not to expect me for dinner. I'll call the air-field at the same time and order them to have the ship ready ...'

'Just a minute! There's no such hurry about it,' he exclaimed.

But she was already gone.

He sighed resignedly and finished his cocktail.

CHAPTER XII

First Appearance of a Green Raincoat

NEXT afternoon, in the tea hour, Dallas and de Cantigny, having driven straight to the hotel from the Le Bourget airport, were at the Grand, asking for Major Hartigan.

'Are you the gentleman that enquired before?' the reception clerk wanted to know.

'No,' said Dallas.

'Pardon me,' the clerk went on, 'it was this gentleman.' A middle-aged individual, very respectably dressed in a brown hat and a grass-green raincoat, had approached the desk. 'It was only to say,' the clerk informed the three enquirers collectively, 'that the major will be back at five — he telephoned that he'd been delayed at the American Express. If you'd care to wait ...'

'No matter,' the stranger replied; and, walking briskly away, he was immediately lost in the crowded lobby. Scarcely had he disappeared when the major himself, gloved and spatted and swinging an elegant malacca, came strolling unconcernedly up the steps from the rue Scribe entrance. '*Zut!*' cried Cant in a stage whisper that rang through the vestibule like a pistol shot. 'Look at the spats! The man's gone *boulevardier* on us!'

The major overheard the aside and, scarlet to the eyes, whipped about. At the sight of them standing there he whooped aloud, flinging wide his arms.

'Robin! Cant! Gosh, it's good to see you! You had my wire, then? Well, are you coming with me or joining Wolf? He's due in Salzburg tonight. Bartels is there. Fellow musketeers,' he went on solemnly, an arm about either, 'wheresoever the carcase is, there will the eagles be gathered together!'

Out of the corner of his eye Dallas had caught a glimpse of a green raincoat in the eddy of people about them. 'Not so loud, old man,' he cautioned. He caught the major's arm. 'That fellow in the greenish overcoat who's moving towards the news-stand, do you know him?'

Hartigan shook his head. 'Not from Adam!'

'He was asking for you just now...'

Ned laughed. 'Then let's get the hell out of it. It's probably a touch. I've only been in Paris for five days, and already the word's gone round that I'm in the money — between them, these bar-flies have taken me for about five *mille* already. Come on up to my room!'

'You've heard from Wolf, then?' was Dallas's first question when they were in the bedroom, littered with traces of the major's packing. 'He probably wired us, too, but we left before the telegram arrived.'

Hartigan took the message from his pocket and handed it over. The wire ran:

BARTELS REPORTED AT SALZBURG TWO DAYS
AGO   STOP   GOING   SALZBURG   IMMEDIATELY
ON   CHANCE   OF   CONTACTING   THE   BIG   BOY
STOP   ADDRESS HOTEL ERZHERZOG
                                        WOLF

'It's a good hunch,' the Englishman commented, giving back the telegram. 'If the negotiations about those plans have temporarily come to a full stop, Bartels would naturally return to headquarters to report. The country round Salzburg is pretty wild and pretty unfrequented at this time of the year, between the end of the winter sports and the opening of the summer season. I wonder whether Clubfoot doesn't make his headquarters somewhere there...'

'Perhaps in this villa of Bartels's Wolf spoke about,' Cant suggested.

'It may well be,' said Dallas. 'But I still think he's headed for the girl and Fane, wherever they are.' He turned to Hartigan. 'Now what about this Baden-Baden trail of yours?'

Briefly the major told his story. 'A pal of mine in the American Express office in Paris,' he supplemented, 'wired at my suggestion to a friend of his in one of the banks at Baden-Baden to try and discover what became of the suitcases after their arrival there. I had the answer not half an hour ago...'

'Well?' Robin and Cant demanded in one breath.

'They were collected on March 9 by a woman driving her own car. The baggage people had never seen her before, but they say the car had German license plates, which suggests to me that Fane and the girl friend must be somewhere in the vicinity. Well, that's all I've been able to find out here — the rest of my enquiries will have to be made on the spot. Are you fellows coming along with me?'

Dallas shook his head. 'I think not, for the moment. Cant and I ran into a spot of trouble in Germany, and I don't want to risk our falling into the hands of the secret police until I know for sure that the hunt has narrowed down to Baden-Baden or the neighbourhood...'

The major looked from one to the other. 'A spot of trouble? What have you two boys been up to?'

'Plenty,' said Cant feelingly.

Between them they related their adventure at the Café Helga.

'It appears there's no direct service by air from Paris to Salzburg,' Dallas went on. 'But the Orient Express leaves tonight: I think the best plan will be for Cant and me to travel by it to Salzburg. If Clubfoot is headed in that direction, we'll be on deck to lend Wolf a hand, and not too far away from you to buzz over into Germany, if you strike a really red-hot scent.'

Ned seemed relieved. 'I guess you're right...'

'We'll be at the Hotel Erzherzog at Salzburg,' said Dallas. 'When do you leave for Baden-Baden?'

'Right away,' Hartigan replied, and added airily, 'I thought I might go by plane...'

'Good! The sooner you get off the better.'

The telephone beside the bed whirred. De Cantigny, who was sitting on the bed, lifted the receiver. They saw his eyes widen. 'One moment!' he said into the mouthpiece — his tone was oddly deferential.

Clapping his hand across the mouthpiece, he announced in a hushed voice: 'It's the little Fane. She asks for you, Ned. She's downstairs.'

Dallas scowled. 'Miss Fane in Paris?' His eyes rested forbiddingly on the major. 'Did you know she was here, Ned?'

Hartigan had changed colour. 'As a matter of fact, I ran into her yesterday,' was the casual answer. 'We were both at a loose end, so we dined together.'

'Tell her you can't see her — here, I'll speak to her!' He reached for the receiver, but the major was before him.

'Hello, there,' he said in his most amiable tone into the instrument. 'Give me two minutes — I'll be right down!'

He hung up and, turning, faced Dallas calmly.

'What's the idea of that?' Robin wanted to know, glowering.

The major shrugged. 'She's paying for this outfit, old man — you can't leave her completely in the dark. Besides, she's worried about her brother.'

'Did you tell her that you were going to Baden-Baden?'

'Well — yes!'

Dallas snorted. 'Fine! Now, I suppose, she'll insist on going with you.'

Hartigan cleared his throat. 'Well, as a matter of fact, old man ...'

The angry voice cut him off. 'You tell her that if she does anything of the kind, I quit!'

The other shook his head at him. 'Don't ask me to say that, old man — she might take you at your word!'

The blue eyes glared frostily. 'Just what do you mean by that?'

With an unhappy air the major fiddled with his tie. 'I'm afraid she's found out about that old business of yours, Robin, and — well, she's kind of upset!'

'Is that so?' His tone was drawling, sarcastic. 'Quite a heart-to-heart talk you must have had about me, the two of you!'

Hartigan sighed. 'Don't be a damned fool, Robin. I didn't tell her. I didn't have to — she knew already. Don't say I didn't warn you! She just went out and made her own enquiries.'

Dallas was scowling. 'May one ask from whom? Or is it a secret between you?'

The major reddened. 'Gosh, you're impossible. From Pinkertons, if you want to know.'

Dallas leaped to his feet. 'Pinkertons? By the Lord Harry, I'll not stand for this.' He made for the door.

Ned stepped in front of him. 'Listen, you lunatic, what are you going to do?'

'Give that young woman a piece of my mind. Get out of my way!'

'Don't be a fool. I've smoothed everything over. She'll not mention that wretched business unless you do!'

'To blazes with her condescension! If you think I'm going to be spied on! Stand away from that door!'

Ned stepped back, his eyes sorrowful. 'Let me come with you at least!'

'You stay where you are!'

He dashed from the room.

CHAPTER XIII

Valse Triste

To WAIT for the major, Patricia Fane had escaped from the turmoil of the lobby into one of the reception rooms that led off it. It was furnished in the solid hotel style of another age, and amid the gilt and plush and potted palms, with her boyish figure and slim, silk-clad legs, she was like a breath of the twentieth century. Her tailored suit of her favourite brown was severely simple, but a bright scarf and a spray of gardenias were a feminine touch relieving its mannish line. She was the only occupant of the room, past the open doors of which the incessant traffic of the lobby paraded. From time to time a prowling male would stop to eye with interest the solitary, graceful figure. But the girl paid no heed to such intrusions, playing with the Sealyham which was perched on her lap. From the distance the strains of the tea-room orchestra were faintly audible.

From the doorway Dallas surveyed her for a moment as she sat there, demure and apparently absorbed with the dog on her knees. She was dandling its forepaws on the arm of her chair and chanting happily,

> Let us see if Philip can
> Be a little gentleman.
> Let us see if he is able
> To keep his elbows . . .

Then she caught sight of Dallas and broke off.

'Oh, hello,' she remarked casually, trying to restrain the dog, which was bounding madly. 'Major Hartigan never told me you were in Paris . . .'

'I've only just arrived,' he told her.

His tone was icy. She glanced up in surprise, then, as she saw the cold blue anger of his glance, rather hastily dumped the Sealyham down on the floor.

'Miss Fane,' Dallas said in his deep voice, 'there's a proverb — you probably know it — "Set a thief to catch a thief!" Let me congratulate you upon your admirable wisdom in selecting a jail-bird like me to run this precious brother of yours to earth. Nothing could be more fitting than to put one traitor to his country on the track of another!'

The anger in his voice disconcerted her. She coloured and answered rather lamely, 'Why do you call him that?'

'I'm just in from Hamburg,' he replied on the same aggressive note. 'Suppose I tell you that Akawa, this man your brother was to have met, was lured to a lonely café there and, as far as we know, murdered?'

The red ebbed from her face. 'And Jimmy? Oh, please tell me — what's happened to Jimmy?'

'You don't have to worry about him — he's alive all right. If that's any consolation to you ...'

She stared at him tensely. 'What do you mean by that?'

'I mean that Doctor Grundt suggests that Akawa was murdered with your brother's knowledge and connivance!'

Her expression became contemptuous. 'Do you expect me to believe that?'

'I don't believe it, either,' he gave her back, bleak and stern. 'But then, unlike you, I don't believe everything I'm told.' She flushed again, her eyes suddenly watchful. 'I don't think your brother knew of the trap that had been set, but I do know that if he hadn't behaved with criminal irresponsibility neither he nor Akawa would have walked into it!'

'Why do you keep on talking about Akawa?' she flared up unexpectedly. 'It's my brother I'm interested in. What's become of him? Will you kindly tell me what you've found out?'

He shrugged indifferently. 'Only that he's off somewhere with this woman...'

'Who says so?'

'Doctor Grundt!'

'You've seen him?'

'Oh, yes!'

Her face was disdainful. 'He was lying.'

'You'll have to let me be the best judge of that!'

A figure had detached itself from the moving frieze, the rustling feet, of the lobby and paused an instant in the open doorway to glance into the writing-room, casually, as though in search of someone. It was an individual in a green-gray overcoat, who carried his brown hat, a placid-looking person with eyes that twinkled alertly behind gold spectacles straddling a long, inquisitive nose. He halted on the threshold so briefly that neither of the two occupants of the writing-room had time to remark him before he drifted on.

Once more indignation burned in the girl's eyes as she cried to Dallas: 'You don't know my brother. If he's gone away with this woman, it's clear proof that he had nothing to do with this trap, as you call it. And, what's more, I don't believe he even knows that Akawa is dead!'

The lean face was unflinchingly hostile. 'You're such a good judge of people, aren't you?'

Her face changed. 'Did you come here to quarrel with me?'

'You give a fellow a mission of trust, then set detectives on him behind his back!'

She laughed on a hard note. 'I see — the major's been talking. Well, and suppose I did? What then?'

'Nothing!' he retorted furiously. 'Nothing, do you hear? I'm an ex-criminal, I was cashiered from the British Army, I'm discredited in your eyes — all right! But you're not sacking me, do you hear?'

Her expression had softened. 'You mustn't mind what I said to Major Ned,' she replied gently. 'I'd only just had the cable about you and — well, I suppose I was rather upset!'

But he dashed this olive branch aside. 'You can do what you like about it,' he went on ragingly. 'But I'm sticking to the job. And I tell you frankly I don't give a damn for your brother, and, if you want to know, I never did. I took this thing on because Grundt ruined my life and I wanted the chance to get even with him. And also, if you're interested, because there was a lot of money in it for me and the other fellows.'

She gazed at him fixedly. 'I don't believe you care anything about the money,' she said.

The blue eyes, wounded and tragic, looked past her. 'It wasn't worth all the money in the world to me to have this old scandal raked up again, I'm with you there!' His tone became bitter once more. 'But I know your type. All your life you've had your own way, and opposition infuriates you. Francis Okewood refused to enlighten you and so did Ned; but that didn't satisfy you. You had to go sniffing into my past life, you and your damned detectives; not because you give a hoot in hell about me, one way or the other, but because you can't bear to be thwarted.'

The distant orchestra was playing the *Valse Triste* of Sibelius. The slow, sad beat of the refrain, every chord a sob, drifted above the hubbub of the vestibule. She was never to hear the plangent melody again without revisualizing the harrowed face that gazed into hers with such enmity.

'Telephone calls to London, I suppose,' he said scath-ingly, 'cables to the War Office and Scotland Yard, ex-pense no object — all this mud stirred up to gratify a vulgar whim!'

She did not speak, but only stared at him gravely, tightly clutching the dog's leash.

He laughed suddenly. 'Did Pinkertons tell you how I passed those two and a half years I spent in stir? — that's what we old lags call prison, you know. I used to sew mail bags — I became quite expert. Such a restful occu-pation — it gives you time to think! I took a course in carpentry, too. Any time you want any knick-knacks for the house, like a corner cupboard or an occasional table, you must let me know. And once a month we'd have a concert, with a bunch of public-spirited amateurs to cheer up the poor, dear prisoners, and the chaplain, ever so breezy and condescending, giving us a batch of carefully selected news. Because at home, you see, Miss Fane, convicts aren't allowed to read the newspapers — in England we keep criminals, convicted traitors, and rats like that in their place!'

'Stop!' she broke in at last, and the tears stood in her eyes. 'I can't bear to hear you talk like that. If I've hurt your feelings, I'm sorry. But why couldn't you have told me yourself?'

He averted his gaze, his face stony. 'The question didn't arise, it need never have arisen. Francis Okewood vouched for me — that should have sufficed.'

'I promised Major Hartigan to forget the whole thing,' she said. 'He says you were unjustly convicted. I'm pre-pared to accept that.' She paused, and added rather timidly: 'We should be working together on this instead of quarrelling. If I say I was wrong in making those enquiries about you behind your back...' She put out her hand. 'Let's be friends!'

For the first time in a long while he looked into her eyes. Her lashes glistened. From her face his glance dropped to her outstretched hand. Then he shrugged and made no further move.

She sprang to her feet. 'All right — I shan't apologize again. I promised Major Hartigan to forget about this business and I shall keep my word. It may be true, as Major Okewood and all of them tell me, that you're the only man for the job; but you're ill-mannered and conceited and stubborn, and the less I have to do with you from now on the better I shall be pleased!' So saying she gathered up the dog in her arms and hurried to the door.

In the doorway she bumped into the major. She would have brushed by him, but he held her arm.

'Robin,' he said to Dallas, 'Cant wants to see you about your reservations on the Orient Express tonight.'

'All right.' He hesitated, looking at the girl. But she had stooped to adjust the Sealyham's collar and, without speaking further, he went out.

The major swung the girl round until she faced him. Her expression was mutinous, obstinate. 'I'm afraid I let you in for that,' he remarked.

Her eyes were sullen. 'He's a rude brute,' she said, and added, 'They're leaving tonight, then?'

'Uh-huh. At seven-fifty-five!'

'Did you tell him I was going to fly you down to Baden-Baden?'

He shook his head. 'He didn't give me the chance.'

She turned over the little jewelled watch that hung from a ribbon round her neck. 'It's late to start today; and the visibility's none too good. But I'll have the bus ready at daybreak.'

He ran his hand dubiously down his cheek. 'Robin'll raise hell!'

'Why say anything about it?' Her eager glance appealed to him. 'Don't be a spoil-sport, Ned — I've set my heart on this trip!'

He smiled back at her. 'Oh, all right!'

'I'll call the airport,' she said, and went out.

At the telephone cabins a man in a green overcoat was poring over the telephone directory. Seeing her waiting there, he not only relinquished the book to her, but also courteously helped her to find the number.

CHAPTER XIV
Wolf Gets to Work

WOLF did not proceed directly to Salzburg. Instead, he quitted the train at the frontier station a few miles outside the city, and, after submitting his passport and modest bag to the scrutiny of the customs officials, prepared to pass out into the little town. It was the last train through: scarcely had it rumbled off into the night when they began putting out the lights in the tiny station. A shrewd nip in the air told of snow yet lying on the hills all around. The customs officers stamped as they folded up their papers: the armed guard at the entrance was muffled to the eyes.

Wolf was the only passenger to leave the train. At the station exit he paused, turned back. 'I wonder if you could direct me,' he said in German to the customs man who had gone through his bag, 'to the Gasthof zur Goldenen Rose?'

The officer gave him a long, significant look. '*Gewiss*,' he said slowly, and Wolf was aware that the other customs men in the station hall had stopped gossiping to stare at him. 'It's the first turning on the left, past the church!'

'*Besten Dank!*' Carrying his bag, Wolf passed out of the station, silent glances following him.

The street was dark and deserted. A wet, cold wind blew from the hills and there was the gurgle of mountain streams in his ears. A sentry paraded outside the station and on all sides searchlights wheeled slowly across the horizon. It was the German-Austrian border — out there in the darkness, behind the lights, Wolf knew, barbed wire, sandbags, machine guns, stores of bombs, guarded the frontier against the raiding Nazi. A clock struck eleven. Wolf sighed and set out along the street.

The inn he was in search of proved to be a small, clean house with a façade decorated with flowers and pictures of saints. It stood in an alley behind the church. Save for a light above the door it was in darkness and the door was fast. There was a large and ancient iron knocker and the visitor let it fall once.

A light footstep sounded, the door opened a few inches, clanking against the chain that held it, and a voice said, '*Ja?*'

Wolf glanced over his shoulder. The lane was dark and empty. '*Freiheit!*' he gave back, hardly above his breath.

A chain rattled, the door swung inward.

A fat man in his shirt-sleeves stood there.

'Herr Maier?' said Wolf.

'Myself,' was the answer. 'Come in!' He closed the door, turning the key and refastening the chain, then led the way into a small taproom off the hall. Silently the visitor handed him a letter.

The man read it, tore it across, and dropped the pieces in the stove. 'What can I do for you?' he asked, coming back.

'A bed. Something to eat!'

He nodded. 'A little moment! Sit down and warm yourself!'

Over the cold ham and beer he presently brought, Wolf said, 'Do you know a man called Bartels, Guido Bartels, round here?'

The innkeeper frowned quickly. 'He's not one of us!'

'But you know him?'

'Surely. He's no friend of the Nazis, either. Or is he another one of their accursed spies?'

The visitor shook his head. 'He's neither the one nor the other. But I have to see him. Where is this villa of his?'

'On the hillside behind the village. But you won't find him there — he hasn't been near the place for an age.'

'He was in Salzburg two days ago...'

The innkeeper shrugged. 'That may well be — he comes and goes. But I haven't set eyes on him for months.'

'Have you ever seen him in company with a big man who walks with a limp?'

The other shook his head. 'No.'

'Have you ever seen a man of that description in these parts?'

'Never. But nowadays on the frontier it's a story of "Here today, gone tomorrow!" If the Herr has finished his supper, my wife's waiting to show him to his room. And in the morning, if the Herr wishes, I can take him to the Villa Friedl, which this Bartels owns — it's no more than a couple of kilometres outside the village.'

'There you are!'

A country lane, deep in mire, wound its way precipitously up the hillside from the main road. The snow had vanished from the valley, but the hills all about glittered whitely with it in the brilliant sunshine. In the valley the thaw was in full swing: from all sides resounded the trickle of water; everything dripped with moisture.

Herr Maier, a stalwart figure in Tirolese dress, with gay green jacket and leather shorts, pointed up the lane. A long, low roof emerged from among the firs that clothed the hillside. Then he started. 'Look!' he cried to Wolf. 'You were right!' He indicated a plume of blue smoke that rose sluggishly in the windless air from the chimney. 'There was no sign of life when I passed by here last week. But there's someone living there now. Does the Herr wish me to accompany him?'

'Thanks, no. I can manage alone now.'

'*Na, grüass' Gott, Kameradl*'

With a cheery wave of his round green hat, the other swung off down the road. Wolf was sorry to see him go. The glory of the April morning was not propitious to gloomy thoughts, but he was uncomfortably aware that an ordeal was at hand. As he trudged up the lane, he rehearsed in his mind the story which he had planned was to gain him the confidence of the man he had come to see.

The Villa Friedl, sheltered by the overhanging mountain, stood a few yards back from the road. Like all the houses in the valley it was clean and neat under its tremendous roof-tree. The shutters were hooked back, and across a yard at the side, the rear end of a big motor-car, deeply encrusted with mud, projected between the open doors of a shed.

An old peasant woman appeared in answer to his ring. She took the card he presented and, leaving him standing on the steps, paddled away. Wolf had had the card printed in Berlin. It was in English and read, 'Wolfgang von König, Attorney-at-Law, Graybar Building, New York City,' which was the address of a lawyer friend of his in New York. Across it Wolf had written in German, 'In the matter of a legacy.'

The woman came back. Without speaking, she ushered him through a hall into a sitting-room with a huge white stove where a man sat at breakfast. He was a gross-looking individual with a red, scorbutic face and a chin that was lapped in folds upon his low collar. He was buttering a roll.

'What do you want?' he demanded without ceremony.

Wolf put down his hat. 'You are Herr Bartels?'

'Yes.' He raised small, malicious eyes to the other's face. 'You're German, are you?'

'German-American, Herr Bartels!'

The man at the table looked as though he were about to expectorate. Instead, he took a drink of coffee and growled, 'Well?'

'You had a friend in America, one Reinhold Führich?'

'Never heard of him!' He bit into his roll.

'Yet he also worked for the German Intelligence in America during the war!'

Bartels shook his head. 'Still I don't know him.'

'He died recently over there. He left a will, appointing you his heir!'

The other looked up sharply, his inflamed face creased in a roguish smile. 'So-o? How much?' He pointed to a chair. 'Sit down!'

The moment was crucial. For the purposes of the interview Wolf had dug up from the recesses of his memory an item he had read in the newspapers some months before, recording the death, at Rochester, New York, of the former enemy agent, and mentioning that he had died intestate and that the lawyers were looking for his heirs to an estate of a few hundred dollars. Wolf hesitated before replying to the question. It must be a good round sum, he decided, but not too high.

'Something over ten thousand dollars,' he answered, seating himself.

'Not bad,' said Bartels. 'You've brought the will?' He held out his hand.

Wolf was prepared for the demand. Unfortunately, he had not as yet succeeded in obtaining a copy of the will, he said. The family were likely to contest it: legal proceedings would be necessary. He would be only too pleased to represent Herr Bartels in the matter and it need not cost Herr Bartels a nickel — just a matter of a little preliminary agreement between them to divide the sum recovered. Wolf was smiling to himself — driving a taxi in New York had familiarized him sufficiently with a certain type of lawyer to make his enactment of the rôle, he reflected, eminently plausible.

Bartels was not pleased. He frowned and rolled his pin-point eyes. But before he could speak, the telephone that stood beside his breakfast tray trilled. With a cross air he lifted the receiver.

'*Ja?*' he snapped, then his manner was suddenly awed. 'One moment, *Herr Doktor*,' he said very deferentially into the telephone, and, raising his voice, shouted 'Maria!'

The old woman hobbled in. 'Show him into the salon!' he ordered, indicating the visitor.

The drawing-room, still enveloped in its summer covers, was across the hall and freezingly cold. Wolf waited until the servant had gone, then noiselessly opened the door and tiptoed to the door of the room he had just left. The person at the other end of the telephone was evidently doing most of the talking. It was a man's voice — Wolf could hear it booming harshly through the silence, though he failed to distinguish any word that was said. Bartels's replies were a series of obsequious '*Jawohl, Herr Doktor!*' '*Gewiss, Herr Doktor!*' '*Aber nein, Herr Doktor!*'

Then the name of Hamburg suddenly struck upon the listener's ear. 'No, not since that night at Hamburg,' Bartels had said. Wolf was shaken out of his customary stolidity: he was trembling with eagerness as he pressed his ear to the door.

At last Bartels seemed to be able to get a word in. 'I will make every enquiry, of course,' Wolf heard him say. 'The *Herr Doktor* may depend on me ... I will do my best ... Naturally ... An excellent plan ... The *Herr Doktor* is never at the end of his resources ..., I cannot guarantee success, but I shall take every possible step . . .'

Wolf was suddenly aware that silence had fallen within the room. Bartels must have hung up — in a panic Wolf scrambled back to the salon. But it was a good ten minutes before Bartels appeared at the door. He found the visitor tramping up and down, smoking a cigar.

Bartels was most *empressé*. 'A thousand apologies, *lieber Herr*, for putting you in this cold room,' he exclaimed. 'But the house has only recently been reopened. Come into the sitting-room where it's warm, and you shall have a glass of brandy.'

Back in the sitting-room he filled two glasses. 'You are stopping at Salzburg, no doubt?' he said, while his visitor toasted himself against the stove. 'You must give me your address before you go and we'll speak of this matter another time, for I must tell you I'm compelled to go out now on urgent business.' As he spoke, there was the sound of a motor outside, and through the window Wolf saw a car emerge into the road. But Bartels seemed curiously reluctant to let his visitor go. He began to speak of New York, and insisted on Wolf's taking another brandy. Then he started to ask questions about the depression. A lot of people had lost their money, he supposed: even the greatest fortunes like the Rockefellers' had been reduced, he'd heard: how had the others fared? The Vanderbilts, the Astors, the Dukes? Wolf answered these queries to the best of his ability, sipping his brandy and wondering what they were leading up to. Ah, now he had it!

'When I was in America,' Bartels said with careful indifference, 'I used to hear of a man called Fane — Cyrus M. Fane — who was supposed to be immensely wealthy. He's dead now, I know, but I was wondering whether his family had kept their money.'

Wolf was so excited that he had to take another drink of brandy before he would trust himself to speak.

'I believe so,' he answered. 'At any rate, they have the reputation of being still extremely wealthy...'

'The children, that is?' Bartels remarked casually. 'A boy and a girl, isn't it? Twins, I believe.'

'I think so!'

The other held out his hand. 'I see the car is there. I would offer to drive you into Salzburg, but I'm going in the opposite direction. You came out by train, I suppose? Where are you stopping?'

'At the Hotel Erzherzog!'

They shook hands. 'Führich, you said the name was?' Bartels wanted to know.

'*Jawohl*, Herr Bartels — Reinhold Führich!'

The other shook his head. 'I can't place him. But there, in our profession, *lieber* Herr von König, names are a secondary consideration, something you change with your collar!' He tittered throatily.

An enormous gray racing car, mud-splashed to the very hood, stood in the lane, a chauffeur wrapped in furs at the wheel. The housekeeper helped Bartels into a vast, fur-lined overcoat, handed him fur cap, fur gloves, goggles — a longish trip was indicated, Wolf reflected. Bartels mounted beside the driver and the car shot off at a reckless pace down the hill.

With despair in his heart, Wolf trudged back to the inn. Here was a turn of events he had not anticipated! With the start they had, by the time he could procure a car — if one were available in that remote village — the lean, gray roadster would be beyond effective pursuit. All he could do was to sit down and await Bartels's return. In the meantime, he supposed, he might as well ring up the Hotel Erzherzog at Salzburg and see if Robin or Ned had replied to his telegrams.

On calling the hotel he had a joyful surprise. Robin came to the telephone. He and Cant had just arrived. They were all for joining Wolf immediately; but Wolf said 'No!' — he was disinclined to stir up local gossip by the simultaneous descent of two more total strangers upon the Goldene Rose — he himself would come in to Salzburg. Bartels was away for several hours, if not for the rest of the day, he reflected, and Maier undertook to keep a sharp lookout and ring Wolf at Salzburg in the event of Bartels reappearing before the other was back. The local postmaster had a flivver, and an hour later Wolf found himself at lunch with his two confederates.

Robin gave the German a rapid sketch of the progress of events since they had parted on the boat. Then Wolf described his interview of that morning. Robin listened with a puzzled air.

'One thing's clear to me,' he remarked when Wolf had finished, 'and that is, that Fane's still alive . . .'

'And enjoying his honeymoon with the little lady at Baden-Baden,' Cant put in.

'And Bartels is off there to find them, no?' Wolf suggested.

'Ned can tell us that,' said Robin. 'We must wait to hear from Ned. He found some air service or other to take him down there this morning — he should be there by this. But it won't harm to wire him that Bartels may be on his way there to see the Lassagne woman. What intrigues me is that, at our interview with the old ruffian, Clubfoot seems to have been telling the truth. To judge by this telephone conversation you overheard, Wolf, Grundt really doesn't know where Fane and the girl are at present, and has ordered Bartels to produce them. If I'm right it means that, in all probability, Bartels intends to bring them back here!'

Wolf grunted. 'It may be. But if Bartels knows where

they are — at Baden-Baden, or wherever it is — why
didn't he say so on the telephone this morning? He only
promised to make enquiries...'

Robin shrugged. 'He may be double-crossing Clubfoot — I wouldn't put it past him: all these professional
agents are as crooked as they make 'em.' He frowned.
'I wish I knew what Grundt's game was. What does he
want with Fane, now that he has the plans?'

'I suppose you realize,' Cant struck in suddenly, 'that
if Bartels brings the young lovers here, Grundt will likewise appear!'

'It's true!' Wolf declared, much impressed.

'I'd thought of that,' said Robin. 'That's why I'm unwilling to dissipate our forces until we hear from Ned.
I'm inclined to agree with Wolf that it's no good attract-
ing unnecessary attention to ourselves for the time being,
so I suggest that he return to his Goldene Rose alone and
await developments, while, as for Cant and me...'

He broke off. A page was at his elbow. 'Baden-Baden
calling you on the telephone, Herr Dallas.'

Robin was a long time absent, or so it seemed to his
impatient companions. At length he came back.

'Well,' he said, 'she's there!'

'And Fane?' Wolf and Cant demanded in unison.

'No sign of him as yet, Ned says. She's at the Hotel
Schlemmer, alone: Ned has taken a room in the same
hotel. He doesn't want me to join him for the present
in case she really is Liselotte: he won't risk her identifying
me until he has found out whether Fane isn't somewhere
in the offing. As soon as he picks up any trace of Fane,
he'll tip us off: meanwhile, I warned him about Bartels.'
He shrugged his shoulders. 'Well, that's all, boys.
We've just got to wait!'

'Ciel!' cried Cant. 'I'm sick of waiting. It's as bad
as the war.'

Robin gave him his wistful smile. 'So it is, old boy. You remember the definition: "Long periods of intense boredom broken by short spells of acute fear"?'

'I'd rather be scared than bored, *moi!*'

Wolf grunted: his air was disapproving. 'And what of Clubfoot? Where has he disappeared to?'

The Englishman veiled his eyes. 'I think we may take it that wherever we run across young Fane, our friend Doctor Grundt won't be far away,' he said.

CHAPTER XV

The Major on the Job

'OF COURSE, I've been to Europe dozens of times before,' said Patricia Fane. 'But it's always been on frivolous sorts of stunts — Paris for the spring collections, London for the season. And I've flown quite a bit on the Continent. Three years ago, soon after I'd passed my pilot's certificate, I spent one whole summer in London, and rather a nice boy in the Guards, who belonged to the Household Brigade Flying Club and had his own Moth, persuaded me to buy one, too. He and I were always flapping over to Le Touquet or Deauville or the Eden-Roc or somewhere...'

'I read about him in my tabloid,' observed the major sedately. '"Love in the Clouds," they headed the story, and he was the ninth — or was it the twenty-ninth? — earl or something. Why didn't you marry his lordship?'

'Adenoids,' was the crisp answer. 'Besides, he had red hair — I decided we had enough red hair in the family. It was all very tiresome, his going sentimental about me, because, of course, it meant that our trips were off. But I kept the Moth on, and the following year when I came over, I made a lot of flights on my own: once, among other places, to the Lido and on to Salzburg for the Festival, once to Berlin and once, even, as far as Warsaw. This year, before this business with Jimmy came up, I meant to try and get as far as Cairo in the new ship, or even India. But the way it's turned out will be ever so much more exciting. I feel I'm going to see Europe from an entirely new angle, flying with you into Germany like this. It's like being in the secret

service — I always thought secret service work in-
credibly romantic!'

They had dined late in the Ritz grill after the major
had seen Robin and Cant off to Salzburg by the Orient
Express. The major did not disclose whether or not he
had told Robin of their plan to fly down to Baden-
Baden together, and Patricia did not raise the point —
it was obvious that she regarded the matter as settled,
for on being shown up to her suite, Ned found her poring
over maps with a very affable gentleman from the French
Aero Club. Everything was arranged, she informed
Hartigan. The plane would be waiting for them at daybreak: the car, already despatched by train, should be at
Baden-Baden the following night.

The major sighed enviously. This was travel *de luxe*,
with a vengeance. In the rare moments of affluence in
his life he had always been wont to do himself well,
and he expanded to luxury like a flower in the sun. He
was uncomfortably aware of having led Robin to believe
that he was taking the French plane service via Bâle;
but it would be time enough to thrash that little matter
out when Robin discovered it. In the meantime he
solaced himself with the thought that, by humouring
Patricia Fane, he was acting in the best interests of the
four, for he gathered, from what the girl had told him,
that Robin had been abominably rude to her.

That night the pair of them sat long over their coffee,
talking. 'I was never in the secret service myself,' remarked the major meditatively, as he sliced the ash
of his cigar against the stem of his brandy glass. 'But
I've known fellows who were in it, and they'll tell you
that it's a mighty dirty business, run as it is by all
manner of tramps, both male and female, double-
crossers and every kind of scalawag. To hear them talk
you'd think there's less romance in it than picking

pockets or pilfering milk bottles, while as for the woman agent, the alluring adventuresses of fiction — well, as far as I can make out, they belong one and all to a profession that's at least as old as that of the spy, and he, as you know, appears in the Bible!'

'You make it sound dreadfully sordid,' said the girl.

'That's exactly what it is most of the time — sordid and dull into the bargain. All the same, when one of the star turns — a fellow like our friend Francis Oke-wood, for example — gets yarning, you're apt to dis-cover that the game has its rare moments of thrill which are all the more exciting for being staged in such ap-parently normal and peaceful settings as this!'

His cigar described a gesture which embraced the restaurant. Save for themselves and a solitary diner, the place had emptied. The other guest, a middle-aged individual with gold-rimmed spectacles, had the *Temps* propped up in front of him — from time to time his long nose appeared above the newspaper.

'Okewood says,' the major went on, 'that there's nothing so incredible that it can't happen in secret service work. And so, Miss Patricia, although, under your expert piloting, we shall in all probability travel down smoothly and securely to our destination to-morrow, don't give up hope — you may yet find your spice of romance!'

The waiter brought the bill. She signed it and said with a sigh: 'I don't believe I want it, really. I guess you can keep your old romance, Major Ned, as long as we find Jimmy. If he's really there with this blonde of his, I know I can make him listen to me.' She pushed back her chair. 'Well, we have an early start — we'd better go to bed!'

The lone diner was also leaving. As they passed his table the waiter was helping him into his green raincoat.

It was all too easy, the major decided. Patricia Fane,
ı vision of workmanlike charm in her canvas flying-
ıuit and leather helmet, brought them expertly over the
ıeeling checkerboard of France, the wooded hilltops of
ıouthern Germany, to the Baden-Baden airfield at
Baden-Oos. The deep blue ceiling, the fleeting earth,
:he exhilaration of their speed, the luxurious comfort of
:he cabin with its silver fittings and soft leather chairs,
ınthralled the major. He was as excited as a schoolboy.
Not so his fellow passengers, those veterans of the air.
Mrs. Evans, the grave and elderly maid, having imbibed
ıome secret specific from a small bottle she took from her
ɔag, never lifted her eyes from her crocheting; while as
ʾor Phil, after an initial bout of restlessness he curled
ıp and went to sleep at Ned's feet. A car, ordered by
:elegram from Paris, awaited them at the aerodrome,
ınd by half-past nine they were rolling into Baden-
Baden.

A little disagreement developed as to where they should
ıtay. Hartigan firmly vetoed the girl's proposal that
:hey should go to the same hotel.

'I'm not going to risk frightening the lady off if she
ıhould discover who you are, and that you and I are in
:his together,' he declared.

'I can give a wrong name — I can call myself Evans
ɔr something,' Patricia proposed plaintively; but the
najor would have none of it. Her passport, the plane's
ɔapers, were in the name of Fane. They must separate,
ɔut he promised to keep in touch with her, and with this
ıhe had to be content. It was the off-season and the
eading hotels were only beginning to open. At one of the
arger ones, off the Lange-Strasse, the major deposited
:he party.

He went on alone in the car to the post-office. There
aboriously, in his broken German, he questioned the

counter clerk. 'I'm looking for a friend of mine, Madame Arlette Lassagne. Do you happen to know where she's staying?'

The man spoke over his shoulder to his colleague at the telegraph pigeon-hole. 'Lassagne? The Hôtel Schlemmer, isn't it?'

'*Jawohl!*' came the answer back. 'In the Lichtentaler Allee,' the first clerk elucidated civilly.

The major was entranced — it was as simple as that! 'Do you know whether a Mr. Fane is staying there, too?' he enquired with bated breath.

But this time they could not help him. They had no record of anyone called Fane, American or anybody else. Hartigan thanked them and took his leave.

The Hôtel Schlemmer stood in its own grounds in an avenue near the Kursaal. The major left his car at the gate and went up the short drive on foot. On a gravelled space at the side, in front of a glazed-in terrace, a number of cars were parked. The letter 'F' painted on one of the rear wings of a smart green saloon caught Hartigan's eye. He glanced at the bonnet. It was a French car; but the license plates were German.

He looked around. At that early hour the parking-place was deserted. The next moment he had the car door open and was peering at the dashboard, congratulating himself on recalling the French regulation which obliges motor-car owners to display their name and address. There it was, engraved on a little metal plate: 'Madame Arlette Lassagne, 79, rue Pichegru, Auteuil.'

He went into the hotel and registered boldly, 'Major Edward Hartigan, Paris.' He forbore to enquire for Madame Lassagne, but, with his most casual air, asked whether Mr. James Fane was stopping there. With a sudden sinking of the heart he saw the desk clerk shake his head. They had no one of that name in the hotel.

'And he hasn't been staying here recently?' Hartigan persisted.

The clerk turned back the pages of the register, then shook his head once more. 'No, Major!'

Hartigan took the register from the clerk and glanced through the arrivals of the past month. Under March 9 he saw, in an extravagant, ornate hand, the entry, 'Arlette Lassagne, Paris.'

There was no Fane in the register.

Somewhat nonplussed, yet with a sense of relief at the thought that he had reached his journey's end, he paid off the car that had brought them from the airport and retired to his room to bathe and change. On redescending to the lounge, his first care was to scan the parking-place for the green saloon.

It was still there. A wizened old fellow, sporting a uniform cap inscribed 'Hôtel Schlemmer,' who was in the act of mounting his bicycle, was the only person in sight. The messenger pedalled off, leaving Hartigan alone. The sunshine was pleasantly warm. The major lit a cigar and stood sunning himself. He was wrestling with a desire to pump the reception clerk discreetly about Madame Lassagne. But he guessed that a lady of her exciting profession must be constantly on the *qui vive*, and, familiar with the gossiping propensity of the average hotel clerk, especially where an attractive woman is concerned, he found himself quite unable to hit upon any form of enquiry which would not be promptly reported back and as promptly arouse her suspicions. Reluctantly he discarded the idea: he would have to rely upon his not inconsiderable experience of scraping acquaintance with engaging and unaccompanied females to get the information direct from the lady herself.

Thus musing, it occurred to him that possibly a closer examination of the car might throw some further light upon the subject. Cigar in mouth, he strolled languidly towards the green saloon. There was a map on the seat which he gathered up through the window and slipped under his coat; a pair of driving-gloves and a duster in the door pocket — nothing else.

He returned to the lounge. The only woman in sight was an elderly person who was writing postcards at a desk. Choosing a chair from which he could survey both the elevator and, through the swing door, the green saloon outside, he sat down and unfolded the map.

It was a large-scale plan of the city and its environs. A small cross in red ink marked a number which he saw, by referring to a table printed at the top of the plan, denoted the site of the Hôtel Schlemmer. Away on the outskirts of the town was another little cross, standing beside a name in type so small that he had to bring out his spectacles to read it.

The name was Hasenberg. Confirming the German suffix, the spidery contour shading showed it to be a hill. A road called the Hasenberg-Weg led up to it — as near as he could make out, from the prolongation of the avenue on which the Hôtel Schlemmer was situated. But the little red cross was on the top of the hill. There were no other marks on the plan.

Hartigan folded the map and went out into the sun·shine again. The coast was still clear and he dropped the map through the window of the green saloon upon the seat. Then he consulted his watch. It was past noon — Robin and Cant should be at Salzburg by this. He made his way to the telephone.

On emerging from the booth, he made his way to the desk again, and after hunting through the register asked the clerk if he happened to know where Herr Bartels was stopping in Baden-Baden. The man shook his head — it was evident the name meant nothing to him.

Save for the stooped, shawled back of the postcard writer, the lounge was empty. The presence of the car outside, Hartigan told himself, suggested that its owner was still in her room. Well, he could wait — it wouldn't be the first time he'd kicked his heels, waiting for a woman. He returned to his chair and sat down.

Puffing at his cigar, he gave himself over to his thoughts. His mind went back over the telephone conversation he had just had with Robin. Poor old Robin, how eager he had been to join him! Ned was glad he had squelched that idea — if the owner of the green car were really Liselotte, Robin's appearance would have given the whole show away. Now his attention drifted to the map. That little red cross, what did it signify? And what exactly, and where, was the Hasenberg?

He resisted an impulse to go to the desk and cross-examine the clerk on the subject. Patience! — too much zeal now might ruin everything. The woman herself should tell him.

Why did women take such an infernal time to get up in the morning? It was nearly one o'clock: he had breakfasted at four; he was aching for food.

CHAPTER XVI

The Pavilion with the Blue Shutters

HARTIGAN was finishing his lunch when, out of a little flurry of waiters, a woman made a languorous entry into the dining-room. All through the meal, which he took in solitary state at a table against the wall, he had watched the door. The Schlemmer was evidently a family hotel, patronized by Germans of the bourgeois class — among the drab and mostly middle-aged women who drifted into the narrow and rather cheerless restaurant, there was none even remotely resembling the one he had come to seek.

The *maître d'hôtel's* deferential *'Bonjour, madame!'* first called his attention to her. One look, and he knew that his search was done; one look, and he knew, moreover, that this must be that same Liselotte who had cost his friend his career. Robin had described her minutely, and a phrase of his came back as, from across the width of the narrow passage between the tables, Ned studied her: — 'dainty as a wax doll,' Robin had said.

The phrase fitted like a glove, Ned reflected, as she sat down at what was clearly her regular table in the window. She was *petite*, and blonde, and adorable, with ringlets, the colour of ripe wheat peeping out from under her jaunty hat and framing dark-fringed, violet eyes, a pert, little nose, a rosebud mouth. Her complexion was pink and white with a sort of high glaze that stressed the doll analogy, and the prettily foreshortened upper lip disclosed a row of pearly, milk-white teeth. She was thirty, Hartigan remembered, but she looked much younger.

She had a rather discontented air as she scanned the menu. When she had given her order, she glanced casually round the dining-room — by this, the two of them had it to themselves. As soon as their eyes met, the major, veteran of such well-tested preliminaries, took his away. But presently he was aware that she was eyeing him again, and this time he let his gaze rest boldly on her face.

With a smile he showed his cigar and said across the gangway, 'I hope my cigar doesn't bother you.'

She smiled back at him. 'I don't mind it.' Her voice was low and caressing, the accent faintly foreign.

'It looks like spring was on the way,' he remarked heartily.

She glanced out of the window, then back at him. 'It seems to be a lovely day,' was the demure rejoinder.

That low voice of hers did something to his heart-beats. He was vividly conscious of the appeal she sent forth. Almost unconsciously, as it seemed — there were no less than two waiters, their faces wreathed in smiles, fussing about her under the officious direction of the *maître d'hôtel*.

'I got in only this morning,' the major returned to the attack. 'This town strikes me as being pretty dead. What's there to do here, anyway?'

She moved her shoulders. 'You can drink the waters, go for walks.' She was looking at him again.

He met her gaze with a quizzical expression in his dark eyes. 'What do you do with yourself all day?' he demanded.

She shrugged once more. 'Nothing. But then I'm here for a rest.'

On that, with the self-possession that characterized

her every movement, she took a magazine she had brought in with her, opened it, propped it against a carafe, and began to read.

It was dismissal — at least for the moment — and the major accepted it. He rose and went out. But no farther than the lounge. He was ostensibly studying a theatre poster beside the porter's desk when the little madame appeared from the dining-room, a natty figure in her short jacket of russet-suède, brown tweed skirt and tiny golfing brogues. She did not stop, but went straight out through the swing door. A moment later the whirr of a self-starter resounded from the parking-place. Hartigan reached the porch in time to see the green saloon swing by, making for the drive.

He gazed about him in despair. Then his eye encountered the messenger's bicycle leaning against the house. There was no sign of the messenger and, thanks to the German siesta hour, no one was in sight: it must be twenty years since he had last ridden a push-bike, the major reflected, as he grabbed the machine.

Perhaps under the influence of the golden afternoon, the little madame drove at a moderate pace. At any rate, the green car was still visible between the lime trees of the *chaussée*, heading away from the centre of the town when, pedalling briskly, he neared the front gate. Rapidly he was left behind; but the road was straight, and when, in the far distance, the car swung to the right and disappeared, he was able to mark the spot by counting the telegraph poles.

It was the eighteenth pole. Opposite, a side road curved steeply upward between the firs. Hartigan's heart sank when he saw the angle at which it mounted. He jumped off his bicycle. Then he caught sight of the name on the finger-post at the corner and his spirits revived. 'Hasenberg-Weg,' he read, and his thoughts instantly flashed back to the cross on the little madame's map. Streaming with perspiration though he was, he set off on foot up the hill, pushing his bicycle beside him.

The climb seemed endless: the hill grew steeper and steeper. He passed one or two villas, but they were shuttered and evidently deserted. He had made up his mind that the green saloon had got away from him when, unexpectedly, round one of the innumerable bends in the road, he came upon it parked alongside the hedge. There was nobody in it, but a lane opposite, winding upward towards a roof rising from the trees, suggested the direction the little madame had taken.

Still pushing his machine, Hartigan toiled up the lane. It ambled to a dead end before the entrance pillars of a small park surrounding the house he had remarked from below. Iron gates disclosed a wooden châlet, ornate and garish, with a gray roof bearing in red and green slates the date of construction, 1898. Above the door a large sign read, 'Pension Hasenberg.'

It was apparent that the place had not yet opened for the season, for every shutter was closed and there was no sign of life discernible. But the road finished there and it was the only house on the hilltop. Dumping his bicycle out of sight in a plantation of young firs that came down to the surrounding wall, the major entered the grounds. The carriage drive stopped at the front door, but a path skirted the house, and, following this, he found himself in the rear of the premises, gazing across a prospect of trees and grassy knolls at the mountain-side. Two or three small pavilions showed red roofs among the trees, and from one of them a chimney sent up a spiral of smoke into the clear air.

Dodging from tree to tree, he went forward. The pavilion whence the smoke was rising was on two floors, with a verandah below. There were chairs and cushions on the verandah and the front door was open. The shutters, a cheerful blue upon a cream background, were folded back. The pavilion was evidently in occupation.

A flight of shallow steps led up to the entrance. But the major remained under cover of the trees which stood thickly about, approaching the house from the side. He was glad he had done so when presently he heard a door bang and perceived a man in a blue apron emerge from the adjacent pavilion, painted a dingy brown and separated from the first by a small apple orchard, and disappear — by the clanking sounds that followed he seemed to be working a pump. Stealthily the major worked forward. Now he was at the side of the pavilion with the blue shutters. Voices struck upon his ear. He glanced up and saw that a window on the first floor was open. A man in what appeared to be a gray woollen skiing cap and a gray sweater stood with his back to the window, his arms about a figure in green.

The man was speaking. Every word drifted distinctly down to the little copse where the major lurked among the firs. Ned's heart thumped as he listened, for the language was English and it was an American voice that spoke there, an educated voice, vibrant with youth and feeling.

'Sweetness,' it said, 'I see you every day, I know, but it isn't enough. If we make this move, do you swear we'll be together all the time, that you'll never leave me?'

The woman laughed, a little crooning laugh. 'But, Jimmy, darling,' she answered with her pretty touch of accent, 'I 'ave promised you over and over again. As soon as it is dark, I shall bring the car, we shall sleep in Basel and next day we shall be at Lausanne and nothing ever more shall separate us. N'est-ce pas, mon chéri?'

'You said that before,' he told her grudgingly. 'But something always came in the way.'

Her hands caressed his face. 'This time it's serious, you'll see, *mon coco*. Max has packed your bags — as soon as I have done one or two commissions in the town, I shall be back to fetch you.'

He drew her to him. 'Honey, I don't know what I'd do without you. Ah, Arlette, sweetheart, I'm crazy about you!' He kissed her passionately.

'*Voilà!*' she exclaimed, gently withdrawing from his arms. 'Now I must really go. You will read your book and Max will give you your supper and before you know it, I shall be back with the car.'

They went away from the window and out of Ned's field of view.

He was aghast. There were not more than two hours of light left and, as soon as darkness fell, they would move. If he were going to act, he must act at once. But how? Fane was clearly infatuated with this woman — short of carrying him off by force, he saw little hope of extricating the young fool from her clutches. But the attempt must be made. As he was debating the point, she appeared suddenly at the pavilion door. At her cry of 'Max!' the man in the blue apron came hurrying through the orchard, and they went off in the direction of the main house together.

It was now or never, the major decided. He paused for an instant to listen. The man and the woman had disappeared: all was silent within the pavilion. Breaking from the copse he ran up the steps and into the house.

It was at this moment he discovered that he did not have his pistol with him — he had forgotten it when he changed his clothes. No matter, he had his fists — at need he would knock young Fane out and hide him in the bushes somewhere until he could return with a car. The important thing was to get it over with before the man in the blue apron came back.

Young Fane was lying on the bed when the major burst in. Hartigan had no more than a fleeting expression of a comfortable, rather prettily furnished bedroom — his whole attention was focussed on the figure that sprang to its feet in surprise as he appeared.

'Listen, Fane,' he said, in a low and hurried voice, 'your sister's looking for you. I've come to take you to her.'

The young man stared. His face was curiously thin and almost devoid of colour — it occurred to Hartigan that the boy looked very ill; but his resemblance to his sister was unmistakable.

'Who the devil are you?' he demanded rather thickly.

'Who I am doesn't matter,' retorted Hartigan sharply. 'But I'm here to tell you that if you don't grab this chance and come away with me, you're apt to be arrested by the Federal Secret Service — I guess you know what for. Come on, Fane, we've no time to lose!'

'Why do you keep on calling me Fane?' the young man demanded — his voice was slurred and Hartigan wondered whether he had been drinking. 'My name's not Fane — it's — it's — well, anyway, it's not Fane. And now will you get the hell out of this and let me sleep?'

The major caught him by the arm. 'Don't be a damned fool! You're coming with me!'

With surprising strength the other flung him off and snatched up a chair. 'Max!' he shouted. 'Max!'

'Do you want to ruin us, you madman?' exclaimed Ned.

But Fane rushed at him with chair uplifted, yelling, 'Get out! Get out!'

The major retreated a pace. Fane, his face distorted with rage, was between him and the window and he had his back to the door. He heard footsteps thunder up the stairs, but he dared not take his eyes from his aggressor.

Then the door behind him opened with a crash — he swung around in time to catch a glimpse of a crimson, pimply face with chins that hung down, of a hand grasping a pistol uplifted to strike. With merciless force the blow descended and Ned Hartigan slumped senseless to the floor.

CHAPTER XVII

Miss Fane Has a Caller

PHIL at her heels, Patricia Fane came in from her walk. Baden-Baden out of the season did not appeal to her, she decided. Already she was bored with the place, bored with her own company, bored, most particularly, with Mrs. Evans, who revealed by a certain deliberate surliness of mien her evident disapproval of their visiting a social centre at such a time — she had long since made the discovery that Mrs. Evans was at heart a snob. She was disgusted with the major, too. She had waited in all the morning in the hope that he would take her out to lunch: not only did he not appear, but he did not even telephone to let her know where he was staying. Unfavourably impressed by the dyspeptic looks of the majority of her fellow guests, she avoided the dining-room and lunched off a salad in her suite. Then she set off for a ramble through the streets with Phil.

It was getting on for dusk when she returned to the hotel. There was still no word from the major, only an advice from the railway that her car had arrived, and she bade the desk clerk send someone to bring it to the hotel.

She was crossing the lounge to the lift when a man stepped up to her. 'Miss Fane?' he said.

Newspaper man, was her first thought. She would have passed him by without replying, but he went on, speaking with a strong German accent, 'Please, it is important. I haf a message for you . . .'

On that she stopped. It was a respectably dressed individual, no longer young. Gold spectacles, a long nose, lent him a sober air — he looked like a lawyer or a doctor. A green raincoat was folded across his arm and he carried a small brown bag. He leaned towards her impressively. 'From Major Hartigan,' he explained in a hoarse whisper.

She was interested at once. 'Oh?'

'He think he find your Herr brudder — he want you to come at once.'

She gasped with excitement. 'He's found him? Not really? I can't believe it. Where are they?'

The other looked mysterious. 'Not far from here. You go wiz me, I take you, yes?'

She hesitated, considering him distrustfully. 'But — who are you?'

He bowed stiffly. 'Excuse! I introduce myself. Doctor Keller — I help Major Hartigan.'

She continued to stare. 'Haven't I seen you before, somewhere? In Paris, wasn't it?'

His smile was benign. 'Possible. I was working for the Herr Major there...'

'I know' — her face cleared — 'you were dining at the Ritz Grill last night when we were there!'

He laughed. 'The Fräulein has a good memory.'

She was still a little ill at ease. 'But why didn't Major Hartigan tell me about you?'

He chuckled. 'The Herr Major is more disgreet than many people realize.' He lowered his voice again. 'He says for you to call the airfield and have the aeroplane ready; ja, and you must bring the aviation papers and your passport with you, he said.'

She frowned, perplexed. 'Why?'

The other's voice sank to a mere whisper. 'I think, maybe, he plan to take your brudder away suddenly.' With an air of extreme caution he cast a glance over his shoulder and put his lips to her ear. 'There's a Federal secret service agent in town,' he breathed.

She started — she had heard from Hartigan all about the adventures of Robin and Cant at Hamburg.

'Not one of these men from Hamburg the major told me about?' She was rather pale.

He nodded solemnly. 'You understand, then, there is no time to lose, Fräulein. If you would have the goodness to arrange about your aeroplane . . .'

'Give me two minutes — the papers are upstairs.'

'I have an automobile — I shall wait for you outside. Horry, Fräulein, please!'

Grasping his bag, he trotted off, a kindly, efficient little man, she thought, as she made for the lift.

In five minutes she joined him at the door. She had changed her hat for a beret and donned a tweed overcoat with a fox collar — she was vibrant with excitement. Phil was in her arms, but Keller made her send the dog back.

'You do not understand,' he told her gravely as they drove away. 'Once we arrive at the house where the Herr Major expect you, we must be on our guard. A leetle dog belling' — she assumed he meant 'barking' — 'might ruin everything.'

'My brother will be there, won't he? I shall see my brother?' she asked eagerly.

They were running out along a leafy avenue. He nodded stolidly. 'Sure, sure. But we must be, ach! so quiet like mouses until I find out what the Herr Major has done about the voman!'

'The woman? Of course. I'd forgotten about her.' She sounded dismayed.

'And this agent from Vashington — we must make sure he isn't anywhere around, no? But don't be scared, Fräulein — I fix eferything.'

His tone reassured her and she began to look about

her. They were climbing the heights that surrounded the town. The evening was chilly and sunless: the light failing fast. Once clear of the city they encountered no one and the villas became rarer as they mounted the ridge — all those she saw seemed to be unoccupied.

'What is this place we're going to?' she demanded presently.

'It is called the Pension Hasenberg,' said Keller, and pointed. 'See, we are there! We go in by the back — it is safer.'

The name was on a sign over an open gate which brought them into a flagged yard. Trees grew all around, and in the gathering gloom some adjacent buildings that spread their low roofs among the branches visible above the wall of the yard were mere blotches of white. Across a vista of trees and shrubs Patricia was aware of the gaunt silhouette of a house outlined against the leaden evening sky. The whole place was enveloped in silence.

Her companion hopped out of the car. A finger on his lips, he signed to her to stay where she was and vanished through a gate at the far end of the yard. Two or three minutes elapsed, then he was beckoning to her from the gate. Without speaking, he led her along a grass-grown roadway that split in two to circle a paddock of apple trees flanked by two pavilions or bungalows, one trim enough with blue shutters, the other much shabbier and painted a uniform shade of faded buff. They entered the buff pavilion and passed at once into a small parlour where an oil lamp burned on the table. A glass partition with a door in the centre separated the parlour from the dining-room behind.

Keller took the girl's hands. 'Wait here,' he said in an impressive whisper, 'and, before all, as you value your brudder's safety, don't show yourself. Whether it is the

Herr Major or anyone else, you must not be seen, until I
come back for you — is it understood?'

She nodded. 'All right.'

'If anyone should come, go into the back room and
make no sound. It is very important, no?'

Alert and tense, she nodded again. 'I understand.'

He smiled at her encouragingly. '*So!* Now I go. I may
be a little time, but you wait for me, *hein?* And you don't
stir from here, is it agreed?' He paused. 'So that I may
find you quickly again, no?'

She tried to smile back, but the hoarse whisper in which
he spoke, his mysterious air, the silence surrounding them
as the shadows deepened in the grounds outside, were too
much for her nerves.

'Must I really stay here alone?' she said unwillingly.
'Where are you going?'

He patted her shoulder and laughed. '*Aber*, Fräulein
— to let the Herr Major and your brudder know that you
are here.'

'You mean, you'll bring my brother back with you?'

'Certainly. But first I must see a little how the land
lies.'

She sighed. 'All right. But be as quick as you can.'

With an expressionless face he crept out.

But for the lamp it would have been already dark in the
little room. She heard the wind rustling the branches of
the apple trees. Then another sound, echoing through the
stillness, came to her ears. It was the clatter of a car
starting up. The sound seemed to come from the direction
of the yard and she felt sure that Keller had driven away.
She laid her hand on her heart in sudden alarm. Where
was he going? Did it mean that Ned hadn't yet arrived
and that Keller had gone to fetch him? And what about
Jimmy? If Ned had sent for her there, it must mean that
he'd traced Jimmy and his girl to the Pension Hasenberg.

She glanced about the parlour and smiled briefly. Somehow, she couldn't picture Jimmy living in a place like this. The room was sparsely furnished with the cheapest kind of furniture and there was an oilcloth on the centre table — not a book or a picture anywhere. Maybe he and the girl were living in the large house she had seen as they drove up.

She was engaged with these reflections when it seemed to her that her ear detected a light footfall outside. The next moment a voice, a woman's voice, called sharply outside, 'Max!' For an instant she was petrified with fear. Then, remembering Keller's warning, she slipped noiselessly through the glass partition into the adjoining room and as noiselessly closed the door. There, flattened against the wall in the darkness, she peered through a clear space in the ground-glass panel into the lighted parlour and, with heart thumping, waited.

She did not have long to wait, for almost immediately the parlour door was thrust open, a voice said in German, 'Max, *wo bleibst Du denn?*' and a woman came in. From the inner room Patricia had only time to remark that the intruder was fair and young and dainty when there was a step in the passage and a man entered swiftly and, closing the door, set his back to it. With a cry the woman whirled about: at the sight of him she fell back, her hands pressed in terror to her face.

'Good-evening, Liselotte!' said the man in English.

It was Robin Dallas.

CHAPTER XVIII

Liselotte

HIS hat was pushed back from his forehead, showing a lock of hair, dank upon it; there was mud on his shoes and a broken twig caught up in the fold of his trousers. His nostrils opened and shut and he breathed quickly, with lips pressed tightly together, as though he had been running. For the rest, his face was a bloodless mask, drained of the last vestige of colour. Only the eyes seemed to live, fixed on the terrified figure that confronted him in a steady, unflinching stare.

There was something frightening about the woman's static pose. She seemed unable to speak or to move, eyes glazed with consternation, while she dug her vermilion nails into her cheeks. At last, in a voice husky with fear she gasped, 'You!'

He said roughly: 'I want young Fane. Where is he?'

The first shock of surprise over, her self-control was beginning to come back.

'Why, Robin,' she exclaimed caressingly, 'is that all you find to say to me after all this time?'

'That's all,' he answered bluntly. 'Where is he?'

She went up to him and laid hold of the lapels of his coat. 'And I thought you had come to see *me!* You have changed, *chéri* — you've cut off your moustache. Tell me, do you think I also have changed?'

He shook her off. 'Answer my question, please. I've no time to waste.'

She stood back affronted and made a little helpless gesture of the hands.

He said sternly, 'You heard what I said. Where's Fane?'

She affected to study her nails. 'You are mistaken, *mon ami*. I have no idea what you are talking about.'

He laughed raspingly. 'Oh, yes, you have. You took him to the Café Helga at Hamburg where Akawa, the Japanese, was murdered.'

Though her answer was a soft laugh, she was on her guard. 'My poor Robin, aren't you being r-rather dr-ramatic?'

'Stop playing the fool!' he said while his dark eyes glowered. 'Where's Fane? I want him.'

She spread her hands. 'But if I tell you I don't even know this man, *mon ami!*'

He pursed his lips and frowned. 'You know him all right. It was you who got the plans that night. Do you wish me to believe that he was murdered, too? If so, I shall know how to act. You're still in Germany, remember — one word to the *Gestapo* and your number's up. The Brown Shirts have the headsman ready to deal with women like you.'

She seemed to shiver. Once more she approached him, with less assurance this time, and put her hand timidly on his arm. 'You wouldn't do this to me, Robin, *dis?*'

A mocking laugh answered her. 'Wouldn't I, though?' Stonily he gazed down at the flower-like face tilted at an appealing angle to his. 'No use making eyes at me, my dear — I'd turn you over to the tender mercies of Hitler and Company without a qualm. But — I'd rather find Fane. Come on, Lise, the game's up. What have you done with the boy?'

Through their long fringes the violet eyes glinted. She sighed heavily and shook her head. 'I don't know where he is. He went away — I haven't seen him for weeks. Oh, Robin, I was so fond of him: I've been so wretched.' She turned away forlornly and pressed a tiny scrap of cambric to her lips.

He gave an impatient ejaculation. 'Will you please stop lying? He's been living here, in this house, hasn't he?'
'It's not true!'
'Then how do *you* come to be here?'
She hesitated, then burst out: 'The man who owns it, he's — he's an old servant of mine. I just looked in to see about — to see about some trunks he has been taking care of for me.'
His laugh rang sarcastic. 'Is that so? Then you weren't waiting for a street car? What are you doing at Baden-Baden out of the season, anyway?' His tone was peremptory.
'I came to take the cure.'
'And our friend, Bartels — has he come to take the cure, too?'
She sprang away from him as though he had struck her. 'Bartels?' she echoed, aghast. Then she darted for the door. 'Let me out of here!'
But he barred the way. 'Not until you tell me where Fane is.'
Her small hands on his shoulders sought to thrust him aside. 'Let me out!' she cried; 'let me out, I say!' And when he stood fast she began to hammer with her clenched fists upon his chest. 'Robin, for the love of God, let me go!' she entreated.
He shook his head, smiling sardonically. 'Nothing doing, my sweet. You don't budge from this room until you answer my question!'
She swung away from him, breathing hard, her cheeks scarlet from the struggle, her fingers tearing at her handkerchief. 'I know you have hard feelings against me,' she said in a suffocated voice. 'I treated you badly, but I couldn't help myself.'
His face clouded over. 'We won't go into that, if you don't mind.'

'I wanted to appear at your trial or, at least, to make a declaration, explaining about that cheque. But they seized my papers, your letters, everything — I could do nothing. This man you saw me with at Munich, the big man who walked with a limp — I was in his power, Robin...'

'In his pay, you mean,' he told her coolly.

From the way she sighed, you would have said her heart was broken. 'Ah, *mon chéri*, you speak like that because you are angry against me. But there was a time when you loved me, Robin — you wanted to marry me. Have you forgotten that night on the Wannsee?'

'That's over and done with,' he retorted angrily, looking away from her. 'All I want to hear from you is where I can find Fane.'

She placed her hands on his shoulders. 'You were expelled from the Army, you went to prison through me — I do not forget that. I have thought often I should try and make — how do you say? — restitution, but I never knew what had become of you. Listen, *chéri*, this young American means nothing to you. If you'll forget him and let him and me go away together, as we had planned for this very night, you'll not find me ungrateful, *allez!* I will give you a full confession. It will exonerate you — you will receive back your sword as an officer. Look at me, *chéri!* What do you say?'

He would not meet her eyes. He made as though to shake her off.

'I want no bargain with you,' he muttered through clenched teeth.

Her voice was low and caressing. 'I will tell,' she said 'how I went to your rooms with a photographer and photographed that code. I'd had keys made — one for the street door, one for the house door, and one for that steel box where you kept your papers: I took wax im-

pressions, one afternoon when I was at the flat with you.
It's not hard, *allez*, when one knows the trick.'

'You were, of course, highly experienced,' he observed.

'Of what use to deny it? When a woman is friendless
and poor, she has to make a living as she can. Besides,
Grundt, this villain, had me at his mercy — at any
moment, he could have denounced me to one of half
a dozen governments whose secrets I had betrayed to
him ...'

He seemed to be staring along the vista of the past
she had unrolled, so fixedly, so sombrely, did he gaze
into space.

'That code,' he questioned hoarsely, 'how did you
manage about it?'

She hesitated, contemplating the unyielding profile
he presented. 'Do you remember the ball you took me
to at Grosvenor House that summer?' she said at last.
'It was a charity affair: the Prince of Wales was there
and you wore your medals. I felt faint, do you remember? and went to the ladies' room to lie down.'

He nodded bleakly. 'Park Street was only round the
corner, wasn't it? It was as simple as that! You'd
warned the camera-man, of course. Sent over specially,
I suppose?'

She inclined her head very slightly. 'One of Grundt's
men — he was waiting in the mews beside your house.
The whole thing didn't take ten minutes — I was back
at the ball within a quarter of an hour.'

'Slick work!' he commented.

She ignored the rancour in his tone and, her hands
cupped about his face, sought to make him look at her.
He resisted, but he did not take her hands away.

'If I put this all in writing,' she murmured caressingly,
smoothing his cheeks, 'and swear to it before a *notaire*,
they'll accept it, *pas vrai, mon petit* Robin, and give

you back your commission? I don't ask much in return — only that you go away and leave this young
man with me. *Voyons, chéri, sois gentil avec ta petite
Lise!*' She stroked his dark hair.

He shook his head. 'No.'

She sighed and dropped her hands.

'I deserve no mercy from you, I know that,' she said
with a little, fluttering sigh. 'But if you ever loved me —
and once you did — you'll be generous, *chéri*. This
young American is madly in love — he wants to marry
me. He's rich, and after the life I've led these past ten
years I cannot do without money. He's going to take me
out of all this' — her hands fluttered — 'out of all the
fear and ignominy I have known with Grundt. I'm
thirty, Robin, and in a little I shall be old. My value to
Grundt will be over and he will cast me aside, if he
doesn't hand me over to the Nazis, or the Fascists, or the
French, for death or life imprisonment. Besides, I could
love my Jimmy — he's so eager, and young, and sweet.
And he idolizes me. He wants to carry me away with
him to America: he says he'll buy a ranch in the West
where the sun always shines and the air is pure and
sparkling like champagne. Robin, *mon petit* Robin, don't
deprive me of this chance, I implore you! See, I go down
on my knees to you!'

So saying she fell at his feet, her arms about his waist,
the tears streaming down her cheeks. Sobs shook her:
her face was woebegone with grief — she looked like a
beautiful child mourning over a dead bird. Now at length
his gaze, tragic and resentful, was fixed upon her eyes that
mutely entreated him: instinctively his arms went out as
though to enfold her. But he dropped them to his side
and shook his head.

'No!' he said again.

'You refuse?' she cried, and this time a note of shrill-ness crept into the insinuating tones of her voice. 'Does it then mean so little to you to regain your honour? What is this young American to you?'

He shrugged sombrely. 'Nothing. But I pledged my word to find him and I must keep it. Stand up now and tell me what I want to know!'

She let him raise her to her feet, then, turning away walked to the table.

'And if I refuse?' she asked mutinously over her shoulder, dabbing at her eyes with her tiny handkerchief.

'You won't refuse,' he retorted.

'How do you know that he'll be willing to go with you?' Her eyes were suddenly watchful.

'I'll take care of that.' His voice was brisk and stern. 'Do you realize that he's accused of selling those plans to the Grundt organization?'

She laughed mockingly. 'You speak like a fool, my friend. As if that were not the best reason in the world for staying with me!'

'You mean that he parted with those plans to you of his own free will?'

Her reply was a ripple of silvery laughter. 'But, of course, my poor Robin!'

'We'll see about that!' he told her grimly.

A new note in his voice brought her about.

'You're a fascinating creature, my dear,' he said, 'and a grand little actress. You've rung the changes on all your tricks, but, you see, I happen to know them through and through, and they leave me cold ...'

She laughed on a grating note. 'I wonder,' she retorted defiantly. Then she saw the pistol in his hand. 'You're crazy!' she cried in a panic, springing back.

'You've done enough harm in your life,' he told her sternly. 'But you're through now. I want you to listen to me, and please don't make the mistake of thinking I'm

bluffing. As there's a God in heaven, Liselotte, I swear
I'll put a bullet into you if you don't take me to where
that boy is. I'm going to find him — if with your help, so
much the better: if not...' He shrugged. 'I shall count
ten. At the word "Ten" this gun will go off and blow a
hole in that pretty head of yours. And it's no use screaming, because there's no one in the place but you and me.
Now, then, I'm going to begin to count...'

In a frenzy of fear she warded him off with her hands.
'Wait! I'll take you to where he is. But I fear we shall
come too late. Max was looking after him, but Max has
disappeared. Put your pistol away! I can't think when
you point it at me.'

He lowered his gun. 'You mean, Fane's here — on the
premises?' he demanded, with a puzzled air.

She nodded. 'In the next pavilion to this — the one
with the blue shutters.'

His eyes blazed. 'I've had enough of your lies, do you
hear? I was in there just now — the place is empty!'

In blank consternation she stared at him, then, heed-
less of his pistol, darted for the door. This time he did not
oppose her, but opened the door and hurried out after her.

In a maze of doubt and fear, shaken by the violence of
the scene she had witnessed, Patricia opened the glass
door and peered out. She was minded to follow them,
but, with Keller's injunction heavy upon her, she
hesitated. She tiptoed to the parlour door and looked out.
As she did so, something stirred in the dark passage.
She shrank back in alarm.

It was Keller. He came into the sitting-room, she re-
treating before him.

'Quiet!' he whispered, his finger on his lips. 'That was
Brewer, the Federal agent. But don't worry! Your brother's not here!'

Like a flash the truth came to her. Dallas had tricked Grundt at Hamburg by impersonating the American secret service man — she had laughed over the story as Ned had recounted it. But Keller had mistaken Dallas for the Federal agent — no one but Grundt could have made a blunder like that: Grundt, or someone associated with him. It could only mean that Keller was one of Grundt's people, his story about helping Ned a ruse to lure her to that lonely house. With a chill feeling in her heart she stole a glance at the vulpine face that confronted her in the lamplight. It seemed to her that its expression was quickened by an underlying air of expectancy. Sick with fear, she wondered what had become of Ned. But her course was clear — she must find Dallas and warn him.

The parlour door had remained open. Imperceptibly she edged towards it. Keller was at the table, poring over his bag. Now she was at the door. But even as she sprang forward an enormous figure loomed up on the threshold, a vast, hairy man with a misshapen foot. With a gasp she shrank back, and at the same moment from behind a hand was clapped over her mouth. She tried to scream, but could bring forth no sound; tried to struggle, but found herself crushed in a grasp like a steel band. Suddenly she felt a sharp prick in her arm — more desperately than ever she fought against the pressure on her mouth, that paralyzing grip. A gentle numbness, starting with a tingling of the finger-tips, was stealing over her — it seemed useless to go on struggling. The shutting of the door, the thump of a heavy foot on the linoleum, were the last sounds she heard before her senses left her.

CHAPTER XIX

In Which the Major Reappears, Followed Presently by Two Old Friends

IT WAS pitch-black outside. A thin rain pattered among the whitened boles of the apple trees stretching away in ranks like sheeted ghosts on parade. The woman scorned the encircling path and plunged straightway among the trees, speeding across the sopping grass towards where the other pavilion loomed up like an inky blot against the hillside. Dallas overtook her at the foot of the verandah steps.

'Too late!' she panted, clutching at her side. 'It is as I feared: he has been before us.' She pointed upward, at the front door flung wide, the dark and silent windows above.

'Bartels?' said Dallas.

She inclined her head. 'Yesterday he telegraphed from Karlsruhe I should bring him there. But I distrust this man and I wire back that Jimmy is no longer with me. I suppose he did not believe me and . . .'

'Which is his room?'

'On the first floor — the door facing the stairs.'

He brushed past her. The whole pavilion was draped in darkness and silence. His torch showed no switches — it was evident that the place was not fitted with electric light. Through the open door of the room at the head of the stairs the beam picked out a large 'H' that detached itself from a crimson ground. It was a Harvard sweater spread over the back of a chair. There was no lamp, but a candle stood beside the bed and Dallas lit it.

Halted at the door, the woman wailed despairingly, 'Gone! His luggage, everything — gone!'

Dallas was examining the bedroom. That Fane had been living there was evident — for some considerable time, to judge from the pile of Paris *Heralds* on the mantel-shelf, the row of detective novels on the chest of drawers. An empty package of a well-known brand of American cigarettes lay in the fireplace where the embers of a wood fire still glowed.

'We were to have gone away tonight,' said the woman. 'His luggage was ready and I was to come back, as soon as it was dark, to fetch him. I left him at four, as I had some things to do in the town — they must have arrived soon after, before it was dusk, because the lamp isn't here. Max always brought the lamp at dusk.'

'Max?' echoed her companion. He was prowling about the room, opening wardrobes, examining drawers.

'The caretaker. He's disappeared.'

'What's this?' Dallas demanded sharply.

He had opened the small wall-cupboard above the fitted wash-basin. There were rolls of surgical bandage on the glass shelf, adhesive tape, a box of cotton wool, a bottle of iodine. When she did not answer, he swung about and found she had disappeared. His ear caught the clack of her heels on the uncarpeted stairs, but when he reached the door, she was gone.

He tore after her, but the night seemed to have swallowed her up: as he stood on the verandah, peering out into the darkness, the rustle of the rain and the soughing of the wind in the trees were the only sounds. He descended to the path and remained there, halted irresolutely in the persistent drizzle, vainly trying to pierce the surrounding blackness.

Then a clatter from behind the house suddenly shattered the silence, the noise of a motor starting up. With a muttered ejaculation he rushed backward along the path in the direction of the sound, hearing as he went the

rising hum of the engine as a car was driven away. A
helter-skelter dash along a short drive brought him to a
flagged yard. It was empty; but a gate on the far side
was hooked back and the beat of an engine, rapidly growing fainter, came to him above the drip of the rain.

He swore under his breath and plodded back to the
pavilion. What a fool he had been not to foresee that she
would grasp the first opportunity to escape! Not that
her concern over Fane's disappearance was not genuine:
he believed that Bartels had kidnapped Fane all right;
but with Fane gone, naturally she had seen no reason to
remain there and submit to further inconvenient enquiries. Absorbed with these gloomy musings, he had
almost reached the pavilion when an untoward sound,
which he subconsciously realized had been going on for
some time, began to force itself upon his attention. It
was a sort of muffled knocking and it came from the interior of the house he had just left.

As he sprinted up the steps and into the pavilion, the
knocking was more plainly audible, a thump, regularly
recurring, that resounded under his feet. A stair led from
the hall to the basement and he hurried down it, lighting
the way with his torch. The knocking issued from behind
a door let into the brickwork of the passage. A key projected from the enormous, old-fashioned lock. Dallas
drew his pistol and with his free hand turned the key and
pulled the door open.

A figure, swathed like a mummy, rolled at his feet. It
was Ned. He presented a terrifying spectacle. His hair
and the upper part of his face were encrusted with dried
blood, the lower part of his face being hidden by strips of
adhesive tape which held in position a gag, consisting of
a towel rolled and stuffed into his mouth. Rope was
wound about him, and, with his wrists and ankles
fastened together at the back, he was trussed up like a

Christmas turkey, while his brown tweeds were smeared all over with plaster and grime.

Dallas had his knife out in a second and slashed the other free. The major grunted, stretched, then, sitting on the ground, began to ease the tape from his face. Meanwhile, Dallas had found an end of candle on a shelf, which he lit, then helped the other to rid himself of his gag.

Hartigan struggled to his feet. 'Thanks, old man.' He put his hand to his head and leaned against the wall. 'Gosh, I'm dizzy!'

'What happened, Ned?' his friend enquired solic-itously. 'You're covered with blood!'

'They slugged me; but I'm all right. Listen, Robin, Fane's upstairs...'

'You saw him?'

'Sure. And spoke to him. He denied his identity when I tackled him. He got quite nasty about it, and, when I suggested taking him away, came at me with a chair. I was fighting him off when the door behind me opened suddenly and a guy knocked me cold with the butt of his gat.'

'At what time was this?'

'Round about four, I guess. I followed the little madame here — I saw her and Fane spooning together in a window upstairs. I waited until she'd gone and ...'

'Did you get a look at the fellow who slugged you?'

'Sure. A fat, red-faced son of a gun.'

'Red-faced, eh? A pimply, unhealthy-looking cuss with a double chin?'

'Add two chins more and it's the bird to the life!'

Robin drove his fist into his palm — the gesture was tense and noiseless. 'Bartels!' he declared sombrely.

With a rueful smile Ned pawed his matted hair. 'I was wondering. And he's snatched Fane, has he?'

The answer was a gloomy nod. 'That's about the size

of it. And, like a damned fool, I let the woman slip through my fingers!'

Ned looked up quickly. 'The little madame? You've seen her then?'

Another nod.

'It's Liselotte, isn't it?' the major asked anxiously.

Robin's face was bleak. 'It only came to me after we spoke on the telephone yesterday. You mentioned that map of hers with this Hasenberg place marked. I thought then that the name seemed familiar — I lay awake most of the night racking my brains to discover where I'd heard it before. At last it came back to me: once or twice, in the old days, Liselotte had spoken of a pension where she sometimes went in the summer — the Pension Hasenberg, it was called. I didn't connect it with Baden-Baden: I only knew it was somewhere in South Germany. After that, I couldn't restrain myself — I left a note for Cant and caught the first train out of Salzburg this morning. I was at the Schlemmer about five, but you were out, and so was she. So I came straight here by taxi to investigate. But, Ned, tell me, are you really all right?'

Through his mask of blood and grime the major grinned cheerfully.

'The old bean's buzzing a bit, but I'm okay. It's not the first time I've been koshed and, anyway, the blow glanced off as I swung round. I bled a good deal, but it's only a scalp wound, I fancy. Good Lord, I was forgetting' — he whipped round to face the cellar door. 'There's another feller tied up in there, a guy in a blue apron with a sack over his head.'

'It's the caretaker, probably. Max, his name is.'

'I don't know. He was down here already when they brought me down, fastened to a ring in the wall. They tied me up, too — it's taken me all this time to wriggle loose . . .'

'We'd better free him, anyway.'

The sack removed and the prisoner, his bonds cut, brought out into the feeble light of the passage, a shaggy man in shirt-sleeves and a denim apron was disclosed. He appeared to be none the worse for his experience, although he was evidently badly scared. Though Robin addressed him in German, at first he could only stare and blink terrified eyes. Gradually Robin coaxed his story out of him. That afternoon, he said in his thick dialect, as he was returning from seeing madame as far as the front gate to the brown pavilion where he lodged, a sack was flung over his head from behind, a voice at the same time threatening him with instant death if he uttered a sound. He thought it was a *Gestapo* raid, although, he hastened to explain, he was only a simple man, the caretaker for Herr Himmelstoss, the proprietor, and had never mixed himself up with politics. There were two of them, although the bag over his face had prevented him from seeing their faces, and they had run him down to the cellar and trussed him up to the wall. About a quarter of an hour later he heard the cellar door open again and 'the *Amerikaner*,' as he called Ned, was flung in beside him.

He would have gone into details of their uncomfortable plight in the cellar, but Robin cut him off short.

'You know Mr. Fane?' he questioned.

The man nodded vigorously. *Gewiss*, he knew Herr Fane.

'How long has he been living here?'

About four weeks, was the reply. Madame had brought the young Herr in her car with a letter from Herr Himmelstoss, who lived in the city during the winter, saying that madame's friend was to lodge in the blue pavilion until further notice. Madame was no stranger — she had often stopped at the pension in the summer. Herr Fane had one of the upstairs rooms and Max looked after him and got his meals. Madame did not stay at the house herself — she lodged at the Hôtel Schlemmer in the town; but she came over every day to visit the young Herr. No, there were no other callers, except, of course, in the first days, the doctor.

The other pounced on the word. 'The doctor? What doctor? A big man, is it, who walks with a limp?'

The caretaker shook his head. It was just a doctor — not so big, either, a young chap with glasses who walked like anyone else. Max had never seen him before and hadn't heard his name. He didn't think it was one of the regular doctors from Baden-Baden or he would have known him. In any case, he didn't come any more, now that the young Herr was able to go out again.

'Able to go out again? Has he been ill, then?'

Max rolled his eyes at him. 'But, Herr, that was why he was here. To recuperate after his accident.'

'What accident?'

'His automobile accident.'

Patiently Robin delved farther. The young Herr had arrived with his head in bandages: he had been in a car smash, madame had explained. Max had had to carry him into the house when madame first brought him. He was over it now, but still wore a bandage, with a cap to cover it. Beyond this Robin was able to extract little. As the young Herr knew no German and Max could not speak English, they had scarcely exchanged a word, the caretaker said: if the Herr required anything, he would ask madame for it and she would tell Max. He had no knowledge of the extent of the young Herr's injuries. For the first ten days he was always in bed and seemed hardly conscious; but for the last week he had walked in the grounds and gone for drives with madame in the afternoons. He and madame were to have gone away that evening. Had they, perhaps, already left?

Robin ignored the question. 'Where were they going?' he asked.

The caretaker had no idea.

'Do you know a friend of madame's called Bartels?' Robin asked.

Max shook his head. No one had been to the house, he repeated in reply to a further question, since the young Herr had arrived, except madame and the doctor.

Robin turned to Ned. 'We must take a look at that head of yours,' he said. 'We'll go upstairs and I'll get Max to rustle up a pan of hot water.'

They mounted to one of the ground-floor rooms. It appeared that Max did his cooking over at the brown pavilion, and he departed to heat some water. Meanwhile, Robin gave Ned the gist of his talk with the caretaker, of which the major had not understood one word.

'Fane was wearing a ski cap when I saw him this afternoon,' Ned remarked when Robin had finished. 'His manner was very odd — at first I thought he'd been drinking. But I guess he was still a bit groggy from the effects of his accident.'

'Accident, my foot!' growled the other. 'Do you know what I think, Ned? I think he was slugged, the same as the Jap, that night at the Helga at Hamburg.'

'Ah!' said Ned.

'I believe that Clubfoot and Company, tipped off by Liselotte about the kid's mission, switched the rendezvous from the Astoria to the Helga. They sent a fake letter to Akawa at the boat and afterwards telephoned Fane in Akawa's name to come to the café. They slugged them as they arrived . . .'

The major furrowed his brow. 'I don't see why they needed to bring Fane down to the Helga. After all, Akawa had the plans, and the moment he told Fane about that fake letter Fane would have smelt a rat . . .'

'Clubfoot had to make sure of Fane. The police were after him, and he wasn't going to risk Fane reporting Akawa's disappearance before he was clear of Germany with the plans.'

'Then why didn't Grundt knock off the pair of them?'

Robin shrugged. 'I don't suppose he meant either to be killed. But some of these Orientals have mighty thin skulls, and I daresay that Ole Johansen, who presumably did the slugging, struck too hard. Fane was luckier, and I now suspect that the bloodstained handkerchief I picked up in the upstairs room, the water in the basin, point, not to Akawa, but to him. I believe that the girl was up there with Fane, trying to bring him round when the police raided the place, and that she and Grundt smuggled the boy out through that trapdoor. As for Akawa, they probably dumped his body in the harbour.'

Hartigan nodded. 'Then if you're right, the kid's cleared?'

'I think so.'

'Then why does he stick around with this jane?'

'He's probably recovering from a fractured skull. He's not been able to travel up till now, remember!'

'He must know that she was back of this business. Yet there he was, up in the window this afternoon, hugging and kissing her to beat the band.'

'And suppose he has no recollection of what took place at Hamburg? Suppose he's lost his memory? It's by no means an uncommon sequel to concussion, you know!'

The major fingered his chin. 'He was certainly all woozy when I talked to him this afternoon. He didn't seem to know what his name was, except that it wasn't Fane!'

'There you are! His mind's a blank!'

Ned grinned. 'All the same, he didn't act so batty up

there in the window, necking with the little madame.'

'Dash it, man, you can suffer from amnesia and be perfectly normal in other respects — everybody knows that. Liselotte hopes to get him to marry her, or did, until Bartels upset the apple-cart: she told me so herself. In his present condition he's an easy mark for any woman, I'd say. He mayn't know who he is, but he sees a devilish pretty woman throwing herself at his head and quite naturally he responds.'

The major chuckled. 'You're telling *me!* The luck that some guys have! I'm knocked cold, and what do I get? A headache. Well, I certainly hope you're right, old man. He looks like a darned nice chap, even with the light of murder in his eyes. And won't his sister be tickled to death?' He broke off, eyeing his friend somewhat doubtfully.

But, before Robin could reply, Max came back with a basin of warm water, lint, and a bottle of iodine. Robin inspected the wound. By the time it was cleansed, it appeared as a large bump with a deep scratch along its surface. Ned would not hear of letting a doctor dress it. A touch of iodine and he'd be right as rain, he protested: he refused even to wear a bandage.

Max had brought a clothesbrush and brushed the major down. With a preoccupied air Robin paced up and down the room while this operation was proceeding.

'The little madame's gone,' said Ned, following his friend with his eyes, 'and Fane's gone. What's the next move, Skipper?'

'Back to Salzburg as fast as possible. If I know anything about it, that's where Bartels is making for with Fane. And it's my guess that Clubfoot's waiting for them at the Villa Friedl ... Hullo, what's the matter with Max?'

Brush in hand, the caretaker had suddenly darted to

the window. Shading his eyes, he was peering into the night.

'*Was ist's?*' Robin cried to him.

The caretaker veered about. His mouth drooped with terror. '*Polizei!*' he gasped, gazing wildly around. There were voices and the crunch of gravel outside and, immediately after, a trampling of feet in the hall. The door was flung open. A figure in a belted raincoat, the brim of his hat turned down against the rain, surveyed them from the threshold. Other figures were behind.

Instinctively Ned clawed at his hip, but Robin caught his arm. Seeing them there, the man in the doorway seemed to start.

'Well, well, well,' he exclaimed in English, 'if it isn't my old pal, Dallas, all the way from Hamburg! Say, what do you know about that?'

The voice was American, its tone loud and threatening, the face under the sodden hat heavy-jowled and red.

Robin flashed a warning glance at Ned who stood close beside him. 'On your toes,' he murmured out of the corner of his mouth, 'It's the Feds!'

Then, with a smile on his lips, he turned to greet Mr. Clarence Wilson.

CHAPTER XX

'The Old Gent with the Whiskers'

MOTIONING two plain-clothes men who accompanied him to stand back, Wilson entered at a run. A pace from Robin he halted and made explosive noises.

'Just a smart guy, huh?' he growled.

'Why, hullo, Wilson,' said the Englishman affably. 'How's the harvester business? Is Brewer with you? Still busy on that banking survey of his, I suppose?'

The secret service man was eyeing the major's dishevelled appearance.

'What's going on here?' he demanded suspiciously. Then, as Max attempted to dodge past, he grabbed him by the necktie. 'Who's this?' he rasped.

'It's the caretaker,' said Robin.

Wilson laughed. 'The caretaker, huh? Then I guess we'd best take care of him.' He called over his shoulder. 'Preuss!'

One of the men in the hall, a broad-shouldered individual who grasped a streaming umbrella, ambled in.

Robin nudged Ned. 'Private detective if I ever saw one,' he whispered. 'As long as it isn't the police, we're all right.' Feet were tramping on the floor above.

'See what he has to say,' Wilson ordered, pushing Max at the plain-clothes man. 'And ask Mr. Brewer to come here.' The unfortunate caretaker had burst into loud lamentations. 'Take him away, Preuss,' said Wilson, 'and shut the door. I'll attend to these two babies myself.'

The plain-clothes man bowed stiffly. 'At vunce, Herr

Veelson,' he replied in strongly guttural English and departed with his charge.

Robin and Ned had not budged.

Jerking his thumb at the major, Wilson said: 'This isn't your team mate from Hamburg. Who is he?'

Dallas shrugged his shoulders. 'Just a friend of mine.' His casual tone seemed to irritate the other. 'What a sweet recommendation that is!' he declared viciously. 'Listen, Mr. Robert Merrall, Esquire, late of the Royal Air Force, we know all about you. Is your buddy in the espionage racket, too?'

The Englishman was silent for a second, moistening his lips — the smile never left his face. 'That, or the harvester business,' he returned smoothly.

Wilson's cheeks trembled and seemed to deepen to a more vivid crimson. 'Like to wisecrack, don't you?' he snarled. 'Well, keep the funny stuff for the Heinies, see? There was an S.S. man bumped off in that little fracas of yours at the Café Helga, my bucko — try and wisecrack yourself out of that!'

Robin laughed. 'I hope they weren't rough with you, when they fetched you out of the hotel that night. I feel we owe you an apology, you and Brewer. A most unfortunate misunderstanding!'

'Unfortunate's the word, as you'll find out when we turn you over to the Nazi police, my lad. Say, what was the idea of you and that frog posing as Department men? What are you mugs mixing in this business for, anyway?'

'I'd like an answer to that question myself,' said a calm voice from the door. Brewer, plump and dapper, came in. 'Well, Mr. Dallas,' he went on briskly, shaking the rain from his hat, 'we've been a long time catching up with you, but here we are.' He proceeded to strip off his wet raincoat. 'Why don't we sit down?' His eyes, unusually keen by contrast with the bland and easy-going

face, rested on Ned. 'Let's see, I haven't met this gentleman, have I?'

There was a moment's silence, then Robin said slowly:
'My friend, Major Hartigan. Ned, this is Mr. Brewer,
of your Department of Justice.'

Brewer smiled amiably. 'Not the Fighting Major, is
it?'

The major grinned. 'Not so much any more.'

The other glanced at the wash-basin and the iodine
bottle, and from them to the major's torn and blood-
flecked collar and chuckled.

'I should have said the contrary,' he observed politely,
and went on: 'I once read some articles you wrote about
your adventures for one of the magazines — "My Sword
for Hire," you called them. Very interesting. Weren't
you a friend of George Ross, who worked for the Department and got murdered afterwards in Holland during the
war?'

'That's right,' Hartigan agreed, and added, 'you have
a good memory.'

Brewer chuckled and dropped into a chair. 'I need it
for this job. Sit down, gentlemen, I want to talk to you.'
And when they had found seats: 'As poor George's friend,
Major,' he said to Hartigan, 'you should know something
of the workings of this outfit of ours. "The old gent with
the whiskers," as the crooks call us — that means Uncle
Sam, you know,' he explained to Robin. 'The crooks
don't like us, Mr. Dallas, because — well, I don't want to
brag, but like your Royal Canadian Mounties, we get our
man. Not always at first, but always, or almost always,
in the end. Preferably alive, but if not, dead.' He
paused. 'I want Fane.'

By contrast with his colleague, his manner was mild,
almost deprecatory. But behind the horn-rimmed glasses
the eyes had a gimlet quality. 'The Lassagne woman had

him here under cover, didn't she? What's become of them, Mr. Dallas?' he said.

Robin laughed softly. 'I'd like to know the answer to that one myself, old man,' he retorted.

With a thoughtful air Brewer bit off the end of a long black cigar. 'You're a convicted spy, aren't you, Mr. Dallas?' he remarked in his gentle way. 'The British sent you up for a long stretch for selling military information to this man Grundt. That's right, isn't it?'

'You're all wet!' the major broke in angrily. 'He went to jail, yes, but now let me tell you something...'

'Ned,' said Dallas, 'shut up!'

'But, my gosh, Robin,' his friend cried excitedly, 'he can't sit there and...'

'Will you kindly shut up?'

The major subsided. Brewer had availed himself of the interlude to light his cigar. Now he blew a cloud of smoke and, as serene as ever, addressed Robin again.

'You were the associate of a notorious secret agent who has worked for Grundt for years, a certain woman called Liselotte Waldeck, but more latterly going under the name of Arlette Lassagne. I don't have to tell you that she and Grundt between them obtained from Fane certain papers, the property of the United States Government.' He glanced at the glowing tip of his cigar. 'It's the showdown, Dallas. You'd better come clean.'

Robin laughed, and his laughter had a joyous note. 'You can't bluff me, Brewer,' he said.

The secret service man looked wise. 'Are you sure it's bluff? The Nazis would like to lay hands on you and that French servant of yours.'

'And who's going to turn us over to them?'

'Well, I might, you know!'

Dallas shook his head. 'You won't and I'll tell you why you won't. You have absolutely no standing here and you know it. The offence young Fane's charged with is not extraditable, and your only chance of fulfilling your instructions from Washington is to kidnap him and run him on board an American ship, where, as it's United States territory, you can arrest him. If you're to do this, you can't afford to have the Nazi, or any other police, butting in.'

Drawing on his cigar, Brewer gazed at him fixedly. 'And what if I tell you I'm already in touch with the *Gestapo*?'

Dallas laughed. 'You conferred with them in Berlin, I know. But you didn't tell them the whole story or you could have picked up Fane four weeks ago. Are you aware that Arlette Lassagne has been living openly at a Baden-Baden hotel all this time? As you doubtless know, foreigners in this country have to register with the police — your *Gestapo* friends could have found her for you. The fact that you've only just traced her here is proof positive to me that you're not working in with the police. And I can guess why. State Department orders — no publicity. Am I right?'

The other was silent for a spell. At last he said: 'I don't have to give anything away to make it darned unpleasant for you, Dallas. I've half a dozen Germans working for me on this job. Any one of them would be tickled to death to turn you in at the first police station.'

Robin cocked his head warily. 'Try it and see. If I were an American subject you might, in the circumstances, get your Embassy to hush it up. But I'm not. I'm British, and if the Nazis arrest me, my Embassy will be compelled to intervene and I'll put up a holler that'll blow you all sky-high. I'll take jolly good care that the whole story comes out. It's dynamite, and you know it. As a good American you daren't risk it — besides, it'll cost you your job...'

The door gaped. Preuss, the plain-clothes man, put his head in. Would Herr Brewer, perhaps, spare him a moment?

Without speaking, the secret service man went out. From his place near the door Wilson kept a stolid eye on Dallas and his companion. Fluttering an eyelid imperceptibly at Ned, Robin produced his pipe and proceeded to fill it from his pouch. He was smoking in tranquil silence, apparently quite indifferent to Wilson's rather forbidding scrutiny, when Brewer came back.

Fingering his watch-chain he stood in front of Robin, gazing at him tentatively. 'Ever play poker, Dallas?' he asked at last.

Robin nodded. 'Rummy, too,' he said.

Brewer smiled fugitively and jerked his chin up. 'How about seeing you?'

The Englishman shrugged. 'What have you got?'

The other took off his glasses. 'Preuss has been grilling the caretaker. So Bartels was here?' He popped his glasses on again and surveyed the man before him.

'Well?'

'We were at Munich yesterday, following up a line we picked up on Grundt, when I was tipped off that Bartels was at Karlsruhe. He must have heard that we were hot on Grundt's tracks, for he seems to have come straight here and whisked Fane away in his car. We missed Bartels at Karlsruhe, but trailed him, through enquiries he made there and at gas stations en route about the Pension Hasenberg, to this house. Unfortunately, we lost the way in the dark and ...' He shrugged and turned to Hartigan. 'You weren't much luckier, I gather. He slugged you, eh?'

The major flushed, but said nothing. 'But he's Grundt's man — why should he attack you?' Brewer demanded, looking from Ned to Robin.

'Because, like you, we're trying to catch up with Fane,' Robin replied.

'If it's those papers you're after...'

'It's not the papers — Bartels has them, I know that.'

'Then why?'

Robin regarded him fixedly. 'To hear his answer to what I believe to be an entirely unfounded charge.'

The secret service man shrugged. 'That don't concern me. My orders are to pull him in. What became of the woman?'

'She was here only a few minutes before you arrived. But she gave me the slip.'

Brewer wrinkled his brow. 'She's gone after Fane and Bartels, of course. Any theory as to where they're making for, Dallas?'

The other moved his shoulders. 'My guess is as good as yours. Frankly, if you expect us to team up with you in hunting young Fane down, that's out!' With a challenging air he stuck his pipe in his mouth.

Brewer nodded sedately. 'Has Grundt been here to-day?' he asked.

Dallas removed his pipe quickly. 'Not so far as I know. Why?'

'He was at Munich, or rather on the outskirts, two days ago. We've been close behind him ever since he left Hamburg that night — he had a plane stowed away on one of the islands off the coast. But he's a slippery son of a gun. We heard of him at Heidelberg and again in the neighbourhood of Stuttgart, and two days since, when we were at Stuttgart, we had word of him at Munich...'

'Well, if you do catch up with the beggar, let me know,' said Robin coolly. 'I'd like to meet him again.'

The sharp eyes rested on his face. 'Just what is your interest in this case, Dallas?'

'I've told you.'

'Brotherly love — the interests of justice — free the Scottsboro boys?'

'If you like.'

He shook his head. 'It don't go with your record, brother!'

Robin shrugged. 'Too bad, isn't it?'

'Then you're not co-operating?'

A firm headshake was the answer. 'Sorry, old man.'

Delicately the other shook the ash from his cigar. 'Okay. But here's a tip. Time don't mean anything to this set-up — we shall get Fane and we shall get Grundt, whether it takes us one year or five. Mark that, son — we'll get 'em. If you're as smart as you seem to be, you'll step out of this case right now and stay out. That goes for the major and your French friend, too. Fresh guys who bump into the old gent with the whiskers are apt to get hurt — in God's country or out of it, it's all one!'

'And where do we go from here?' said Robin, faintly ironical.

'You can go plumb to hell, as far as I'm concerned,' retorted the secret service man, without raising his voice.

Robin jumped up and snatched his hat from the table. 'That takes us off, I think, as they say in the theatre.' He clapped Brewer on the shoulder. 'Thanks, old top. If you don't mind my saying it, that's a wise decision of yours. Coming, Ned?'

The major raised his hand to Brewer. 'So long, old man!' They went out together.

Wilson sprang forward. 'Have you gone nuts?' he exclaimed wrathfully to his colleague.

Brewer cocked his head at an angle. 'He had us cold, stupid. But he's not done with me yet. I want Preuss and one of the other Dutchmen to tail those two until further orders. Report to me every twenty-four hours. Jump to it, will you, Clarry, before they get away again!'

CHAPTER XXI
Disaster

IN THE hall two plain-clothes men propped themselves against the wall, gossiping in whispers by the light of a stable lantern planted on a chair. When Robin and Ned sought to pass, with a brusque '*Nein! Nein!*' one of the detectives, a fierce-looking personage with bristling moustaches, barred the way. Robin burst into German, but the man refused to budge until Preuss, emerging at the end of the passage, roared in stentorian tones, '*Durchlassen!*' and they were free to leave.

'Touch and go!' said Robin as they hurried down the steps. 'We're well out of that, Ned, my hearty. This Brewer person puts the wind up me. I never did like these quiet blokes!'

'Bah!' was the major's comment. 'That's the last shot out of that gun. You called his bluff, old hoss, and how!'

'Don't be too sure. He's right about the Department, you know. If all I hear is true, these fellows stick to the scent like a pack of ruddy foxhounds. Brewer has all sorts of difficulties to contend with, but he's obviously a first-class man with lots of guts and resources, and, take it from me, we're not through with him yet. I told you from the start, back there in New York, that it'd be a question of who reaches Fane first, we four or they. Well, the race is on with a vengeance!'

They were under the dripping trees now, following the path that skirted the shuttered boarding-house.

'How do we get back?' Robin demanded. 'Have you a car?'

The major stared at him aghast. 'Haven't you?'

'I came by taxi. I sent it away.'

Ned explained about the bicycle.

'It must be a good four miles,' said Robin. 'Well, we'll have to foot it — that is, if you think you're good for it, old man!'

It was evident that his adventure was a sore point with the major. 'I'm all right,' he growled. 'Thank Heaven, it's downhill nearly all the way.'

Outside the gates he retrieved his machine from among the firs and they set off down the lane. The rain fell pitilessly. Robin, his coat collar turned up, plodded along in stolid silence.

'Anything on your mind?' said Ned.

'I was wondering what chance we have of getting a train to Salzburg tonight.'

The major cleared his throat. 'Why don't we fly?'

'At this time of night? Don't be an ass! There's no direct service, as far as I know. And certainly none at this hour.'

'And if I told you that Miss Fane is here with her plane?'

There, it was out now! The major could not see his companion's face in the dark: apprehensively, he awaited the expected outburst. Instead, with a sort of joyful incredulity, Robin cried, 'No?' and stopped dead.

Ned concealed his relief under a casual air. 'Sure. As a matter of fact, she flew me down here. It was quicker than the regular service, and — oh, well, I didn't care to disappoint her, she was so keen to come.'

Robin was jubilant. 'What marvellous luck!' he exclaimed, as they resumed their tramp. 'Bartels is travelling by road — even with the start he has, we should be at the Villa Friedl before him. I haven't taken a bus up very lately — the last time was in Quebec last fall; but I ought to be able to handle that Lockheed of hers.'

His companion grunted. 'Aren't you forgetting that she's an experienced pilot? If we go, she'll do the piloting. You may as well be clear about that, old man.'

'Rot! What does a girl like that know about night flying?'

'Plenty! She's flown all over Europe — to Salzburg, too, she told me. That young woman will fly anywhere at any time.'

'That may be. But I'm not taking her with us — as a matter of fact, you had no business to bring her down here in the first place, although, as it happens, it's turned out for the best. This is the kill, Ned. You don't know Clubfoot. He's as savage as a wild boar and, like a wild boar, he's never so dangerous as when he's at bay. We're in for a proper rough-and-tumble, old boy. You're out of your mind to suggest dragging a girl like Patricia Fane into it.'

'Well, you tell her,' Ned suggested ominously.

'I will. Where's she stopping?'

'At the Excelsior.'

'We'll go there straightaway.'

Ned said suddenly, 'There's someone behind us, I think.'

They halted and looked round. Between high hedges the lane was like a trench snaking its way down the hillside. Their eyes, habituated to the dark by this, could discern the gaunt shapes of trees rising from the hedgerows. No one was in sight.

'I could swear I heard footsteps,' Ned averred.

But the gurgle of water and the lisp of the wind in the branches were the only sounds that came out of the dense surrounding blackness.

'It must have been the echo of our own feet,' said his companion, and they went on.

They had hoped to pick up a taxi on reaching the main

chaussée; but rare cars or trucks, roaring over the concrete in a spray of water, were the only vehicles they
encountered. Robin's mood grew more and more morose.
As though urged by the endless vista of highway stretching arrow-straight before them, he kept increasing the
pace until at last the major, plodding beside him with the
bicycle, protested.

'Why don't you ditch the darn thing?' said Robin
impatiently.

'I was going to return it,' the other pointed out.

His companion stopped. 'We're not going back to the
Schlemmer, if that's what you mean. We haven't time.'

'I can ride on and meet you at the Excelsior.'

'If you think I'm going to hang about, waiting for you!
What we have to do is to pick up Miss Fane and beat it
for the airfield as quick as we can. Besides, who knows
what you may walk into at the Schlemmer?'

'But my suitcase is there!'

'I can't help that.'

They almost had a quarrel about it, wet and cold and
hungry as they were. In the upshot the major dumped
the machine by the roadside. They resumed their trudge
in a resentful silence on either side.

It lasted until the lights of the Hôtel Excelsior greeted
them. Robin was hastening towards the entrance when
Ned's sharp 'P-st!' called him back. Unwillingly, the
other turned and saw the major examining an elegant
car, extravagantly stream-lined, which was parked there.

'Her car,' the major explained. 'She sent it down
from Paris. I see it's ready for the road — German
license plates and all. And she has triptychs for every
country in Europe, except Russia, in a case in the pocket
— she showed them to me.'

'Fine,' said Robin dryly. 'She can drive herself back
to Paris in it after she's dropped us at the aerodrome.'

Ned grunted. 'You don't know that young woman,' he observed; but Robin had disappeared into the hotel.

He had left the desk and was making for the lift when the major overtook him.

'Six-fifty-three and four,' Robin told the operator.

'Did you announce us?' Ned asked his friend.

'No time,' was the curt rejoinder.

At the suite the door was opened by an elderly woman, an austere figure in shiny black, who grasped a flatiron.

'Miss Fane?' Dallas demanded eagerly.

'Not back yet,' was the abrupt reply.

Hartigan thrust himself forward. 'Did she say where she was going, Mrs. Evans?' he asked.

The woman regarded him severely. 'You should know that, sir, since she went to meet you.' Her manner was exceedingly blunt: there was an air about her when she opened her tight lips as though she were perpetually seething with indignation.

'Went to meet me?' said Ned. 'Where?'

'You sent for her,' Mrs. Evans declared, seething more than ever. 'Or so she told *me!*' She tested the heat of the iron against her cheek.

'At what time was this?'

'As near as I recall, about five.'

Ned turned to Robin. 'This is devilish odd. I never sent for her.'

'Are you sure you're not making a mistake?' Dallas said to the maid.

Mrs. Evans came to the boiling point. With a faint creak of whalebone she shuddered.

'Well, sir, I hope — I hope as I understand plain English. Turned five, it was, when Miss Fane come in. "Evans," she says, and throws her arms round my neck, which is her 'abit when excited, "Evans, Jimmy's found" — alludin' to her brother, Mr. James, gentlemen.

"Major Hartigan's sent for me." And with that she asks
me to fetch the satchel with the aeroplane papers and get
out her béret and her Chanel sports coat.'

Dallas frowned. 'The aeroplane papers. Has she gone
off in the plane, then?'

'Such is my conjecture, sir, since, while I was finding
her things, she tells the hotel operator to get her the
airfield.'

'And she ordered the plane?' the major asked.

'Indeed, she did, Major!'

With a bewildered air Hartigan shook his head. 'This
beats Banagher! How am I supposed to have sent for
her? By telephone, or what?'

'From what my young lady let fall, I gathered you'd
come to fetch her yourself. "Hurry, Evans," she kept
saying, over and over, "the gentleman's downstairs with
his car."'

The major was excited. 'But I've not seen her since I
dropped you both here this morning. Whoever said I'd
sent him to fetch Miss Fane was telling a lie. This is
serious, Mrs. Evans. Miss Fane must be found.'

Mrs. Evans was unruffled. 'If you'll permit the
familiarity, sir,' she observed with her habitual air of
protest, 'I shouldn't worry. Once the young lady gets
up in that blessed ship, as she calls it, there's no knowin'
when she'll be seen again. I've known her go trapesin'
off for two or three weeks at a stretch, and not even a
postcard to tell me or Mr. Tupper when to expect her
back. If you'd care to leave your telephone number...'

Robin broke in sharply. 'That's all right, thank you.
Good-night!'

The door closed. Ned turned blankly to his companion. 'From four o'clock on I was locked up in that
damned cellar,' he said in a voice husky with alarm.
'Robin, what does it mean?'

'It means they've snatched her, too, that's what it means,' was the savage answer, 'and it's all your doing. I warned you: I did my damnedest to keep her out of danger. But you disobeyed my orders, and now, what's the result?' The lean face blazed with anger. 'By God, Ned,' he cried, 'if anything's happened to her, I'll never forgive you!'

CHAPTER XXII

Grundt Scores Again

WITH that, Robin Dallas turned and swung off along the broad corridor. The suite they had left was remotely situated in a *cul-de-sac*, and from it, enclosing an interior court, the corridor bent off at a right angle, to turn twice again upon itself before the lift and main staircase were reached.

He was rounding the second bend when he felt his arm grasped. Ned's voice spoke explosively in his ear: 'Quick! We're followed!' He forced his companion to a run. 'One of those dicks of Brewer's from the pension — you walked right by him. When I trickled along, he ducked out of sight — service stairs. Probably got a buddy watching the elevator — these babies always hunt in couples.'

Now they were in sight of the old-fashioned lift and, facing it, the main staircase with its plush rail and faded pink drugget.

'What's the name of this pub where Bartels has his villa?' the major demanded abruptly.

'The Goldene Rose ...'

'The village?'

'Rodenbach. It's just over the frontier.'

Robin's hand was warmly gripped. 'Don't you wait,' said Ned. 'Take the girl's car. Leave word for me at the Goldene Rose.' He broke away, headed for the main staircase.

Robin raced after him. 'But what are you going to do?'

'Try and head him off — main staircase. I'll take a stab at holding both, if there's two.' He fluttered his hand. 'I'll be seein' you ...'

'Ned! Wait!' cried Robin.

But the major was halfway down the first flight. From the head of the stairs Robin watched him reach the second landing, bolt back along the corridor, disappear from view. With a thoughtful air he rang for the lift.

As he emerged into the lounge, an extraordinary turmoil broke out in the near distance. There were whoops and shrieks, punctuated by a series of ear-shattering bangs as though an iron vessel were briskly bumping down a stone staircase. With a muttered '*Um Gottes Willen!*' the lift attendant rushed from his cage: all over the lounge heads were raised in alarm. The porter came racing from the front entrance, one of the clerks from behind the desk, a waiter and a brace of pages joined them, and the whole party made helter-skelter for the swinging service doors at the back of the lobby. The excited yelping of a dog added to the uproar.

The telephone cabins flanked the lift. A broad-shouldered individual, an umbrella hooked over one arm, was in the act of telephoning. The din evidently penetrated the booth, for he came bouncing out, mouth agape. At the sight of him Robin quickly dodged behind a palm. It was Wilson's henchman, Preuss, the plain-clothes man they had seen at the pension. The hubbub continuing, the detective dashed off on the heels of the pack sweeping across the lobby. The noise from the rear of the premises was terrifying: howls, and shrieks, and clangings, mingled with the dog's yapping, rent the air: from all sides people came running. Robin Dallas smiled rather grimly and went composedly to the main entrance.

A small white dog, tethered to the porter's desk, was bounding up and down, barking madly. Dallas

stooped and glanced at the name on the collar, then
unfastened the leash and took the dog in his arms.

'All right, Phil,' he murmured, 'all right, old man.
You and I are going to find her.'

Outside it was dark and raining fast. The coupé
was still where they had seen it. Robin's deftly groping
fingers found the dashlight. The key was in the switch.
He hauled his long legs in behind the steering-wheel,
dumping the dog down on the seat beside him. 'A long
road, Phil,' he told the Sealyham. 'We shall be lucky
if we make the Goldene Rose by dawn.' Phil whined with
excitement and sought to poke a wet nose in his face.
'You'll be glad to see her again, won't you, old chap?'
the man said caressingly, switching on engine and head-
lights. 'And she'll be glad to see you. Lucky dog!' he
added with a wry smile.

The falling rain made a silver curtain in the head-
lights' glare: the clock on the dash marked twenty-five
minutes past eight. The engine purred on a deeper note,
and no one appearing from the lighted porch to stay
them, the car shot away into the darkness.

In the modest tap of the Goldene Rose, Captain de
Cantigny was finishing his breakfast when the door
leading into the passage was unceremoniously thrown
open.

The Frenchman sprang to his feet. 'Ned!' he cried.

With chin unshaven and trousers and boots thickly
coated with white mud, the major was not an impressive
sight. His face was seamed with fatigue. He came in
with a flagging step and, dropping hat and raincoat on a
chair, said abruptly, 'Where's Robin?'

'Robin? Didn't you see him? He went to Baden-
Baden yesterday.'

'He left me last night to come here. Where's Wolf?'

'He and Maier — that's the *patron* of the inn — went out two hours ago. There's been a hold-up on the other side of the frontier. Do you want some breakfast?'

'Just a cup of that coffee of yours. What news of Bartels?'

Cant fetched a cup from the dresser, filled it from the large blue china pot, passed it across. 'The Villa Friedl's been closed ever since he went away,' he declared. 'The moment anything budges in that quarter, however, we shall know it. The excellent Maier has a scout watching the house day and night. He has a regular organization of peasants — something to do with the smuggling of refugees from Nazi Germany over the frontier. What news do you bring, *mon vieux?*'

The major put down his cup. 'Bad,' he said and wiped his mouth. 'They've kidnapped Miss Fane!'

The other's dark eyes widened with dismay. 'But surely we left her in Paris?'

'She persuaded me to let her fly me down to Baden-Baden in her plane. It seemed harmless enough. But Robin blames me, and he's right. He's raging!' With a heavy sigh he cut a roll in two and began to butter it.

'Tell us!' said Cant and replenished the major's cup.

In brief, staccato sentences, punctuated by the process of eating and drinking, Ned described the events of the previous day. His breakfast seemed to revive him, and by the time he had reached the moment of his parting with Robin on the staircase of the Hotel Excelsior, he was warming to his tale.

'It was the damnedest thing you ever saw. By the time I reached the back stairs this Dutchman who'd followed us to the suite was past my landing and tearing down three steps at a time. So I let out a couple of yells and rolled an ashcan down on him. He saw it coming and squawked like a good 'un. But he couldn't avoid it and it knocked him endways and gave me time to catch up with him. Just as I reached him a perfect rabble of waiters and people came galloping up the stairs, and with them another of these plain-clothes dicks we'd seen at the pension. You never saw such a shemozzle!'

Cant was laughing. 'But what did you tell them, *bon Dieu?*' he demanded.

The major chortled. 'I knew that this bird couldn't explain what he was doing, snooping about upstairs on the floor. So I went straight into my act. I said I'd been calling on Miss Fane and that, coming away, I'd caught sight of this baby behaving suspiciously. I kept them all arguing there on the stairs for a good five minutes which I reckoned would give Robin time to get clear . . .'

'And they let you go?'

'Sure, they let me go. You know how these hotels are about a scandal. We all adjourned to the office, where I showed my passport, told 'em I was at the Schlemmer. They called the Schlemmer and confirmed it, then I had Mrs. Evans — that's Miss Fane's maid — down and she corroborated my statement that I'd been calling on her mistress — well, and there you are!'

The Frenchman whooped delightedly. '*C'est magnifique!* And what happened to the dick?'

Ned grinned. 'I left him there explaining. I bolted back to the Schlemmer and packed my grip to catch the night train, with the other dick at my heels . . .'

Cant looked worried. 'He followed you here?'

'I don't believe so. He was on the train with me, in the next compartment. But as we neared the frontier I went to the lavatory and stayed there until I felt the train slackening speed. Then I took a chance and dropped off. I didn't wait to see what the other fellow was up to, but ducked straight into the woods. I must have crossed the frontier without knowing it, for when I came out on a road I found myself in Austria. I've been two hours getting here...'

The sound of a car outside interrupted him.

De Cantigny sprang to the window. 'Here's Robin now.'

Dallas entered the bar, Phil at his heels. He flung down cap and raincoat, nodded to de Cantigny and, espying the major, said curtly, 'Ah, Ned. So you got clear?'

Hartigan nodded. 'Sure. I thought you'd have been here before me.'

'I missed the way in the dark. Besides, the roads are frightful — I had two blowouts. Where's Wolf?'

'He went out,' said Cant. 'There was a hold-up.'

'I know — I heard about it at the Customs just now. No sign of Bartels, I suppose?'

The Frenchman shook his head. Robin sank wearily into a chair. He looked exhausted, his face darkened with stubble, his eyes sunk in his head.

'Well, Ned,' he said, glowering at the major who was playing with the Sealyham, 'it may interest you to know that, thanks to you, Patricia Fane is in Grundt's hands.'

The major raised his eyes from the dog. 'You've news of her?' he asked in a husky voice.

'I went to the aerodrome at Baden-Oos before starting off last night. Around half-past seven last evening, they told me, three men arrived by car and asked for her plane — it seems she'd telephoned three hours before to have it ready. One of the men, who was in flying-clothes, produced the ship's papers. They explained that Miss Fane was ill, that they were rushing her to hospital at Vienna...'

'Ill?'

'They spoke of an overdose of drugs: she'd been doped, of course — they had to carry her from the car to the plane.'

Ned groaned, staring miserably at Phil's black nose. In a matter-of-fact tone Robin went on:

'One of the men, a fellow in a green raincoat, seemed to be a doctor, they told me. The other was Grundt — at least, he's described as a huge man who walked with a limp. Their story about making for Vienna was a blind. I called Aspern — that's the Vienna airport — and they have no word of any American plane arriving. Maxglan — that's the Salzburg field — reports hearing a plane over the aerodrome about ten o'clock, last night.' His voice shook a little. 'We've got to trace that plane of hers — it's the only clue left to us.'

'Here's Wolf,' Cant announced from the window.

Wolf strode in out of the wet, his heavy boots ringing on the stone floor. '*So*, Ned — and Robin?' was his greeting, as phlegmatic as ever. He walked over to the big iron stove and tapped out his pipe in the woodbox. Turning to warm himself, he rumbled, '*Nu*, what brings you two back?'

'Tell him, one of you,' Dallas exclaimed irritably and went to the window, where he stood dejectedly, staring out at the rain. Ned remaining silent, it was the Frenchman who burst excitedly into the tale.

When he had done, Wolf demanded abruptly, 'And why does Grundt have to kidnap the young lady when the brother's already in his hands?'

'That's where you're wrong, he isn't,' Robin declared, coming forward. 'At least, I don't think so. I believe Bartels has double-crossed our clubfooted friend. Grundt couldn't get his price for those plans from Uncle Sam, so he thought he'd get it from Fane.'

Wolf wrinkled his forehead. 'From Fane?'

'Because he's found out that Fane has money. His idea is that the boy would be glad to buy those plans back, in order to clear his name. At least, that's my theory. What do you fellows think of it?'

Wolf puffed stolidly at his pipe. 'It may be,' he conceded cautiously and looked at Ned. But the major, apparently absorbed with the dog, offered no comment.

'Not bad!' said Cant. 'And Bartels had the same idea; is that what you mean?' he asked Robin.

Robin nodded. 'Clubfoot made the mistake of confiding in Bartels,' he said. 'It was a mistake, because Bartels evidently knew where Liselotte had the youngster hidden away and Clubfoot didn't. Bartels raced to Baden-Baden and snatched Fane. Grundt was on his heels, but got there too late. So, to recoup himself, he seized the sister and is now holding her for ransom.'

The Frenchman laughed rather derisively. 'Then we're not likely to see the engaging Monsieur Bartels back at the Villa Friedl, since, of course, the Herr Doktor knows the address. The chase begins all over again, it seems to me, only this time we have two hares instead of one. And not the *soupçon* of a scent, *que diable! Eh bien, les amis,* the prospect is not gay!' With the slightly supercilious air which was habitual to him he regarded Dallas. 'What does the gallant d'Artagnan say?'

Robin shrugged miserably. 'For the moment I'm at a loss, I confess. This business about Miss Fane — it's bowled me over completely.' His manner was so distrait that, for the moment, it seemed to them he spoke no more than the truth. 'If we could only get hold of Liselotte, she might lead us to where Bartels has gone to earth with the boy — there's no love lost between her and Bartels, obviously.' He repeated: 'If we could only get hold of Liselotte...'

Wolf broke a long silence. 'Others have the same idea, *mein lieber...*'

Robin glanced up sharply. 'What do you mean?'

'I mean, about your friend Liselotte knowing where Bartels may be found.'

'I still don't follow ...'

'There was a hold-up this morning ...'

'I know. Beyond Freilassing. What of it?' His tone was increasingly impatient.

'Two masked men stopped a car coming from Germany and carried off the driver. A woman driving herself — she was alone.'

The lean face paled beneath its mask of grime. 'A woman? I didn't know this. Wolf, it wasn't — Liselotte?'

The other nodded sombrely. 'They left the car. We saw it by the roadside, Maier and I. A green saloon.'

'She drives a green car,' said Ned.

'Her name is on the dash — Arlette Lassagne,' said Wolf.

A melancholy silence descended.

Robin broke it. 'Clubfoot's trick again,' he rasped, 'and our last chance gone!'

The innkeeper put his fat face in at the door. 'Herr Wolf! A little piece of news — about the gentleman from the Villa Friedl.'

Robin sprang forward. 'Bartels?'

The man appeared to hesitate; but Wolf said: 'You can speak freely, Herr Maier. We are all friends here.'

The innkeeper came in. 'Frau Eigl, a woman in the village, works for Herr Bartels at the villa,' he declared confidentially. 'Word has just come to me that a car called for her at her house at three o'clock this morning. It was the gray car of Herr Bartels.'

'*Na*, and ...?' Wolf prompted.

Herr Maier's shrug was expansive. 'That's all I know for the present. Her husband will be able to tell us more, but he works on the railway and won't be back until this afternoon. As soon as he returns, I'll let you know.'

'Let's talk to him about that plane,' Dallas proposed to Wolf. 'Besides,' he added, picking up the dog, 'I want to get Phil some breakfast.' The two men followed the innkeeper out.

The rain streamed down the windows.

Cant looked at Ned, hoisted his shoulders. '*Eh, bien,* we can only wait,' he remarked resignedly.

'We can also have a drink,' was the somewhat sour reply. 'This infernal damp has got right through to my bones.'

A bottle of cognac stood on the bar. Ned crossed to it and, the Frenchman declining, poured himself out a tot.

CHAPTER XXIII

Schloss Baltasar

PATRICIA FANE was dreaming. She dreamed she was flying. Somehow, things wouldn't come right in her dream. At one moment she seemed to recognize the familiar interior of her 'ship,' then the background would fade, and keep fading. One thing she was certain about, she wasn't at the controls: queerly enough, for she couldn't recall ever having seen a bed on the plane, she was lying in bed; also she was feeling exceedingly sorry for herself.

She felt so wretchedly ill and they were bumping about so much (or so it seemed to her in her dream) that she asked who the pilot was, because she couldn't remember giving anybody leave to take the bus up in her place. A voice replied in guttural English: 'Don't worry, Fräulein! He's doing fine!' And when she murmured feebly, '*I* think he's terrible, letting her roll like that,' a great laugh, 'Ho, ho, ho!' boomed through the cabin and the voice said, 'Nevertheless, the good Hermann flew with Richthofen in the war!' and the laugh rumbled again. She could hear it still, though no longer, as before, in her ear: it rang echoless, as though it came from outside.

She opened her eyes. It was a dream, after all! She wasn't up in her ship, soaring above the clouds, but on *terra firma*, well and truly in bed. But where was she? What was this pompous bed with silk curtains looped back from gilded posts and a cherub at each corner? And what was the matter with her head? She was always moderate about liquor — she disliked it for what it did to people and because she considered it fattening.

To get drunk was not her idea of gaiety — Jimmy had often chaffed her because, he would say, she didn't know what a hangover was. But this was a hangover, all right, she told herself — her head seemed ready to burst. She groaned aloud and, burying her face in her pillow, called faintly, 'Evans!'

When no brisk tread, no cheerful rattle of tea-things, no slightly disapproving 'It's gorn nine' — or ten, or eleven — 'Miss Fane!' answered her, full consciousness came and she raised herself up. Propped on one elbow in the great bed with its canopy of silver brocade, she gazed about her. The bedroom was quite large. Green shutters filtered to a restful *eau de nil* the light rimming the two windows: a gold ceiling, elaborately moulded and frescoed, walls clothed in silk, furniture ornate with the protuberances and quirks of the baroque, met her eyes. Everything revealed traces of neglect, the canopy ragged and tarnished, the silken hangings tattered, gilding and frescoes peeling.

A bell-sash hung down beside the bed. She gave it a vigorous tug. It came away in her hand; but out of the distance a cracked bell jangled. Glancing down at herself, she perceived that she was wearing a borrowed nightgown — a cotton one, at that, high at the neck, with long sleeves. Her Chanel coat and béret were on one chair, the rest of her clothes on another. The sight of the overcoat with its fox collar did something to her memory. She had a sudden vision of Mrs. Evans bustling in with it in one hand, the satchel with the ship's papers in the other. Where had that been? Not in Paris, surely? In a sudden rush the events of the previous afternoon came back: Doctor Keller, the brown pavilion, Robin Dallas and Liselotte, the figure that had barred the way as she had tried to flee, the suffocating pressure of that hand on her mouth . . .

She sat up in the broad bed, hugging her knees, her eyes bright with the effort to concentrate. Why, then, her flight was not a dream! Details were beginning to emerge — she remembered awaking to the bitter cold, the shaded lights, of the cabin, with the roar of the propellers, the beam of a night beacon striking upward through a window, warning her that they were in the air; her dire sensation of nausea, of prostrating weakness; someone holding a medicine-glass to her lips; a frightening, hairy face bending over her chair, coming nearer and nearer...

Rocking there under the silver canopy she was again aware of the laugh that had reverberated through her memories of the night. It mounted from below the windows now, mingling with the murmur of voices, the faint aroma of cigars. She started violently. The face still haunted the dark places of her mind: somehow, that laugh seemed to be linked up with it...

Grundt! Crying the name softly under her breath, she sprang out of bed and stood barefoot on the worn Aubusson rug, her fingers pressed against her temples. Terror assailed her. Like a djinn escaping in a cloud of vapour from his imprisoning bottle, the image of the apelike figure which had confronted her at the Pension Hasenberg was invading the bedroom, seeping into the remotest crannies of her consciousness. Now she knew the truth. It was Grundt into whose hands she had fallen, who had kidnapped her and carried her off in her own plane — Grundt, the notorious man with the clubfoot of whom even Major Okewood, so matter of fact, so English, stood in awe. Dallas had warned her: how he would gloat when he discovered that she was missing! She wondered what had become of him, of the major, too.

In a sort of despair she ran to the window, pushed the

shutter open. The shutters were of iron and immensely heavy. The voices she had heard had died away: she found herself looking out upon a vista of trees, a panorama of snow mountains behind. She was at the window staring out when, with an icy sensation of fear, she heard the door behind her creak. For the moment she was so scared she was unable to stir.

But when at last she looked round, it was to perceive a woman standing there, a short, pudgy woman, no longer young, with a bathrobe and some towels across her arm and a pair of bedroom slippers in her hand. The woman dropped the slippers on the carpet, and holding out the bathgown said gruffly, in fluent English, 'So, you rang for your bath, eh? It's all ready, if you'll follow me.'

Patricia was thinking that never in her life had she seen such a terrible-looking old harpy. The face was heavy, in hue a dead, fish-belly white, with lashless eyes as hard as a snake's, the hands gnarled and yellow with fingers like talons, the body gross and shapeless in an outmoded confection of soiled mauve taffeta topped off by a skittish-looking little apron. An ingratiating smirk on her lips, the woman stared at the girl as she stood there in her thin cotton nightgown.

As though resentful of her scrutiny, Patricia suffered herself to be helped into the bathrobe and thrust her feet into the slippers. Her courage was coming back. She wasn't scared of an old image like this, she told herself.

'And who are you?' she asked the woman.

'I'm Frau Schratt,' was the answer in a syrupy tone. 'But you can call me Anna, dearie, the same as the rest.' Her accent was decidedly cockney — she had obviously learnt her English in London.

'What is this place?' Patricia demanded.

'This place? It's Doctor Keller's, dearie.'

'Why was I brought here?' Her tone was peremptory. The woman gave her a sly look. 'Why are people taken to sanatoriums?'

'Sanatoriums?' She was aghast. 'But this isn't a sanatorium?'

The old harridan chuckled. 'I'd like to know what else Schloss Baltasar is' — she chuckled again — 'or used to be.'

'But there's nothing the matter with me.'

Frau Schratt grunted. 'You should have seen yourself last night. I could have stuck a pin in you and you wouldn't have known.'

Patricia stamped her foot. 'I was drugged.' She put out her hands appealingly. 'Look here, be a sport and help me to get out of this place. I'll make it worth your while, Anna — I've plenty of money.' She began to hunt through her things spread across a chair. 'Where's my bag?'

The woman veiled her lizard eyes sullenly. 'I never saw no bag,' she declared with a truculent air.

'But I had it with me when I left the hotel. All my money was in it. Some French mille notes, three hundred-dollar bills, my cheque-book, my passport.'

'You had no bag,' said the woman.

Patricia gasped, pointed a denunciatory finger. 'You stole it!'

Frau Schratt shot out a bony hand and, clutching the girl's wrist in a grip of steel, drew the flushed face close up to hers.

'You keep your trap shut about that bag, dearie, and we won't quarrel,' she snarled. 'The boss has the other things, but the cash, that was a little gift for old Anna, wasn't it? Wasn't it? As she repeated the question, she drove her fingers deeper into the wrist she clutched until

Patricia cried out. 'It's worth while being friends with old Anna, my sweet,' the cajoling voice went on, 'because old Anna can give you good advice, see, my pretty? She can tell you, for instance, to stay quietly here at Schloss Baltasar like a good little girl and not to think of running away.'

With an effort Patricia wrenched herself away. 'I'll do no such thing,' she retorted hotly, rubbing her wrist. 'They can't hold me here against my will.'

The hag chuckled. 'Tell the boss. But don't go out in the park after dark.' She cackled again and added: 'Best get your bath now. The boss wants to see you soon as you're dressed, and he don't like to be kept waiting. I'll have a cup of coffee ready for you when you're out. Hurry, lovie! I'll show you the way.' She hobbled out into the corridor.

For a Schloss the place seemed very small, Patricia reflected, no more than an eighteenth-century mansion on two floors. And there was no suggestion of a sanatorium about it. The corridor smelt of dry rot, not disinfectants, and there was not so much as a glimpse of a doctor's white coat or a nurse's cap. Her bedroom was on the top floor, and to judge by the glimpses she had of the other bedrooms along the corridor, hers was the only one tenanted. A staircase with an elaborate gilt balustrade led, past the first floor, to the ground level. Everything seemed to be in a state of progressive decay, with walls and ceilings peeling.

The bathroom was as dilapidated as the rest of the house, with a tub as vast as a sarcophagus and heated by a little tile stove at the side. But the tub was clean and the water hot, and her bath, followed by the coffee and rolls which awaited her on her return to the bedroom, went far to restore her to a more normal frame of mind. She felt that she was approaching the radius of her missing brother and the prospect buoyed her considerably. As she grew calmer, a sense of indignation supervened. She'd been drugged, robbed, deprived of her liberty — she'd show them they couldn't do such things to a freeborn American. When Frau Schratt came to fetch her, she followed the old woman downstairs in fighting mood.

The staircase descended to a little atrium, chastely frigid in the eighteenth-century manner, pillared on three sides, the front door on the fourth. A voice, harsh with rage, filled the echoing space with its bellowings. It stammered, it blustered, it trumpeted on an ever-rising note, pouring forth a cascade of German words that seemed to bump and jostle each other like tree-trunks swept along by a mountain stream in spate. Frau Schratt went under the arcade and stopped at a door from which the raging voice issued forth, waited until it had subsided, then knocked. The same voice roared, '*Herein!*'

It was a small library lined to the ceiling with books along one wall and lit by French windows giving on the park. The ceiling was gilded and lavishly frescoed with sprawling nymphs, the furniture consisted of enormous pieces, heavily ornamented with bronze. A large bust, in which Patricia recognized the martial features of the ex-Kaiser under a helmet, stood on a marble pedestal, and there was a glass case of decorations on the wall. An immense desk littered with papers occupied the centre of the room, and behind this, his back to the bookshelves, the huge man she had seen at the Pension Hasenberg towered erect. His hairy hands clutched a document and he was glowering at two men who faced him across the desk. Behind him a third man lounged at the bookshelves, idly inspecting the titles of the books.

The air in the room was thundery. The perspiration

gleamed on Grundt's beetling forehead and his bulbous lips were trembling.

Frau Schratt called from the door, '*Die junge Dame, Herr Doktor!*' and for a moment the cripple's eye, hot and wild under the jutting brows, rested on Patricia. The next moment it had shifted back to the two men before him.

They were an oddly assorted pair, the one with a twitching, livid face, stooping shoulders and glasses, the other, fat and swarthy, clearly terrorized as they stood there, clutching their hats. Grundt flung out his hand and pointed to the door. '*Heraus!*' he roared at them with such unexpected violence that Patricia jumped. The sallow man began to speak in German — by the way he cringed, he seemed to be pleading; but another bellow from Grundt cut him off. On this the second of the two became violently excited. He launched into a long speech, jumping from German to Italian and gesticulating extravagantly.

He kept appealing to his companion, and was so absorbed, waving his arms about and declaiming, that he failed to note the signs of storm gathering again in the savage countenance that glared at him from across the writing-table.

Suddenly Grundt shouted '*Basta!*' in a voice that made the windows rattle, and when, notwithstanding, the fat man continued to spout, he hurled the document, which he still held in his hand, straight at the speaker's head.

It was an affair of many pages typed on stiffish paper and bound in cardboard covers, and as heavy as an average book. The fat man tried to dodge the missile, but the hard edge caught his cheek, gashing it deeply. With a shrill cry he whipped backward, the blood welling out between his fingers. But Grundt paid no heed.

'*Heraus!*' he trumpeted again and, hobbling round the desk with stick uplifted, he drove the couple from the room.

A laugh rang out behind him. The man who had been at the bookshelves lounged forward. He was plump and well-groomed and wore a monocle.

'You frighten our charming visitor, *Herr Doktor*,' he said in stiff German-English, ogling Patricia unashamedly through his glass. 'Will you not present me? I should like to talk with her about America. It will be good for my English.'

Grundt frowned. 'Miss Fane will have to defer that pleasure,' he retorted cuttingly in the same language. 'If you're to catch that train, you should go and pack.'

The man with the monocle consulted his watch, whistled. 'In truth, if I'm to be back in Berlin tonight...' He leered engagingly at Patricia. 'What a pity!' He made her a formal bow. 'Fräulein!' then nodded to Grundt. '*Auf wiedersehen, Herr Doktor!*'

Patricia was looking at Grundt — indeed, she felt as though she could not take her eyes from him. She saw the shadow of a smile hover round the thick lips. '*Adieu!*' the cripple answered softly and the man with the monocle went out.

Frau Schratt had not waited for her dismissal, but had disappeared. Grundt limped heavily back to the desk and sat down. Silently he pointed to a chair and, with a sinking sensation at the heart, the girl took it. A self-starter whirred outside and through the window she saw the sallow man and his companion enter a car and drive away. Grundt saw them too, for he grunted and said, 'Now that we're rid of those rats, Fräulein, we can talk.'

He stared at her balefully. 'Rats,' he reiterated, 'vermin. Faugh!'

Under their fantastic eyebrows his eyes had a yellowish gleam, and she felt a quick stab of fear.

CHAPTER XXIV

The Master Spy

Now that she had leisure to study him, her consternation deepened. It was not so much his monstrous ugliness as the sense of power this man conveyed that appalled her. With his flat, Mongoloid features, his barrel chest, his flail-like arms, there was something definitely animal about him — at any rate, she was very sure he responded to no human impulses as, rigid in her chair, she watched him chattering to himself like an angry ape. 'Rats! Vermin!' he growled, pushing about the papers on the desk with angry flicks of his tremendous hand. Though she said nothing, too scared to speak, he glared at her as though she had contradicted him.

'You never met a secret agent before, I'll be bound!' he declared at last in his harsh but fluent English.

She shook her head. 'No.'

He laughed raucously. 'Well, you saw a couple of beautiful specimens, museum pieces, here in this room just now. This Castellotti, for instance, the fat pig who dared to raise his voice at me, he used to be a commander in the Austro-Hungarian Navy. All through the war he was in the pay of the Entente — he sent hundreds of his fellow countrymen to their deaths. And that old ruin with him, he was once professor of higher mathematics at the University of Lausanne. Now he'll betray anybody for a hundred-franc note. Morphine's his trouble — did you notice his hands? But he's still one of the best cipher experts in existence. And to think that I, Grundt, who have been the personal confidant of one of the mightiest of sovereigns' — he pointed at

the bust on its slender pedestal — 'should have to pass
my life among such scum!'

He stopped, and once more brought his glance to bear
on the girl.

'They have no country, no roots,' he cried. 'Their
one thought is money. They come to me with their
wares, most of them spurious, and expect me to buy —
plans, blueprints, formulae, secret reports. Scientific
warfare is the rage today and every agent has his portfolio filled with plans for making war on land, at sea,
in the air, more terrible. Shall I tell you there are fash-
ions in such things, Fräulein, just as there are in the
clothes you wear? It's a fact. Yesterday it was tanks,
submarines, poison gas: today it's the ray, the obstruc-
tive ray, as they call it, for putting aeroplane engines
out of action. That was an alleged secret report on ray
experiments in the Italian air force which that creature
Castellotti was trying to sell me just now, the sixth I've
had this year, and every one a swindle, a fake. Bah!'
He narrowed his eyes at her. 'Have you ever seen a
rubbish dump?' he demanded abruptly.

Her curiosity was getting the better of her fears. His
frankness towards her, a stranger, intrigued her. She
discerned in him elements that reminded her of a certain
type of American business leader — the same ruthless-
ness, the same indifference to the opinion of others, the
same simplicity. There was nothing petty about this
man. The strangeness of his question took her by surprise, but without waiting for her to answer he went on:

'There's an island in the East River at New York:
I forget the name, but the city's rubbish has been deposited there for many years — I was taken to see the
place when I visited your country. Sometimes I think
of that island as a — what do you say? — a symbol
of the world today, a great mass of matter always in

disintegration, always in ferment and wreathed with the smoke of hidden fires, steaming, seething, bubbling with the gases of national hate and suspicion and ready to burst into flames at half a dozen points simultaneously.' His voice took on a savage ring. 'And everywhere you look,' he cried, 'the rats are swarming, nibbling, gnawing, fighting among themselves, burrowing and scurrying in the dark, like the Castellottis and all their kind.' Furiously he ground his teeth together. 'Rats, that's what they are! Like rats, when caught they deserve no mercy, and like rats, *bei Gott*, they get none from me!' Then his mood changed. 'Did you see his face when I laid his cheek open?' he demanded roguishly.

His outburst appeared to have relieved him, for his features cleared and, dipping his hand into a box on the desk, he helped himself to a cigar, nipping off the tip with a wrench of his strong, yellow teeth. Lighting up, he blew a cloud of smoke, contemplating his visitor through half-closed eyes.

'Now that I have the chance to make myself financially independent, of cutting loose from this riff-raff,' he told her, 'you'll understand I intend to take it.' He wagged his head. 'Oh, *ja!*'

Although he spoke softly, there was something faintly ominous in his tone.

Her uneasiness revived, and to repel it, because she was resolved to betray no fear, she said boldly: 'Why have I been brought to this place? And why am I held here against my will?'

Cigar in mouth, he picked up a paper-cutter and began to play with it. 'See, Fräulein, I will lay my cards on the table.' His voice was silky. 'You know about the plans your brother was sent to fetch? *Na, gut!* Originally, it was only the plans I wanted, but now it appears that your brother is more important than the plans...'

She was frankly puzzled. 'How do you mean "more important"?'

He rolled his eyes at her. 'Your State Department accuses him of treason. Secret service men are looking for him, to arrest him ...'

She made an effort to keep her voice steady. 'Well?'

With an air of finality he laid the paper-knife aside. 'Well, he'd like to clear his name, no? Supposing' — he leaned across the desk — 'supposing he could restore those plans to the Department?'

Her face lit up. 'You mean, you're willing to return the plans to Jimmy — to my brother?'

His bold eye held her. '*Jawohl* — for a consideration.'

'You mean, you want to be paid?'

'I thought he might be glad to buy them back.'

Cyrus M. Fane's daughter spoke up. 'What price are you asking?'

The broad face hardened. 'I want half a million dollars.'

She shrugged disdainfully. 'Now, of course, you're joking.'

He shook his head. 'Not by any means. You remember your *Othello*? "Who steals my purse, steals trash": how goes the rest of it in English? It seems to me that your brother can well afford himself the luxury of a good name.'

'Where is my brother?' she said.

He frowned Olympically. 'I shall still be frank with you. The agent I sent to bring him to me played me false. Instead of conducting him to me ...'

He broke off, the fleshy lips pursed, the tufted eyebrows a straight bar above eyes that darted fire. 'But have patience, Fräulein! In the course of the day this double-dealing rogue of a Bartels, together with your brother, will undoubtedly be in my hands. Until then' —

he smiled craftily — 'may I hope you'll honour my house by being my guest?'

'Your house?' she said. 'I thought it was Doctor Keller's.'

'A figure of speech,' he answered. 'I find it convenient to have this haven handy to the German border where at need I can merge myself in the character of a scientific acquaintance of the good doctor, who, I may tell you, occupies himself with problems related to the science of flight.' He grinned expansively and added: 'Which satisfactorily explains to the inquisitive the presence of a small aerodrome in the Schloss park, an indispensable arrangement for one who, like myself, travels extensively by air. By the way, your plane — what a superb machine, Fräulein! — is safely housed in one of the hangars there.'

She stood up. 'Will you please have someone take me to where it is?'

He laughed easily. 'There's plenty of time for that.'

She squeezed her palms together. 'I wish to leave immediately.'

He shook his head. 'No, Fräulein.'

She stamped her foot. 'If you think you can drug people and kidnap them in their own airplanes and detain them against their will ...'

He shrugged. 'I regret ...'

'I'm leaving, I tell you! You can't stop me!'

He bent his gaze at her. 'Do you know what this place is?'

'I don't want to know and I don't care!'

'Before the war,' he remarked blandly, 'this house, once the summer château of the Counts Baltasar of Salzburg, was purchased by old Professor Keller, father of our good friend the doctor, and conducted as a sanatorium for mental cases — paranoiacs, dipsomaniacs, drug ad-

dicts. Most of the patients belonged to the nobility
— even archdukes were treated here, I believe: they
were all of the very highborn, and it was extremely
expensive. The war came, the professor died, and there
were no more archdukes, and Doctor Keller found himself unable to carry on the place as a sanatorium. But
while patients are no longer received, the Schloss is still
equipped to deal with such cases.' He chuckled. '*Ja*,
Fräulein! Iron shutters which can be locked, bars on
the windows, a twenty-foot wall round the park —
frankly, you'd find it quite a business to get out. And
at night, let me warn you, the grounds are patrolled by
four police dogs, very savage, trained to bite first and
bark afterwards — *na*, *ja*, it would be quite risky for
you to try wandering out in the park after dark.'

She had paled. She was reminding herself that one
thing she mustn't do was to show that she was afraid,
and returned to the attack.

'But since it's my brother you say you want,' she
told him haughtily, 'what's the idea, holding me?'

He bared his teeth in a gold-filled smile. 'My old
friend, the famous "C," probably the ablest British
secret service head in the war, had a favourite maxim:
"Always have two strings to your bow!" Supposing
your brother continues to elude me, who shall pay me
my half-million dollars? You, *liebes* Fräulein, are my
second string. *Ja*, *Gott*' — he shrugged his enormous
shoulders — 'it's a matter of indifference to me who pays,
you or your brother.'

She looked at him fixedly. 'You mean, if Jimmy
doesn't turn up, you hope to get the money from me?'

He gave his dry, creaking chuckle. 'Your perception
does you credit, Fräulein.'

'And if I tell you that you won't get a cent?' she retorted, but not very steadily.

'I would warn you,' he gave her back gently, 'that I'm a bad person to defy.' He paused, and in the ensuing hush the throb of a car drifted into the room. He rose and, supporting himself on his stick, limped to the window. 'Come here a moment,' he invited her, parting the curtains.

A car stood outside the porch. A figure leaned out giving instructions to the driver. It was the man with the monocle.

'That gentleman,' said Grundt, 'is an officer on the staff of the German Reichswehr. He is the source of most of the information I receive about Germany's secret armaments, for which, I would add, I've paid him very considerable sums of money, chiefly from French sources. But the gentleman is greedy: the gentleman grudges me my modest commission: and so, behind my back as he imagines, he has recently put himself in direct touch with the French General Staff.' He made a little break, and, with a brusque gesture of the hand, said, 'Take a good look at that head, my dear, because before long it's going to roll in the sand.'

She recoiled in horror. The expression on Grundt's face as his victim, smug and jaunty, had taken his leave was fresh in her mind — in the light of this revelation she perceived the significance of the curt '*Adieu!*' which had greeted the other's cheerful '*Auf wiedersehen!*'

Grundt was speaking again. 'It's true,' he affirmed. 'In half an hour he'll reach the frontier. The Nazi authorities have chapter and verse of his treason — I've seen to that. He'll be arrested — the rest I leave to your imagination.' He dropped the curtain and they heard the car depart.

'A foolish fellow,' Grundt remarked placidly. 'You, *liebes* Fräulein, I'm sure will be more reasonable. As soon as your brother arrives, we'll have a little conference, the three of us, to decide on the best method of paying me the sum I ask for the plans. Should your brother not appear, then you and I will settle the matter alone. In the meantime, do nothing headstrong, Fräulein. Don't try to escape from Schloss Baltasar — it might be bad for your health.' He chuckled. 'And before all, don't attempt to bribe the good Schratt!'

'I'm likely to do that,' Patricia retorted with spirit, 'seeing that your good Schratt has lifted all my available money.'

The big man cackled joyously. 'No? Excellent! She was taking no risk of having her loyalty tampered with. A faithful soul, old Anna! You wouldn't think to see her that, years ago, she was an ornament to a profession even older than mine and one of the most successful woman decoys I've ever employed. But what have we here?'

A car had flashed past the window. Grundt drew the curtain aside. The car had stopped at the porch and two men got out, followed by a woman wrapped in a dark mountaineer's cloak. Grundt dropped the curtain and hobbled swiftly to the door, shouting, 'Anna! Anna!'

The old woman trotted in. Grundt barked an order in German and went out limping to the vestibule.

'Back to your room, lovie!' Frau Schratt told Patricia. 'Guv'nor's orders.'

The girl wavered, then let herself be led away. Grundt had planted himself on the threshold of the library in an aggressive attitude and was staring into the hall. A gloating look in his face caught Patricia's attention, and, following the direction of his glance, she perceived that the front door was open and that the woman in the cloak was coming in.

It was Liselotte, her face ashen. Before Patricia could see more she found herself hustled by Frau Schratt upstairs.

CHAPTER XXV

The House on the Lake

To THE four cooped up in the tiny tap of the Goldene Rose the morning passed with desolating slowness. Frau Eigl's husband did not appear, and sundry enquiries which Maier, the innkeeper, set on foot by telephone or otherwise regarding the missing plane bore no result. Frau Maier produced a pack of greasy cards; Ned, the cognac bottle at his elbow, and Cant sat down to écarté, while Dallas paced eternally to and fro, from door to window, like a caged lion. Outside the rain descended in sheets: within the room the stove made the temperature unbearably oppressive. A dispute developed between the major, who insisted on keeping one of the windows open, and Cant, who declared he was freezing to death. Then the major objected to Robin's restlessness. There were words between them, and Wolf, who was the only placid member of the party, posted by the stove with a book, had to intervene to keep the peace. The midday meal was a diversion; but all nerves were on edge and Frau Maier's roast pork and red cabbage was eaten in gloomy silence. Wolf brought his book to the table and when addressed answered in monosyllables.

The major drank beer with his lunch, but when the coffee appeared started in on the brandy again. Dallas looked vexed and at last said, 'When we started on this trip you promised to lay off the liquor, Ned!' to which the other replied bluntly, 'Yeah, but I wasn't taking the pledge for life.'

Robin flushed. 'Just what do you mean by that?'

The major laughed. 'Well, we're not exactly making progress, are we? At this rate, we shall still be looking for Fane a year from now.'

'And his sister, too — don't forget the sister!' Dallas rapped back.

The major slammed his hand down on the table. 'I've taken all I'm going to take from you, Robin Dallas!' he cried. 'I ran her into this mess, sure. But it's done now, so what? And let me tell you this! The girl would never have been snatched if you and Cant had had any guts in the first place. You had this big palooka at your mercy, that night at Hamburg, but instead of blowing his ugly head off, you let him slip through your fingers. Now let me tell you something...'

'Oh, hell!' said Dallas and, springing up from the table, he strode from the room. It was raw and miserable out-of-doors, but it had stopped raining. He began to walk up and down the road.

In a moment Cant joined him. 'You mustn't mind Ned,' he said. 'You were pretty hard on him and — well, he drinks to forget.'

The other nodded. 'I know; but I couldn't help myself, Cant. When I think of that girl in that ruffian's hands, Lord, I feel as if I should go mad.'

'Do you think you're the only one?' was the sober answer.

'We're all on edge and no wonder. It's this hanging about that does it. If only something would happen! What's the matter with Wolf?'

His companion looked at him curiously. 'Why do you ask that?'

'A fellow can't get a word out of him. And did you see what he's reading?'

Cant nodded. 'The German Scriptures, I know. It was the same yesterday. He read his Bible all day —

he'd scarcely open his lips to me. And when I told him
he was damned poor company, he nearly bit my head off.'

The other smiled. 'He's not what you'd call chatty
at any time, but I've never seen him like this before.'

The Frenchman glanced at him impressively. 'Do
you know what I think?'

'What?'

'I think he has a presentiment.'

Dallas laughed. 'You don't believe in that stuff,
surely?'

His companion's expression was enigmatic. 'Such
presentiments were by no means uncommon in the war
which you, my little one, are too young to know anything about,' he said soberly. 'Men who were destined
to be killed often knew it in advance. It made them —
how do you say? — grumpy, nervous. I saw it several
times in the case of friends of mine, brother officers.'
He tilted his finely moulded face towards the sky as
though to read the future behind the gray and swollen
rain clouds massed there. 'We're not at the end of the
adventure yet, my Robin. Who knows what tomorrow,
or it might even be still today, has in store for you, for
me, for any one of us?'

Dallas shivered in the wind that went blustering down
the muddy road, blowing the raindrops from the firs
in their faces.

'You give me the horrors when you talk like that,'
he said. 'This inaction is bad enough, but when I think
of Patricia Fane, drugged and helpless in the power of
that savage, I'm almost afraid of what the future may
bring . . .'

The other caught his arm. 'I think there's some news.
Look!'

Wolf had appeared on the porch. 'Robin! Cant!'
he called through his cupped hands.

They ran back to the house. 'We've traced Bartels,' said Wolf, and led the way inside. A sturdy man in a short hunting-coat with a fur collar was in the tap talking to Maier while Ned looked on. 'This is Franz Eigl,' Wolf explained. 'Bartels is at a place called Wildsee. It's about half an hour by car from here on the way to Ischl. He sent his chauffeur in the middle of the night to fetch Frau Eigl to look after him and some young man who's stopping with him . . .'

'A young man who's sick,' said the innkeeper. 'Eigl will go with you. Without him you'd scarcely find the road. Eigl has been to Wildsee before — he fetched his wife back from there last year. The Wildsee is one of the smallest lakes in the region, very remote and inaccessible, he says. Bartels has a little summer place there, the only house on the lake — it seems he was there for a few days last year with a lady friend of his and Frau Eigl went up to look after them.'

Dallas pricked up his ears. 'What was the lady called?' he asked Eigl in German. 'Not Frau Liselotte Waldeck, was it?'

The man nodded stolidly. '*Ja*, Herr, so was the name.'

The weary face lit up. 'Everything now depends,' Robin said to the others, 'on whether Grundt has been able to persuade her to reveal this hiding-place of Bartels, and if so, how long it will take him to get to Wildsee from wherever he is with Miss Fane. With any luck we may kill two birds with one stone.'

His air of depression had evaporated: his tone was firm and brisk. Glancing out of the window at the coupé parked in the lane, he went on: 'We can all fit in her car. Eigl will ride with me in front and Cant, who's a little fellow, can squeeze in between us. You and Ned, Wolf, will have to squash into the rumble. Bring your guns!' Something gently nipped his trouser leg and looking down, he perceived the Sealyham. 'Oh, hullo, Phil,' he said, 'we can't leave you behind, old boy.' He picked up the dog and gave it to Cant. 'Cant,' he cried gaily, 'we'll make you dog man! Are we all set? Come on! Let's go!'

Spring was on the way in the Salzkammergut. Under the bridge at Salzburg the river was brimming, its green glacier water racing over its pebbly bed. There were buds on the trees, the grass was bright green, and the villages had a clean-washed look after their long winter night. The great Kaiser-Strasse from Salzburg to Vienna, coiling round glassy lakes, in and out of majestic valleys ringed by the snowy-breasted mountains, unrolled itself like a shining black ribbon before them. There was little traffic and the surface was magnificent — there were stretches when the speedometer needle touched the seventy-five mile mark.

As they drove along, Robin, in his accentless German, made his plan with their guide. He noticed that Eigl asked no questions: he assumed that the man was a member of Herr Maier's mysterious organization and therefore accustomed to obey without demur. Robin's proposal was that, on reaching their destination, Eigl should bring his wife out to them so that they might cross-examine her as a preliminary to further action. If it should prove that Grundt had not yet arrived on the scene and that Bartels was alone in the house with Fane, Robin's idea was that Wolf, who was already known to Bartels, should go boldly to the front door and thus gain peaceable admittance for the four of them. Dallas explained this over his shoulder to Wolf in the rumble, and with a gruff 'Sure!' the German agreed.

They soon quitted the main *chaussée* for a network of roads that wound their way through a region of lakes and woods. Concrete gave way to macadam and macadam at

long last to what was little better than a farm-road, soft
and deeply-rutted. They were climbing steadily now,
and there were patches of rotting ice on the lake they
circled and snow on the lower slopes of the hills. The lake
at their backs, they dropped down through a wood,
roared through a wee hamlet, and beyond, at their guide's
direction, took a road that clambered steeply between
alpine pastures to a dense belt of forest. This they
traversed and saw, as they topped a rise beyond, a tongue
of water darkened by the reflections of the stately firs that
hemmed it about and, in the foreground at the foot of the
hill, the roof of a house. Eigl pointed. 'Wildsee!' he said.
He made them stop and park the car out of sight along a
forest track.

He indicated a belt of woodland that flanked the road.
'Go through the wood,' he bade them, 'and wait for me
under the trees at the bottom and I'll bring my wife to
you.'

Then he set off down the road. Cant still had Phil in
his arms: Robin made him go back and put the dog in the
car.

The wood thinned out at the end of the incline, so they
halted about a hundred yards from the house. It was no
more than a small frame shack: evidently occupied, for
the windows were open and a pencil of smoke curled aloft
from the brick chimney. No movement was audible from
within: the only sound was the clatter of Eigl's footsteps
as he swung down the hill. They watched him round the
front of the bungalow on his way to the back and vanish
from sight.

There was a moment of absolute silence. Then a
woman screamed.

CHAPTER XXVI

The Vengeance of Clubfoot

NOT once, but again and again, the scream resounded. Vibrant, agonized. As one the four burst from the shelter of the trees. At the side of the house a door banged in the wind. Within was the kitchen where Eigl was making desperate efforts to cope with a frenzied woman in peasant dress who, in the broad pâtois of the region, was shrieking, '*I' muass weg! I' muass weg!*' Vainly the man sought to pacify her, saying, 'There, there, Mariechen, don't be frightened! It's Franzerl! Tell Franzerl what's the matter!' But she only clamoured on, 'Let me out of here!'

In a scared voice Eigl spoke over his shoulder to Dallas: 'I found her crouched in the passage back there. She started to scream the moment I touched her. She kept pointing along the passage as though she was afraid of something beyond the door at the end. The devil knows, there's been mischief done here. If the gentlemen would take a look round, while I get her into the air...'

Already Robin, pistol in hand, was making for the door at the end of the short corridor giving access to the rest of the house. He opened the door, then recoiled so violently that he collided with Cant who, with the others, was at his heels. 'God!' he gasped.

They saw a small entrance hall with a staircase on one side, on the other double doors folded back on the living-room. In the doorway two figures dangled from the transom below the fanlight, two figures that oscillated gently in the draught from the passage, heads drooping, hands fastened at the back with straps.

One was a man, gross of body, bald-headed, double-chinned. The other was a woman. Her face was not visible from that angle, but her silhouette was slim and young, and a mass of golden ringlets gleamed in the hard afternoon light. On the threshold of the living-room a little slipper lay where it had fallen, and the small feet and slender legs above it emerged, silk-clad, from a natty tweed skirt. The transom creaked faintly as the bodies swayed: the sound of helpless sobbing drifted in along the corridor.

Dallas was the first to recover himself. 'Too late!' he cried in a terrible voice and darted into the hall. Then he caught a glimpse of the face framed in yellow curls, and halting abruptly, he covered his eyes with his hand.

The others swept past him. Pale as death, Cant felt, first the woman's hands, then the man's. 'Dead for hours,' was his curt report. Wolf had drawn a hunting-knife and now, stretching his arms to their full length, he cut one rope after the other, and between them he and Cant lowered the bodies to the ground. The major came forward with a flask, but Wolf, who was on his knees, waved him back. 'Their necks are broken,' he said, and stood up.

The four of them went into the living-room. It was a simply furnished parlour done in bright peasant tones. Just across the threshold the two bodies lay side by side on the floor. Cant whipped the cover from the centre table, a gay thing of red and white check, and would have flung it over them. But Robin said, 'One moment!' Dropping to his knees he went through the dead man's pockets. 'Stripped bare,' he announced hoarsely and rose to his feet. 'I thought that perhaps those plans ...' He shrugged. 'I might have known — Clubfoot ...' He broke off.

'What about the other?' said Cant, looking down at the woman.

'Search her, one of you,' Dallas answered, and brusquely turned aside. Wolf went down on his knees again. 'Only one pocket, and that's empty,' he informed them and stood up. Cant came forward with the tablecloth, but Robin took it from him. For an instant he stood, contemplating the face of the dead woman, then, with a sort of lingering tenderness, spread the cover over her and her companion.

A cry rang through the hall. Eigl was there, stammering with excitement. 'She says,' he clamoured, 'she says...' Then he perceived the severed ropes hitched about the door-beam, the bodies on the ground, and his eyes grew saucer-wide. '*Grosser Gott!*' he faltered, 'then it's true?'

'As you see,' Wolf growled, and added, 'Has Frau Eigl recovered sufficiently to tell us what happened?'

The man nodded. 'She's calmer now. She says three men came — apparently they brought the woman with them. The young man who was sick they took away. There was no chance to resist — Herr Bartels had sent the chauffeur into Salzburg to have some repairs done on the car. Very soon after the chauffeur left, the men appeared — they were watching the house, I shouldn't wonder. But the wife will tell you...'

In the kitchen, shuddering and still racked from time to time by sobs, the woman gasped out her tale. It was about eleven o'clock and she was in the kitchen, getting the midday meal, when suddenly Frau Lise burst in. She knew the lady well, Frau Eigl explained: not only had Frau Lise been at Wildsee the previous summer, but she had sometimes called to see Herr Bartels at the Villa Friedl.

'Pale as a corpse she was, the poor thing, and all out of breath. Is there a young man staying there, she wants to know, and when I say, yes, "Quick, Maria," she cries.

"Don't let Herr Bartels see you, but run to the young man and tell him to save himself. Let him hide in the wood," she says, "and I'll join him there. Hurry, for the love of God!" she tells me and says something about breaking away from some men who brought her in a car and how they're close after her. With that she throws a hundred-schilling note on the table and goes to run out of the door. But now, oh, *Gott*, oh, *Gott*, there's one there who catches her in his arms, a great ogre of a man with a twisted foot. She screams and I scream and Herr Bartels rushes to us from the living-room. But two more of these wretches have come in who seize my poor gentleman and Frau Lise and drag them into the hall, the lame man hobbling behind. I go to run after them, but one of the men puts his head in, not the lame one, a smaller man, who wore a green raincoat. If I stir from the kitchen or make a sound, he tells me, I'm a dead woman. And with that he goes out.'

'And after that?' Wolf asked.

'They seemed to be all over the house. I listened at the door and heard them trampling above-stairs and voices, angry voices, in the living-room. I opened the door a chink and saw the man in the green overcoat who threatened me descending the stairs with a young man in a jersey. The young man was pale and had a bandage round his head — I think, perhaps, it's the young man who's been staying with us.'

The four friends exchanged glances. 'Did he appear to go willingly?' Cant enquired.

'Yes and no. He went willingly enough, but they were arguing.'

'What became of him?' Wolf questioned.

'They went out by the front door together and I heard an auto start up. I ran to the window. Two autos were there at the foot of the hill and one was just driving away.

I was still at the window when I heard someone cry out within the house ...'

Dallas spoke for the first time. 'Frau Lise, was it?' he said huskily.

Frau Eigl shook her head and shuddered. 'It was my master — gentlemen, it's an awful thing to hear a grown man scream. I crept to the door, but now there was a man in the passage and he drove me back. "Stir out before it's dark and your old man can get himself a new wife," he says. With that he slams the door in my face and at the same moment Frau Lise — God rest that poor creature's soul! — began to shriek ...'

She gave a convulsive sob. 'She cried "Mercy!" and "Save me!" and "Pity!" sobbing and crying like a mad thing. I put my fingers in my ears and prayed — there was nothing else I could do. After a time, there were footsteps and voices and the sound of the other auto starting. I was too scared to move. For aught I knew they'd kill me, too. But all remaining still, at last my courage began to come back and I told myself I must see what they'd done to my master and that poor lady. So I ventured to peep out into the hall and, oh, *Gott*, oh, *Gott!*' She flung her apron over her head and began to rock herself in mute agony.

Eigl spoke soothing words in her ear.

Dallas said to him, 'Has she any idea where they went to on leaving here?'

The man repeated the question. Frau Eigl shook her head. They had gone away in the autos, that was all she knew.

'Didn't you overhear any conversation between them?' Robin persisted. 'For instance, between the young man and the one who brought him downstairs. You said they were arguing. What about?'

The woman wiped her eyes on her apron. 'He wanted

to know where they were taking him. It was to see madame, the other said ...'

Wolf puckered his forehead. 'Madame, what madame?' he growled to Dallas.

'Liselotte, obviously,' came back in a stage whisper. 'They knew he was crazy about her — don't you see, they were using her as a decoy?'

'The young man was foreign — he spoke German badly,' Frau Eigl went on. 'But from what I could make out he was complaining that Herr Bartels had deceived him. Herr Bartels had promised him that madame — whoever that might be — would be at Wildsee, but she hadn't arrived. "Don't let that bother you!" says the other. "Didn't she send us to fetch you? She's at Schloss Baltasar, waiting for you."'

Dallas flashed a glance at Eigl. 'Schloss Baltasar?'

'Isn't that the sanatorium — old Keller's place?' the man asked his wife. 'I thought it was closed when the old professor died.'

Frau Eigl shrugged. 'I'm telling you what I heard them say.'

'How does one get to this place?' Robin demanded.

Eigl spread his hands. 'I was never there — it's north of Salzburg, close to the German frontier. But it should be on the map, an old house like that. Or anyone in Salzburg ought to be able to direct you.'

Wolf was already pulling a map from his pocket. 'The old Austrian General Staff map,' he announced with a professional air, 'the best of its kind ever made.' It was a large-scale map of the area of the Salzburg command. He spread the map on the table and donned his glasses. After a moment he looked up, his finger pointing to a name printed across the contour shading. 'Schl. Baltasar,' they read. 'We'll find it with this,' he promised, and folded up the map. Then, with a glance at the bodies on the floor, he added, 'The authorities will have to be notified . . .'

Robin nodded. 'But not until we're gone — we don't want to be dragged into any enquiry. Eigl will attend to it as soon as the chauffeur returns.'

He spoke to the man in German. The others were already outside. With a backward glance at the bodies prone beneath their gaudy pall, Dallas hurried from the house.

The three were waiting for him at the foot of the hill. Cant's face was bloodless: he was trembling with rage.

'Did you see her eyes?' he demanded between clenched teeth. 'Let's hurry, all of you, because this man must die!'

The major was swearing under his breath and mopping his mottled cheeks. 'A girl like that! I could tear the black heart out of him,' he said thickly. 'And, please God, I, or one of us, will!'

Wolf shrugged. 'It is better, I think, first to rescue the girl and her brother,' he suggested stolidly. 'Then we settle accounts!'

Robin said nothing, but ran furiously up the hill to where the car was hidden among the trees.

CHAPTER XXVII

'Du glaubst zu schieben und Du wirst geschoben'

THIS time it was Cant who took the wheel, saying, when Robin would have forestalled him, '*Laisse!* I'm in better shape than you — at least, I've been to bed. We've got to step on it, my little ones, and for that one needs a clear head. This time, let's see what I can shake out of her!' He raced the engine. '*Zut*, but she has a good snort, the *douze-cylindres* of the little Fane!' he cried gaily. '*En route, messieurs* — we must not be late for the last act!'

Ned, nursing the Sealyham, mounted beside him, while Robin, who had clambered into the rumble, said to Wolf, 'Get in here with me, Wolf. I want to talk to you.'

It was close on four o'clock of a mild afternoon, the air soft after the rain, the roads drying under the combined influence of a brisk breeze and the thin spring sunshine, when they set off from Wildsee. It would be between fifty and sixty miles to Schloss Baltasar, Cant announced after poring briefly over Wolf's map, while the engine ticked over silkily. Thereafter, he handed the map back, nor asked to refer to it again, as though in that summary glance his mind, the highly specialized mind of the French General Staff officer, had absorbed all the information required to bring them as directly as might be to their destination.

He drove as only a Frenchman can drive, taking every risk but minimizing them by a skill and *sang-froid* that never deserted him. In his hands, the light hands of the fender, the powerful car became a live thing, responding to the slightest touch of hand and foot like a hunter to rein and knee. Almost without slackening speed and, as

It seemed, with the merest flick of those slender wrists, they rounded the innumerable curves of the mountain roads, pulled out to pass the rare vehicles they overtook, threaded the traffic of the villages, scattering cows and pigs and chickens before them. Even after they had left the broad Kaiser-Strasse where it swung west to Salzburg and, crossing the Salzburg-Linz *chaussée*, plunged into a network of secondary roads leading north, the Frenchman continued to push the coupé along at the same reckless gait, his eyes cool, a smile hovering about his finely chiselled lips.

In the rumble Robin and Wolf conferred together.

'The last act?' said Robin. 'I should like to believe it was.'

Wolf grunted. 'At least, we know where young Fane is now. He's at this sanatorium place, or whatever it is, with his sister.'

The Englishman gazed haggardly at the fleeting landscape. 'He was; but how do we know that he, that the two of them, are still there? Grundt has a good four hours' start of us. And he has the plane — I can't forget the plane.'

His companion shrugged. 'The frontier region is lonely, especially at this time of year, between the seasons, before the summer visitors begin to arrive. No doubt this Schloss, too, is suitably remote: why, then, should Grundt trouble to move his prisoners, as long as he doesn't suspect we have located him?'

Robin frowned. 'That's the point — does he suspect? If he doesn't, although the house is probably well guarded, our best plan would probably be to walk up boldly to the front door and demand admittance. But I can't make up my mind to run this risk. I can't help feeling that our best plan will be to wait until dark and then try and sneak into the house and surprise him.'

The major, who from the front seat had been listening
to their conversation, spoke up.

'Aw, nuts!' he cried bombastically. 'We're four to
one, aren't we? I'm all for busting straight in on that big
gazeebo, knocking him cold and rescuing the two kids.'
He appealed to the Frenchman at his side. 'What do you
say, Cant?'

Cant smiled happily. '*De l'attaque*,' he murmured,
'*toujours de l'attaque!*'

'Snooping about till it's dark — anyone would think
you're scared of the big cheese!' Hartigan told Robin
disgustedly.

The Englishman flushed. 'I'm not afraid of a fight;
but it mustn't go wrong. If we bust in, as you call it and
are beaten off, what becomes of Miss Fane then? We
daren't risk it, I tell you, until we know something of the
lie of the land and particularly how many of his people
Grundt has with him at the Schloss.'

'And the only way to do that is to bust in,' the major
insisted.

Wolf shook his head and said; 'Robin is right, Ned.
We shall do well to be cautious. Caution is always a good
thing.'

But the major was in a quarrelsome mood — the
brandy he had drunk had not improved his temper.

'Caution, my foot!' he rasped back. 'You guys give
me a pain in the neck. If you ask me, there's been a darn
sight too much caution about this show already. But
I'm warning you — if you think I'm going to hang around
doing nothing while the General Staff's trying to make
up its mind how to act, you're all wet. To hell with
caution — let's have some action!'

Dallas was about to make an angry rejoinder when
Wolf stayed him with a hand laid on his and a deprecatory headshake. Meanwhile, the major, closing his eyes,

proceeded to fall asleep, and they sped on in silence.

For some time now they had been dropping down from the heights to the lower level of the valley of the Salzach, Salzburg's river, which, marking the frontier of Austria and Bavaria, rolls its green waters along between the Bavarian mountains on the one hand and the Austrian on the other. A gentle melancholy seemed to brood over this half-forgotten region where, in the curve of the river, the once far-flung dominions of the Habsburgs drive a wedge into German territory. Time was, Wolf told Robin in his pedagogic way, when all this country had been Bavarian land, and in the villages they thundered through he showed stately churches in the ornate German-Italian baroque which had long since outlived their fast-disappearing communities and survived only as crumbling monuments of fallen splendour. One day, maybe, it would be German again, said Wolf, for at Braunau-on-the-Inn, away at the top of the wedge, separated only by the river Inn from Bavarian territory, Adolf Hitler was born.

It was five-fifteen by Robin's watch and the light was golden on the flying foothills when Cant, turning, flung out a hand towards a roadside sign that whizzed by. In scarce decipherable lettering they read: 'Zur Heil-Anstalt Schloss Baltasar. 2 Kilometer.' Presently, round a turn of the road, they sighted it across a belt of scrub which the road traversed — a line of windows gleaming in the western sun against a yellow façade above a long, dusky avenue. The avenue was closed by a gate set between pillars topped by heraldic lions, and just beyond the gate, on a notice-board half obliterated by time and weather, the words were still distinguishable. 'Heil-Anstalt Schloss Baltasar.'

They had halted in the lee of a group of farm buildings which, bordering the road, had, at some remote date, evidently been destroyed by fire, for blackened walls emerged from a jungle of weeds on three sides of a small yard.

'Better we leave the car out of sight,' Cant remarked, and backed the coupé into the yard. He switched off the engine and instantly, against the little sounds of hot metal that came from under the bonnet, a deathly silence enveloped them.

Cant shivered. 'How quiet it is!' he murmured. 'One would say we had reached the end of the world!'

Robin and Wolf had already descended, but Ned slept on. Cant would have roused him, but Robin said, 'Leave him!' and stepped out on the road. Phil was whining and jumping about on the driving-seat. 'We don't want the dog to get out,' Wolf lingered to tell Cant. Cant raised the car windows and the two men joined Dallas on the road.

'And what now?' the Frenchman demanded.

'Reconnoitre,' Robin retorted curtly.

At the entrance to the Schloss avenue, beyond the patch of common, the road branched right and left to run parallel with the fence of a dense thicket which separated the Schloss from the road. From the outer gate the avenue, darkened by the branches meeting overhead, drove arrow-straight through the thicket to a massive door set in a high wall. Immediately behind the wall and rising above it, the Mansard roof and the pediments of the upper windows of a mansion of the rococo period were visible. The wall, lofty and fashioned of rough-hewn masonry with a frieze of broken glass along the top, and the great doors, oaken and studded with iron, gave the exterior the air of a prison. Like a prison it presented a blank face to the outer world, and the hush that prevailed within and without gave no clue to what might be going on behind those unrevealing gates, that grim masonry. Halted there, the three men strained their ears in vain for any sound.

'It can't be that the place is empty,' Robin murmured with a haggard air.

'Someone's been here in a car,' said Cant, and pointed through the gate to tire marks under the trees where the roadway of the drive was still spongy from the day's rain.

The gate was padlocked, but they vaulted over and, swinging right, were instantly merged in the gloom of what had clearly once been a plantation of young trees bordering the avenue on either side. Now the trees were full-grown, and shrubs and bushes, which had sprung up between their orderly rows, had transformed the plantation into a wilderness through which the three had to force their way. To keep out of sight of the avenue, they deliberately continued to bear right, so that when at length the limits of the plantation were reached, and the Schloss wall towered before them, they emerged considerably farther away from the entrance than they had intended. And so it happened that the three, each ensconced behind his separate tree, panting with their exertions and peering towards the Schloss doors, were cut off by the woods about them from a view of the avenue and were thus powerless to avert the imminent disaster.

It came in the shape of a stalwart figure which without warning shot out from the mouth of the avenue, making for the Schloss entrance. It was the major, pistol in hand, with Phil joyfully gambolling about him. Before one of them could move, he had grabbed the iron bell-pull that hung down beside the gateway and tugged it vigorously. A bell clanged furiously and clanged and clanged as the major, with a sort of blithe fury, tugged.

Robin sprang out from behind his tree, his eyes blazing. 'Ned,' he called in a cautious undertone, 'Ned!'

If the major heard him, the paid no heed, but went on savagely pulling the bell.

Dallas darted back to cover as, without warning, one half of the great doors was cautiously opened, but almost in the same instant slammed to again. At the top of his voice the major roared: 'Hey, what's the idea? Open that door, will you? *Offnen*, I tell you!' at the same time hammering on the solid oak with the butt of his gun.

Some twenty paces from the gateway, where the wall bent back at a right angle, a slender turret projected with a narrow, shuttered window like a loophole, commanding the whole open space before the Schloss entrance. Suddenly the shutter swung outward, there was a streak of flame, an ear-splitting report, and the major fell flat.

Wolf was nearest. Immediately he whirled forth to Ned's aid. But already the major was on his feet, scurrying for safety. A rain of bullets came from the wood, splintering the shutter, shivering the window glass — from behind a tree-trunk Cant had emptied his pistol at the unseen sniper. At the same moment a figure flashed out from the trees. It was Dallas. Gaining the shelter of the wall, he ran along it and vanished from sight round the corner.

Wolf, left in the open, had swung about at that burst of fire from the wood. For an instant he halted, irresolute. In that split fraction of a second there was a movement at the loophole behind him, a glimpse of a livid face. A hairy hand protruded, a pistol roared, and Wolf, spinning half round, pitched forward on his face and lay still.

Head down, his gun smoking in his hand, Cant burst into the open. Deliberately, the figure at the loophole fired at him, a lightning succession of shots, regardless of the spatter of bullets that sprayed the window from the other side of the avenue, where the major in full view was seeking to cover his comrade's advance. The bullets kicked up the pebbles about the Frenchman's feet and spat savagely among the tree-trunks, but Cant still kept on until, gathering Wolf up in his arms, he began to drag him to safety. For the moment Ned's fire had silenced the fusillade from the window, and in the lull the major, sprinting forward, helped Cant to carry Wolf into the shelter of the trees. Between them they bore him deep into the thicket.

He was still alive and conscious. But his chest rattled as he breathed and every breath he drew brought scarlet bubbles frothing at his lips. They had reached a spot where, in the shade of a lofty fir, the wood was less thick, when the wounded man stopped them.

'So, it is enough,' he gasped. 'Set me down here. All my life I have loved the trees. If I have to die, I should like it to be in a wood.'

They were not sorry to comply, for the wounded man was no light weight, the going rough. But they paused an instant to listen before putting him down. Silence had fallen upon the woods again: the only sound was their own hard breathing, that eerie rattle from Wolf's chest.

They propped him against the tree-trunk. His features had a pinched look in the forest twilight and his eyes were clouding over: the grizzled moustache trembled to his rapid, laboured breathing. Ned dropped to his knees beside him and would have opened his waistcoat, but the other stopped him.

'Don't trouble!' he murmured faintly. 'It's the lung. You and I know what that means, old friend — we've seen it before. An hour at the most...' The blood bubbled at his lips and he broke off.

Ned put his arm about him. 'What can I say to you?' he cried brokenly. 'I ran you into this, old man. I must have been crazy, but you know what I am when the drink's in me. If you die, Wolf, I'll never forgive myself.'

Wolf smiled. 'It was written, Ned — three days now I have known it. Do you remember what I told you that night at Schulte's? *"Du glaubst zu schieben und Du wirst geschoben"* — we're all in the hands of Fate ...' His voice trailed off. Cant wiped the blood from the pallid lips with his handkerchief, but Wolf did not appear to see him. With an anxious air he was gazing about him. 'Where's Robin?' he panted.

'The last I saw of him was just before you were shot,' said Cant. 'He bolted across the open and followed the wall along. It sounds crazy, for the place is a regular fortress and God knows how many people Clubfoot has with him, but if I know anything of Robin, he's gone to try to find a way into the house.'

The wounded man nodded imperceptibly. 'So, it would be like him,' he murmured. The dimming eyes smiled at the major. 'You told him you wanted action, didn't you, Ned?' Then he suddenly grew agitated. 'Don't let him be slaughtered like the others,' he gasped. 'Never mind about me. Go after him. Or, better, find Maier at the Goldene Rose — he'll bring help. To fail now might cost Robin his life.' A fit of coughing caught him and he closed his eyes.

Ned seemed utterly broken, staring tragically at the dying man.

Cant beckoned him aside. 'I don't believe that Robin will manage to break in,' he said in a low voice. 'But if he has been fool enough to run his head into this hornets' nest, we shall do no good by following his example. They're on their guard now — it would be madness to try to get in while it's still light. You stay here with Wolf. I'm going to take the car and fetch Maier and some of his men.'

The major nodded abstractedly. The wounded man had joined his hands together — his lips moved silently as though he were praying. With sorrowful eyes the Frenchman stood and contemplated him for a moment, then, turning on his heel, strode off rapidly through the trees.

The evening was very still. A blackbird whistled in the branches of the fir; in the distance lambs were calling. The Fighting Major dropped to his knees beside his dying friend and, bowing his head, wept unashamedly.

CHAPTER XXVIII

Phil to the Rescue

PATRICIA FANE had plenty of spirit; but she found it oozing away as, back in her bedroom, she heard the key turn in the lock and the old woman's shuffling footfall die away along the corridor. For most American girls of the leisured class, life is made easy, and while Patricia Fane had sought to vary the monotony of what she felt was a rather useless existence by deliberately courting danger — motoring, flying, speedboat racing — she had been spared all contact with such methods of violence as those she had just witnessed.

The unfamiliarity of it all disarmed her. As long as she had been with Grundt, her natural pride had come to her · aid. No one was going to bully her: she was an American, she must keep her chin up. But once more alone in the depressing surroundings of her dilapidated bedchamber, a sense of despair came over her that seemed to paralyze her instinct to rebel. Self-willed as she was and unused to having her slightest wish gainsaid, she let Frau Schratt lock her in and leave her there without the least show of resistance. For the first time in her life she felt cowed, less by fear of Grundt than by the realization of the utter helplessness of her position.

She felt as though civilization had forsaken her. It was a bewildering sensation to realize that you could be carried off like this to a place about which you knew nothing, not even in what country it was situated, and held a prisoner, without being able to walk out or even telephone the police. As she stood in the centre of the floor and let

the silence of the upper regions of the ancient house in-
vade the room, she found her mind reverting with horror
to what Grundt had told her about the former character
of the Schloss.

In her ears seemed to ring again the maniacal cries and
peals of laughter which might once have resounded under
those golden ceilings, perhaps in that very room, and she
realized that with as little result she, too, might cry out in
terror — in pain, even, if torture — she shivered — were
in Grundt's plan: she thought of the glimpse she had just
had of this girl of Jimmy's, whom Dallas called Liselotte,
eyes glassy, features distraught with fear, and her
consternation deepened. She had a foreboding that the
crisis was approaching. What would the next move be?
They had captured Liselotte: then Jimmy, too, must be
in their hands. Was he a prisoner in the Schloss as well?

She stole to the door and listened. There were voices
and footsteps in the hall below, but nobody came upstairs. After a little she heard the throb of a motor engine, the noise of a car door slammed, the grinding sound
of tires on gravel as a car — no, it was two cars — departed. Then silence once more, this stagnant silence
that seemed as much part of the atmosphere of the house
as the faint, sour odour of decay that hung over all.

Her watch had run down. She had no means of telling
the time, for it was raining and the sun was hidden—
there was nothing to be seen from the window but a
huddle of dripping trees, masses of mist obscuring the
mountains behind. She pulled the window open. The
room was on the second floor, too high from the ground
to make jumping feasible, and there was no rain-pipe or
any other available means of descent. Still she lingered
there, staring blindly out at the cheerless scene, until her
growing sense of panic, invading her in great waves, made
her fear that under the goad of some unreasoning im-

pulse she might be tempted to throw herself out. She closed the window and turned away.

The silence fretted at her nerves. She longed for a cigarette; but her cigarettes were in her bag which the old woman had stolen. She began to pace the floor, wrestling with the terrors that seemed to dog her footsteps. She halted at last, her heart thumping. This would never do, she told herself. She must keep calm. She would shut Grundt from her thoughts, concentrate on her chances of rescue.

She lay down on the bed, tried to relax. By this they must have missed her at Baden-Baden: surely, Major Ned would have looked her up at the Excelsior and found her gone. He would know that he had never sent for her, that she had been kidnapped: more than this, however, he was hardly likely to discover. She wondered what he, what his friend Robin — for Dallas had certainly gone to Baden-Baden to meet him — would do: she had a feeling that, however completely she might seem to have vanished, Robin Dallas would, sooner or later, track her down. He was like that. Direct. Tenacious.

Her mind travelled back to the conversation she had overheard between him and Liselotte at the pension. Hadn't Liselotte offered to clear his name in that old espionage affair, provided he would abandon his hunt for Jimmy, and hadn't he refused? That was decent of him. His private honour must mean a great deal to a man like Robin Dallas, yet he had turned down this chance of winning it back, in order to keep faith with her and his mission.

Despite her night's rest, she was still inexpressibly weary and her head was aching again. She closed her eyes and went on thinking about the man Dallas. It was strange, but he had left her with a sense of confidence in

him that endured even now, when she was so far beyond
his ken. He had been odiously rude to her and she had
called him ill-mannered and conceited. So he was, and
she had done nothing that wasn't completely within her
rights in having his past investigated. Then why did she
feel so sorry for him, why was she conscious of a stab at
the heart as she recalled their parting in Paris and the
hurt and angry look in his eyes?

The colour came into her face. How savagely he had
spoken to her! Men back home in America didn't speak
to women like this — at least, not the men she played
around with. But of course they belonged to her set, rich
men's sons — friends of Jimmy's, for the most part —
who, in the natural course of events, would marry money
— some day, by the same reasoning, she supposed she
would marry one of them. They were not poor devils with
nothing to lose, like this rough-tongued, arrogant Dallas
person — she was definitely a 'marriage prospect,' as
Willie Hastings had once put it, and it stood to reason
that they courted her, made much of her. Of course she
was self-willed and spoilt. Dallas had been right there —
she knew because he had wounded her, and the truth always wounds. The tears came into her eyes. She would
like to be friends with him, but to be friends with a stubborn brute like that you would have to let him boss you,
and of course she wouldn't stand for that. Still, it must
be rather thrilling to have a man like Robin Dallas in
love with one, to see that iron reserve of his melt, his eyes
light up as one came into the room. No chance of that.
He didn't give a damn for her — he had as good as told
her so. Suddenly she felt very friendless and forlorn.
She began to cry in earnest and, crying, fell asleep.

Someone was shaking her feet. The tears wet on her
face, she opened her eyes, then sprang up in terror.

Grundt stood at the foot of the bed. The heavy face was set in grim lines, the great jaw jutted rock-like.

She had swung her legs to the ground, sitting on the edge of the bed. 'I was asleep — what time is it?' she asked confusedly, rubbing her eyes — she was aware of Frau Schratt in the background.

'Past five,' came the gruff reply. 'You've had no lunch, Anna says. She brought it, as I ordered, but she couldn't rouse you.' He swung to the woman. 'All right — you can fetch it now.'

Frau Schratt began to grumble. 'I let the fire out. You said you'd be leaving before dinner. It'll take time.'

'No matter. Get out!'

The door closed softly. Grundt hobbled to the window, turned and came back. 'I have had your guardian telephoned to in New York . . .'

Patricia looked at him apprehensively. 'My guardian?'

'*Na*, this man Hastings — there were two cables from him about business matters in your bag.'

'You spoke to him?'

He laughed dryly. 'You surely don't imagine I called him from here so that he could trace you to this house?' He laughed again. '*Nee, nee*, Fräulein. My Vienna agent attended to it. Herr Hastings understands that the cash must be remitted to my account at the Crédit Lyonnais in Paris within the next twenty-four hours.'

'The cash?' she faltered.

'*Gewiss* — the half-million dollars which is the price of your and your brother's release?'

She jumped up. 'My brother? He's here?'

Grundt ignored the question. 'Herr Hastings requires proof of your identity. It appears that you have a secret indicator word, known only to the two of you, which guarantees the authenticity, as coming from you, of any cable prefixed with the word in question. Am I right?'

She stared at him affrighted, her breath coming and going quickly. 'What did you tell Mr. Hastings about me?'

'The facts,' was the crisp answer. 'That you have found your brother, that the money is required to clear his good name.'

'I know of no such word,' she answered with a little defiant air, 'and in any case, I don't believe Mr. Hastings would consent to have any dealings with you.'

He growled at her. 'Don't waste time. Your friend Hastings tried to parley until he realized we mean business. Come, give me the word!'

She was trembling. 'There's no word!' she said.

This was a different Grundt from the man she had seen that morning. His bantering air was gone and a lowering frown clouded the beetling forehead. His manner was unspeakably menacing, his eyes glinting with a yellowish reflection, the nostrils twitching like those of an angry ape. He seemed to take a deep breath and his grip tightened on his crutch-handle stick until the tendons stood out on the back of the hairy hand like ropes. 'Don't lie to me, you baggage!' he snarled. 'Hastings spoke the truth because he knows that it's your life and your brother's against the money.'

'Bluff,' the girl cried with heightened colour. 'You daren't touch me and you know it. I'm not so friendless as you think. I've friends at Salzburg, at Baden-Baden, who have come to Europe for the express purpose of finding my brother . . .'

He laughed mirthlessly. 'I know. This adventurer Hartigan, who flew down with you from Paris and the jail-bird, Robin Merrall. I shouldn't count on them, if I were you. They'll never find you here. And if they did, they wouldn't get farther than the outer entrance.'

Her courage was ebbing. 'That doesn't mean that

you'd dare to do anything to me,' she said unsteadily. 'I don't know whether you realize it, but I'm not just anyone. If I were to disappear permanently, the newspapers would never rest until they'd found out what had become of me. And that's altogether apart from Major Hartigan and the others who are hunting for my brother.'

'I'll chance that,' was the terse rejoinder. 'But don't *you* go taking chances, *liebes* Fräulein. People don't take chances with Clubfoot.'

To keep herself in countenance, because she was so desperately afraid, because her hands were damp with fear and her heart lay like an ice cube within her, she made a contemptuous mouth. Like lightning striking, rage flamed suddenly from him.

'You think I jest?' he roared. 'I'm bluffing, *ja?* Then let me tell you this. The charming little lady who captivated your brother, she took a chance with me. And where is she now? Dangling from the end of a rope, the double-crossing slut, and her accomplice beside her!' And when the girl gazed at him blankly, the colour flowing out of her cheeks, he thrust out his great, hairy paws and, shaking them in her face, trumpeted, '*Ja*, this very morning, I strung her up myself with my own hands. Now do you think I'm bluffing? Answer me, *verdammt!*' With stick upraised, he came lurching at her, his misshapen foot clumping on the threadbare rug, while he screamed: 'Do you want to be served alike? The word, *verflucht*, the word!'

At that instant there was a loud hammering below. He stopped dead. A shot followed and, with a furious imprecation, he hobbled with incredible swiftness to the door and was gone. A regular fusillade ensued, voices called and doors were banged while she, asking herself vainly what the hubbub portended, sank down, petrified with fright, on the bed. When at last, the shooting over and the turmoil abated, she glanced towards the bedroom door, she perceived that Grundt had left it ajar.

She sprang to her feet. From the threshold of the room she saw that the staircase was empty. Noiselessly she ran down the shallow steps. But as she reached the first-floor landing, she heard Grundt's strident tones in the hall below.

A gallery stretched its length before her, broader and more imposing, with its busts and cabinets, than that on the floor above, with a line of rooms giving off it. At hazard she darted along it, no plan in her mind except to get out of earshot of that terrifying voice. As she sped along, something white and fluffy came hurtling out of the open door of one of the rooms and began leaping about her, filling the air with frantic barks.

It was Phil. In a panic she snatched up the Sealyham, trying to stifle his barks with her hand. A voice cried joyfully, 'Patricia!' and, looking up, she saw, in the doorway of the room from which Phil had come bounding out, a figure in a gray woollen cap who held out his hands to her.

It was Jimmy.

CHAPTER XXIX

Hope Flares up and Dies

WITH a quick glance behind, one hand still firmly clamped about the writhing Sealyham's jaws, she whisked into the room and closed the door. It was a bedroom no less dilapidated than hers, but larger and, if anything, more ornate. Two suitcases, one of them partly unpacked, stood on the floor.

For a long moment she was unable to speak. Her eyes grew misty, as she gazed at the man before her. He on his side was regarding her with a bemused, incredulous air. His face was thin and worn, his hands emaciated, as though he had only just emerged from a long illness.

She gave a little sob. 'Jimmy,' she faltered, 'Jimmy, darling!' And, dropping the dog, she flung her arms about him, burying her face against the old gray pullover he wore.

In a strained voice he said: 'How did I get here? What is this place? Patricia, honey, what's happened to me and what are you doing here?'

But she only hugged him closer, murmuring, 'Oh, Jimmy, Jimmy!'

'This doctor guy who brought me here from Wildsee — Keller, his name is — was with me,' he went on in the same halting fashion. 'Suddenly a lot of shooting started and he rushed off. I sat on here because — well, because I was afraid to go out, I guess — besides, noise kind of hurts my head. Then I heard a scratching at the door and there was Phil, dear old Phil. Do you know, until I saw him, I believe I'd forgotten about your very existence? I think I'd forgotten my own name until I saw "Patricia

Fane" engraved on his collar, the collar I sent you from London. Then everything started to come back.' He broke off. 'What's the date?'

'It's the fourteenth — no, the fifteenth,' she said, glancing up at him anxiously.

'The fifteenth of what?'

'April, honey. You've been ill — you wouldn't know.'

His eyes were deeply troubled. 'April?' he repeated with dismay. 'And I left London — when was it?' He brushed his hand across his forehead. 'Everything's so mixed up.'

She pressed him to her. 'Don't worry about it now, Jimmy.'

'I went to Hamburg,' he said with growing agitation. 'What became of the man I was to meet? He couldn't come to the hotel — he sent word that he was waiting for me at some café on the waterfront. I remember taking a taxi there, going upstairs, but after that...' He clasped his head in his hands.

She lifted a tear-stained face. 'Don't bother trying to think back, Jimmy boy. Nothing matters, now that I've found you again.'

His bewildered air was clearing. Now his eyes snapped angrily and he squared his jaw, sticking out his underlip in a way she remembered of old. 'But it does matter,' he retorted obstinately. 'I had to collect a packet from this man — I'll get his name in a minute — and bring it back to London. It was most important, the Ambassador told me.'

She had run to the door and opened it a fraction, listening. Now she closed it hurriedly and came back. 'It'd take too long to tell you now,' she said. 'We haven't any time — we've got to get out of here.'

He grabbed her wrist. 'Not until I know what became of that packet.'

Impatiently she caught her breath. 'You were robbed, Jimmy.'

He glared at her. 'Robbed? By whom?'

'This girl of yours, Arlette Lassagne, she was a spy.'

His face was blank with consternation. 'Arlette? It isn't possible. Why, she was with me only ——' Violently he pulled his sister towards him. 'Is that why she's run away?' And, Patricia remaining silent, he went on, frowning: 'It's true, she was the only one who knew I was going to Hamburg. She followed me there — she said her brother had been arrested by the Nazis.' He glanced wildly about him. 'Where is she? They kept on telling me they were taking me to her.'

Patricia put her arms about him again. 'You must forget about her, Jimmy.'

He shook her off. 'Whose house is this?'

'It belongs to a man named Grundt. Arlette betrayed you to him.'

'I've heard that name quite lately. Wait!' He pressed his fingers to his temples. 'Is it a big man who's lame and bawls at you?'

She gazed at him aghast. 'Oh, Jimmy! You've seen him?'

'He was up here with the doctor chap this afternoon. He asked me a lot of questions, but I can't think what they were. Anyhow, I told him to get the blazes out of it and he went away.'

'It's he who has those plans you were sent to fetch,' she said, watching him anxiously. 'He intends to sell them back to you — for half a million dollars.'

'Half a mil——!' He broke off. 'Like hell he will! Where is he? Take me to him — I've got to get that packet.'

She had returned to the door and was listening again. Now she stepped in front of him as he came storming towards her.

'Jimmy,' she cried, clinging to him fast, 'you don't understand. We're prisoners here, you and I, and the house is full of this man's people. There's someone moving in the corridor outside now, but once things quiet down, we'll slip out of this room of yours and hide somewhere until we see a chance to escape.'

By this he had thrown off his lassitude. 'Escape, nothing! I'm not leaving without that packet.'

She stamped her foot. 'You've got to do as I say. Help's on the way. I sent four men over from America to find you. I believe that shooting we heard just now means that they've arrived. I know because of Phil. I left him at Baden-Baden, where two of these men, Robin Dallas and Major Hartigan, and I had followed you, and since Phil has turned up it must be that one of them, or perhaps both, have traced us here. As long as those shots we heard don't mean that they're dead...' She shuddered. 'But we can't afford to wait for them, Jimmy. As soon as the coast is clear...'

The words died on her lips, for without warning her brother had clapped his hand over her mouth. The door was softly opening. Inch by inch it gaped until an unkempt face was visible, peering in. The next instant the door was noiselessly shut and a tatterdermalion apparition stood before them.

The strong growth of beard, the layer of dust and grime that obscured the features, the gaping rent in the sleeve of the jacket, the mud-encrusted shoes, suggested a tramp. But the eyes, cobalt blue in the swarthy face, and a certain pantherlike swiftness as the newcomer advanced were unmistakable. He was hatless, and a bloodstained handkerchief was wrapped about his left hand. A smile wrinkled his face as he caught sight of Patricia.

'It's a regular fortress — I'd quite a job to get in,' he

observed. 'But here I am!' His glance shifted to Fane.
'This is the brother, isn't it? He's very like you.'

'Who's this?' said Fane gruffly.

'It's Robin Dallas — one of the men I spoke of,'
Patricia replied.

Dallas nodded coolly to Fane. 'You've had a rough
time,' he said to him. 'I'm glad to see it's no worse.
How do you feel?'

'I'm all right,' was the rather ungracious reply.

'His memory's come back,' the girl explained in an
aside to Dallas. 'But he's got to take it easy. We must
get him out of here.'

Fane overheard her. 'I've told my sister,' he broke in,
'I'm not going until I've recovered that packet that was
stolen from me.'

Dallas laughed dryly. 'Don't let that worry you. It
was hard enough getting in; but it's going to be the devil's
own business getting out.'

The girl was staring at his hand. 'You're wounded —
they've shot you?' she exclaimed.

'I'm all right. It's only my hand,' he answered. 'I
nicked it on the broken glass, shinning over that infernal
wall. But they got poor Ned, I'm afraid.'

She clasped her hands tightly together. 'The major?
You don't mean he's ...'

The light had gone out of his eyes. 'I'm afraid so.
They opened on him from a window as he was ringing at
the front door — I saw him drop.' His voice was sombre.
'Poor Ned! I didn't wait to see what happened: I made a
dash for the back in the general confusion and managed
to swing myself from a tree over the wall.' The Sealyham
was sniffing at his trousers. Gazing down at the dog,
'Phil was with Ned —he got in at least,' he concluded
wistfully.

'That was how I knew you were here,' said Patricia,

and drew out her handkerchief. 'Let me look at that hand of yours, won't you?'

He thrust it behind his back. 'No time now — besides, it's nothing. Has Grundt talked to you yet?'

She nodded. 'He wants half a million dollars for the plans.' She told briefly of the interview.

'But this guy Grundt, or whatever his name is,' her brother broke in excitedly, 'he's crazy. He can't get away with this sort of thing.' He sprang forward. 'Come on, you,' he cried to Robin. 'Let's you and I lam hell out of the . . .'

But Dallas, with head bent, was listening at the door. 'Softly!' he told Fane. 'I hear voices.' He faced the two of them. 'Listen, you two, before we decide on any plan of action, we've got to discover how many of them we have to tackle. Poor old Ned, the gallant madman that he always was, gave the show away by trying to rush the front door, and I think Grundt's getting ready to bolt. There's a private airfield in the grounds here and that plane of yours is drawn up on the runway ready to take off — I saw it as I came by. Three men — a husky-looking fellow in flying-clothes and two mechanics — were working on her. Apparently they've been having some trouble with the engine. Grundt himself went down, after the shooting, to hurry them up — that's how I managed to slip upstairs after getting in through a window in the basement. With these three assistant murderers down at the airfield, as far as I know only Grundt and Doctor Keller are left in the house — oh, and an old woman I had to dodge in the kitchens, a nasty-looking piece of work.'

'Frau Schratt,' Patricia explained. 'She's my jailer. She stole my bag with all my money.'

Fane had swung to Dallas. 'And you think that you and I can't take on a couple of Heinies and an old woman, is that it?' he demanded truculently.

Swiftly the other rounded on him. 'All that matters
to you is to recover that packet and complete your
mission. You can't do that if you get shot like my poor
friend Ned Hartigan. And I don't suppose you're anxious
to cough up half a million dollars, either. Very well,
then! You keep out of this and leave it to your sister
and me.'

The young man flushed angrily. 'You can't give me
orders,' he cried in a high-pitched, hysterical voice.

Dallas glanced at Patricia. 'You haven't told him —
about the Feds?'

She shook her head, and the Englishman spoke to Fane
again. 'You don't realize it,' he said quietly, 'but you're
in a mess. The State Department believe you sold those
plans to Grundt.'

With fists clenched Fane sprang at him. 'It's a filthy
lie!'

Anxiously the other's glance travelled backward to the
door. 'Will you pipe down, for the love of Mike, and not
waste time? We know it's a lie, but the fact remains
that United States secret service men are at Salzburg,
only a matter of twenty-five miles from here, looking for
you to arrest you.'

'To arrest me? You're kidding!' The boy was aghast.

'What we have to do is to get you out of here together
with those plans before these G-men can nab you and run
you back to London, where you can hand the plans over
and report to your Chief in the ordinary way. Now, will
you kindly shut up?'

'But they've nothing on me,' Fane wailed. 'I can't
seem to remember just what happened to me at Hamburg, but I'd never do a thing like that, as my sister will
tell you. Won't you, Patricia?'

Gently she put her arms about him and made him sit
down on the huge four-poster.

'We know you're innocent, Jimmy, darling,' she soothed him. 'But all the same these people are after you and you must do as he says.' She turned to Robin again. 'Go on!' she bade him.

Dallas was once more listening at the door. Now he came back — the girl quailed at his grave look. Fane had flung himself full length on the bed, his face to the wall.

Robin said, 'Grundt hasn't finished with you yet, you realize that?'

She bowed her head. 'I know.'

'He's bound to return to the charge. When he does, temporize with him. If the worst comes to the worst, give him his code word, but not the right one. I believe he's planning to take you and your brother away with him in your plane to Paris to keep you as hostages there until the money's paid over. Well, he mustn't — you'll have to try and hold him. There are three of us here, if we leave poor Ned out, but two are on the wrong side of the wall and we must give them time to break in. Is that clear?'

Her brief nod assented. 'What are you going to do?' she asked huskily as he turned once again towards the door.

'Get those plans back before Grundt sends for you again.'

'Alone?'

He shrugged. 'It depends on what the situation is downstairs.'

She shuddered. 'You're crazy. He's raging.'

He nodded. 'I know. He's tasted blood.' His mouth twitched. 'Liselotte...'

'It's true, then?' Her voice trembled. 'He told me, but I couldn't believe it, it was so horrible — I thought he was trying to scare me.'

Under its caking of grime the haggard face was mask-like.

'Stay here with your brother,' said Dallas. 'Don't let him do anything silly. The house is buzzing with them, for all we know. If I get the plans, I'll try to come back and the three of us will have to make a dash for that plane of yours. Meanwhile, if you do see Grundt, remember — play for time!'

A finger to his lips, he opened the door, holding it slightly ajar. From somewhere close at hand a shambling footfall came to their strained ears.

Patricia caught his arm. 'Frau Schratt!' she whispered.

He did not close the door, but set his foot against it, bracing it by the handle. The shuffling footstep came nearer, its faint rustle mingled now with the chink of crockery, but did not stop. A second of breathless expectancy and he softly swung the door inward, peered out. He whipped his head in again, closed the door without a sound.

'You're right,' he said softly. 'She came up by the service stairs at the end of the gallery. The way I came up. She has a tray — she's stopped for a breather before going on up the main staircase.'

'Grundt sent her to fetch me some food,' said Patricia in dismay. 'She'll go to my room on the floor above this and find me missing.'

He laughed noiselessly. 'So much the better if she has to hunt for you. Give us more time.'

'Stay here with me!' she pleaded. 'It's insane to take this risk. Wait till the others show up!'

He shook his head. 'I've got to get those plans.' Inch by inch he eased the door towards him, peeped out. 'The old trout's still there,' he reported humorously, holding the door.

Her agitation was growing. 'This man's a monster. If you fall into his hands...' She looked desperately about her. 'When I think of Major Ned...' She broke off. 'I'll give him the indicator word — he can have his ransom. It's a lot of money, but I can afford it, I guess...'

He stared at her in horror. 'Not on your life...'

'Money isn't everything. Enough blood has been shed. It's bad enough about poor Major Ned. If anything happened to you, I should never forgive myself.'

'Give in to that bloody-minded ruffian? You're crazy!' he cried. 'Besides, the money isn't all, not by a long chalk. You're forgetting that the four of us have a score to settle with this man, and now poor Ned's death on the top of it. For more than three years I've been waiting for this opportunity — if you think I'd let you rob me of it...'

'And if they shoot you down, as they shot Major Ned?'

'There are the other two, aren't there? We swore an oath to settle with him, whether we found your brother or not, and, by God, we're going through with it!' He opened the door gingerly, poking his head through the opening, then swiftly withdrew. 'Damnation, will she never move?'

The girl sighed. 'If you're determined to do this,' she told him, 'there's something I must say before we separate. I want to apologize...'

'To me?'

Her nod was almost imperceptible. 'You know — for that Pinkerton business.'

He smiled at her. 'I'd already forgotten it.'

'At the Pension Hasenberg, the other afternoon, while you and Liselotte were talking,' she said hurriedly, 'I was hidden in the next room.'

He was astonished. 'You *were?* How?'

'It doesn't matter now. But I overheard your conversation. I know now that you were betrayed. I also know that this poor creature offered to clear your name if you'd let her take Jimmy away and that you refused.' She put out her hand. 'Thank you.'

For an instant he retained her hand in his. 'I'm sorry, too — about everything. But we were bound to quarrel.'

Her nod was wistful. 'I know. The trouble is we're too much alike in character. You told me, the very first time we met, that I always wanted my own way.' She checked herself, then took her hand away. 'Well, and so do you!'

He grinned at her through his grime. 'I expect you're right,' he replied apologetically.

'Besides, you're looking for something under the surface, too, the same as you say I am, aren't you?'

'Looking for what?'

She averted her eyes from his steady gaze, colouring slightly. With a listless shrug she answered, 'I don't know. Sympathy, perhaps!'

'Or love?' He made it sound like a question: she did not know whether he spoke of himself or of her.

She met his glance. 'You were very much in love with her, weren't you?' she hazarded timorously.

'With Liselotte?' He shrugged. 'Once, perhaps, but all that died in prison.' He turned from her: her eyes followed him as, with infinite caution, he peeped round the door. 'All clear!' he announced, withdrawing his head. 'Well, here goes!'

His gaze hung on her face.

'Take care of yourself!' she murmured huskily.

'You said that as though it mattered,' he told her, staring sombrely before him.

'You know it does,' she answered in a low voice.

Her eyes brimmed over. As though to encourage her, he put his two hands gently on her shoulders. At his touch, with a little, sobbing cry, she fell forward and clung to him desperately. 'Oh, my dear!' he murmured and caught her to him.

But only for an instant. The next moment he had stood back, contemplating with a sort of dismay a tear that rolled slowly down her cheek.

'Go if you must,' she told him brokenly, 'but, oh, Robin, come back to me!'

He did not speak, but his smile, encouraging, confident, seemed to say, 'Trust me!' The next instant, he had slipped out into the corridor. Never had she seen eyes that shone so fearlessly, she told herself as he disappeared.

He had closed the door behind him. Beyond it, silence reigned once more, razor-sharp with suspense, boring into her taut nerves like an auger. Jimmy, prone on the bed, lay like a log, and she perceived that he had fallen asleep. Posted at the door she strained her ears for any untoward sound beyond the fringes of the stealthy hush about her. Her mind reverted to her plan of taking Jimmy with her and stowing away somewhere in the fastnesses of that rambling barrack of a house. It wouldn't be difficult — she thought of the rows of empty rooms — and they would gain time by disappearing, even if they should be dragged to light again. Somewhere not too far away — she must be able to intercept Robin if he should come back. She laid a hesitant hand on the door-handle ...

Like a stone flung through a window-pane, a shout, a crash, a medley of violent, confused noises on the floor below shattered the stillness. She opened the door and, like the trumpet notes of an organ, Grundt's tremendous voice, screaming with wrath, came rolling upstairs to her. Then, with a clap that made the windows dance, a door slammed and abruptly, as though a tap had been turned off, the hubbub died, and she was left there, torn with fear and indecision, her heart pounding in her ears. What did that sudden outburst signify? Could it be that Robin had taken Grundt by surprise, disarmed him? Or was it that...? She felt her dwindling stock of hope slowly running out.

She glanced towards the bed. Jimmy still slept on. She faced the door again. As she did so, the blood seemed to grow cold in her veins — a stealthy, shuffling footstep was audible, coming along the corridor.

Frau Schratt's squat and toadlike figure was framed in the doorway. She was wheezing with short puffs and her bleary eyes were venomous. She cackled stridently.

'So there you are, my pretty?' she croaked 'You thought you'd pay the brother a little visit, did you? And who gave you permission to leave your room?'

As she spoke, deadly with menace, she advanced upon the girl, dragging her splay feet in their black list slippers over the floor. As though to shield the sleeping figure, Patricia fell back until the bed stayed her farther progress,

'So I should cart yer grub up and downstairs like I was your negro slave?' the old woman grumbled wrathfully. 'I could bust my bloody bellows, waiting on yer, yer 'aughty slut, and you wouldn't give a damn, would yer?' With a sudden, fierce pounce the clawlike fingers pinned the girl's wrist. 'You try and give me the slip again, my beauty, and I'll cut the livin' lights out of yer! Come on out of that!'

So saying she began to haul the girl towards the door. Patricia resisted, crying in a low voice, as though afraid to disturb the sleeper, 'Let me go! Where are you taking me?' Vainly she tried to free her wrist.

'Stow it!' the hag snarled, jerking the wrist round so that the girl gasped with pain. 'The Guv'nor wants to see yer.' She tittered spitefully, screwing up her blood-shot eyes. 'He's got a little surprise for yer.'

A figure swung into view in the doorway, long-nosed, bespectacled. It was Doctor Keller. In his hand he had a sort of leather cuirass with strings that hung down.

'We gif her the chacket if we haf any trouble, Anna,' he cried excitedly; and added to the girl, 'We know how to handle violent patients here, yong leddy, yas, by golly!'

'She knows what's good for her — she'll come without that,' Frau Schratt rejoined ominously, giving the wrist another jerk, and Patricia let them lead her downstairs.

Between them they brought her to the ground-floor study where Grundt had interviewed her before. Doctor Keller knocked and went in, then called in German to Frau Schratt, who promptly pushed the girl across the threshold.

Patricia had never seen a strait-jacket before. But now she was to realize the purpose of the odd-looking contrivance in Doctor Keller's hand. It was a replica of the stout leather jerkin, pulled down over the arms and pinioning them to the sides, in which Robin Dallas confronted her, roped to a chair in the gathering dusk of the library.

CHAPTER XXX

'*Stone Dead Hath No Fellow*'

WITHOUT looking at the desk, she knew that Grundt was there — the atmosphere of the room was thundery with his presence. She could picture him gloating over his victim with that blandly sardonic air she had learnt to associate with his most terrifying moods. Then and there her mind was made up. Robin had wanted her to bluff; but now that he was out of the game, bluffing was too dangerous.

Hadn't Grundt himself warned her: 'People don't take chances with Clubfoot'? Let him suspect her of trickery and he would be capable of wreaking on the pair of them a vengeance as merciless as that he had exacted from the unhappy Liselotte and her companion. Grundt should have his code word, she resolved: but at her price, and that would be Robin Dallas's release.

As though he could read what was passing through her mind, Robin's eyes signalled her an unspoken warning. He bore himself with a defiant dignity that made her heart ache — there was a lump in her throat as she turned towards the desk. Ensconced in his big chair, his bulbous lips pressed firmly together upon a freshly lighted cigar, Grundt was contemplating her through a haze of smoke, his chin sunk on the barrel chest, his eyes glittering through half-closed lids.

With a jerk of the head towards Dallas, he growled out in mocking tones: 'Such a clever gentleman, *ei, ei!* So softly, pit-a-pat, he went creeping down the stairs and never knew that my faithful Anna was at his heels every step of the way.' His deep laugh rumbled through the

room. 'Old Clubfoot may not be as young or as active as
he used to be, but he still knows how to defend himself,
ja, and while this English rat was skulking in the hall,
the good Anna pressed the danger signal that rings here
in my study, and when he came sneaking in at the door,
hey, presto! friend Keller and I were ready to receive him.
Ach, Gott, Gott!' The huge torso shook with mirth.

Dallas remaining silent and aloof, after a pause he went
on:

'*So*, Fräulein, everything is prepared. The plane
awaits us: you, your brother, and I leave for Paris immediately. It is still banking hours in New York: all that
remains for you is to give me the code word. I will call
my Vienna agent' — he indicated the telephone on the
desk — 'he will put the matter in hand at once and by
tomorrow the transfer of funds to my account in Paris
should be accomplished and you two young people will be
at liberty. The sooner this little business between us is
completed, the sooner, I would point out, you will be rid
of a presence which, it desolates me to observe, is not
wholly grateful to you.' With a flash of gold-filled teeth
he beamed at her.

Her heart was in her mouth. 'And if I give you the
word,' she said tremulously, 'what guaranty do I have
that you'll carry out your part of the bargain?'

He smiled amiably. 'None. You perceive,' he added,
'that I am not so simple-minded as to offer, or expect
you to accept, my word of honour.' He chortled. 'But
old Clubfoot is not greedy. Half a million dollars is the
price: with half a million dollars I shall be content. Once
the money is in my possession, you and your brother go
free.'

'And the plans?'

'These will, of course, be restored to you.'

Her eye dropped to the littered desk, to the orderly

bookshelves behind. 'How do I know that you have them?'

He narrowed his eyes until they were mere slits. 'Again you must accept my simple assurance, I fear.'

'I should prefer to see them.'

He shook his head. 'They are safer where they are,' he rejoined, with a whimsical glance at Dallas. 'But come, Fräulein, we must be off. Albeit this house is remotely situated, I am unpleasantly aware that the exchange of shots you heard may have alarmed the countryside, and I am loath to be delayed by unwelcome official curiosity. Besides, I wish to be on our way before nightfall. The word, if you please!'

The thought was in her mind: perhaps, after all, I can stall along, as Robin suggested, until the others arrive. She listened for any sound from outside, but all remained still. Grundt was regarding her expectantly, and it seemed to her that his urbane mood was perceptibly waning.

With as much confidence as she could muster, she broke in quickly, 'Wait! There's another point.'

He frowned impatiently. 'Well?'

'You'll release Mr. Dallas, of course?'

His scowl deepened. 'Out of the question!'

Her eye sought Robin, who continued to remain disdainfully mute.

'I'm sure he'll give you an undertaking to do nothing to interfere with your receiving the money.'

Ponderously Grundt shook his bullet head. 'I'm taking no chances with this gentleman. He has caused me considerable trouble: moreover, he has obtained an insight into my methods and organization which is likely to prove inconvenient. I should be glad to oblige you, but in the circumstances . . .' He shrugged and drew thoughtfully on his cigar.

Her eyes grew stubborn. 'Then just what do you mean to do with him?'

He laughed softly. 'I have read in the life of Oliver Cromwell that the English Parliament was confronted with a similar problem in the case of the unfortunate Strafford. There were those on the side of the Parliament who would have saved his life; but one of the parliamentary leaders — Essex, I think it was — came forward with a proverb which sealed his doom. An excellent proverb, Fräulein, and strictly practical, like everything English.' Balefully, his eye rested on the man in the chair. '"Stone dead hath no fellow,"' he quoted, and added, 'Doctor Keller will attend to him after we have gone.'

There was the glitter of spectacles in the background and Patricia was aware of Keller standing there. The blood had drained out of her cheeks.

'You must be joking,' she exclaimed to Grundt. 'You can't mean . . .' Then she met his glance, stony and unsmiling. 'But he was acting under my instructions,' she cried wildly. 'If there's anyone to blame, it is I. It's solely on my account that he's here now.'

The big man grunted. 'I know all about that,' he said impatiently. 'His late lamented lady-love told me. Perhaps you were not aware that our plausible young friend is a convicted spy, a traitor to his country? You should be more careful of the people you employ, young lady. In any case, he's not worth bothering your pretty head about. Come, give me the word and let us depart!'

She was trembling, but she stood her ground. 'Not until he's released,' she replied firmly.

With a gesture ominous in its slow deliberation, Grundt laid his cigar aside.

'So?' he muttered thickly while a sort of spasm shook him. 'You'd dictate to me, would you?'

She quavered. 'I'm not trying to dictate to you. But I feel responsible for Mr. Dallas, and if you want the indicator word, you'll have to let him go.'

On that he turned his head and from under his beetling eyebrows stared at her without speaking. She was aware that the whole expression of his face was changing. The eyes were suddenly aflame with a murderous light, the pendulous cheeks shook, the mouth slavered with little beads of foam that bubbled at the gross and pouting lips. Then without warning he roared, 'Anna!'

Obediently Frau Schratt bobbed out from among the shadows at the door. Grundt had shifted his gaze from the girl to Dallas. He barked an order across his shoulder in German. Patricia did not understand what he said, but she was watching Robin, and it seemed to her that he had suddenly grown rigid under his bonds.

With a shrill cackle the old woman had shuffled to where a tall stove, tiled with white porcelain, straddled a dusky corner of the library. She stooped to the brass door. There was the glimmer of red coals in the gloom, the clatter of iron on iron. The sound caught Patricia's ear. She swung about and saw Frau Schratt, a pair of tongs in her hand, withdrawing a glowing coal from the oven.

Grundt had risen to his feet. Hirsute and forbidding, he towered above the writing-table — his eye never quitted Dallas. Still Dallas remained silent, but Patricia saw a drop of moisture ooze from his forehead and roll down his unshaven cheek.

Frau Schratt shambled forward, a fiery coal smoking in the tongs she grasped. Grundt lurched out from behind the desk, his hairy hand extended to take the tongs.

Patricia was too late to stop him; but she flung herself in front of Robin. 'Stop!' she screamed as Grundt came at her, the tongs in his hand. 'Stop! You shall have the word!'

The lame man halted. 'Then quickly!' he growled. 'My patience is at an end!'

'The word is "Valhalla"!' she gasped.

With a contented grunt, the big German handed the tongs to Frau Schratt and hobbled to the desk. Dropping into his chair he was in the act of drawing the telephone towards him when, for the first time Dallas spoke.

'Just a minute, *Herr Doktor!*'

He had turned to Patricia. 'It's no good trying to deceive him,' he told her sulkily. 'For my part, I shall have nothing to do with it. Give him the right word! I'm not going through with this torture business again.'

She ran to his side. 'But it *is* the right word!' she cried breathlessly. 'Oh, Robin, don't you know I couldn't sit there and ...'

'Stand away from me!' he barked at her suddenly and called to Grundt: 'She's lying, *Herr Doktor*. I don't know what the word is, but it certainly isn't "Valhalla." because I hear her and her brother arranging it between them — their idea was to give you any word but the right one so as to gain time.'

Grundt, his hand on the telephone, was clearly disconcerted. There was something extraordinarily simian about him, as with a puzzled, suspicious air, his short neck poked out, he rolled his head from side to side.

'Her brother?' he rasped. 'He's out of his mind. I tried to get the code word from him this afternoon, but he didn't seem to know even his own name.'

'That was because you scared him,' Dallas replied glibly. 'He'll talk sense for his sister all right and I tell you again it was he who proposed to her this plan. She asked him what word she should give and he suggested "Valhalla" — I heard them myself. She said, "All right.

Jimmy, I'll do as you say. But what word shall I tell the old devil?" And he ups and says . . .'

Grundt's fist, descending on the table with a crash, cut short this flow of talk. 'Shut up!' he roared. Then, leaning across the desk towards him. 'You're smart,' he snarled, 'but you can't hoodwink me. "Valhalla" is the word, all right. I know when a woman's telling the truth. She was scared out of her life when she gave it to me.' He glared at Patricia. 'Well,' he trumpeted, 'were you lying, or weren't you?' And when she only stared at him in terror, he hammered on the desk and shouted, '*Himmelkreuzsakrament*, will you answer me?'

Dallas laughed quietly. 'You'll get no change out of her, *Herr Doktor*. Ring Hastings in New York, why don't you? and hear what he says. Of course a transatlantic call's an expensive business, and if I'm right you'll have wasted your money for nothing, not to mention the fact that the deal will fall through, because, naturally, once you give him the wrong word, he'll think that you're just a cheap crook, "a chiseller," as they say over there . . .'

'*Ruhe!*' the big man trumpeted, exasperated beyond measure. 'Another word out of you and I'll knock your teeth down your lying throat.'

But Dallas was not to be quelled. 'I'm not lying,' he declared indignantly. 'I wouldn't deceive you, *Herr Doktor*, honestly, I wouldn't. Miss Fane got me into this mess and I don't see that I owe her anything. Her brother knows the word. Why not send for him? If she won't talk, he will. You see!'

There was a moment of tense silence. Then Grundt snorted, 'Get him!' to Keller and pushed the telephone away. Without waiting to see whether his command was obeyed and paying no further attention to Dallas and the girl, he hauled his unwieldy body out of the chair and, leaning on his stick, began to pace restlessly between desk and window.

Then only did Patricia venture to steal a glance at Robin. He was smiling — as their glances met his right eyelid fluttered at her. On that, with a contented air, he closed his eyes and she, groping blindly for a chair, sat down to await her brother's coming.

CHAPTER XXXI

The Last Throw

THAT clandestine wink set her heart beating faster with revived hope. She had disclosed the right word: she now realized that Robin had guessed it was the right one and had struck swiftly to repair the consequences of her moment of weakness. What a fighter he was, always full of resource, never acknowledging defeat! He was still playing for time, yet she wondered what shred of hope could be left to him as, in the silence that followed the doctor's departure, she listened in vain for any sound that should tell of help on the way.

A minute, two minutes, passed, and Keller did not return. It was twilight outside, but the library was almost dark, and Frau Schratt, having switched on the light in the central chandelier, drew the curtains. Grundt seemed to arouse himself from a brown study and, halting, blocked her path as she came away from the window.

'Where's Keller, *zum Teufel?*' he growled. 'Find him, Anna! If the young man's not dressed, let him come down as he is! *Schnell!*'

A prod of his stick and she shuffled out. The heavy boot thumped the parquet as he resumed his pacing. In the distance a door slammed, but still no one came.

'*Herr Gott*, are they all asleep?' the lame man cried at last and stopped by Patricia's chair. 'Out of that!' he ordered. 'You and I will go and find your brother!'

At that moment the door opened quietly. Fane, in his cap and sweater, looked in. He was alone. Closing the door deliberately behind him, he was drifting over to the desk when he caught sight of the trussed-up form in the chair and stopped.

'Hullo, Jimmy!' said Robin.

'Another sound from you and I'll blow your head off!' Grundt roared at Dallas, and they saw that he held a pistol in his hand. 'Keller!' he shouted, then glanced about him. 'Where's Doctor Keller?' he barked at Fane.

The American turned a vacant eye on him — his manner was listless and distrait. 'Doctor Keller?'

'I sent him to fetch you. Where is he?'

Fane did not answer. He only giggled and, pointing at Dallas, said, 'What's he doing, tied up like that?'

Grundt made an irascible movement of the shoulders. 'Can you understand what I say?' he bellowed at Fane.

The young man grinned. 'Sure. You don't have to bawl at me.' He smiled at Patricia who was watching him wide-eyed. 'Hello, there!' he greeted her blithely.

With a visible effort at self-control, Grundt resumed his seat.

'Come here!' he said to Fane. Obediently the American went forward and stopped in front of the desk. 'I wanted to ask you a question,' observed the big man suavely. 'You know Mr. Hastings in New York?'

A vague look. 'Hastings?'

'Your sister's guardian. She cables him sometimes for money.' His tone was studiedly even. 'These cables have a prefix, a code word. Do you remember what it is?'

'A code word?'

'You know about it, don't you?'

'Sure.'

Grundt drew a deep sigh. 'Then what is it?'

'I might remember it, only my head feels so funny.' His tone became suddenly fretful. 'What do you want to point that gun at me for? How can I think when you frighten me? Put it away, damn it, or I shall never remember the word.'

'*Gewiss, gewiss*,' was the honeyed answer. 'Why should

I want to frighten you, *um Gottes Willen?* See, I'll put it down here and we will talk like friends...'

So saying he laid the gun gently on the desk and lifted his face, wreathed in an oily smile, to the American. He found himself looking along the barrel of a Mäuser pistol.

'One move for that gun and I drill you,' Fane commanded sharply, all trace of vagueness gone from voice and manner. 'Now put 'em up and keep 'em up, do you hear me?'

For a fraction of a second the German's glance, stung to instant vigilance, dropped to the desk as though to measure the distance to where he had deposited his weapon.

'You heard what I said,' Fane snapped. 'Up!' Slowly the tremendous arms were lifted. 'Grab his gun, Patricia!' Fane called over his shoulder and, as the girl ran forward, 'There's a pair of scissors on the desk. Cut Dallas loose!'

A quiet voice said behind him, 'Good boy, Jimmy.' Already, with the scissors, Patricia was severing the ropes. The strait-jacket was a tougher problem, but at last she got it unfastened and Robin was free.

'Touch and go,' he said in his quiet way, smiling at her, as he stood up. 'What happened to Keller?' he demanded of Fane.

The American chuckled. 'Who's loony now? I crowned him with a chair, gagged him with a towel and locked him in the bedroom closet. Then the old girl breezed in. I was waiting for her behind the door and threw her with a football tackle. She fought like a cat, but I tied her up the same way and pushed her in with Keller.' He nodded towards Grundt. 'Frisk him, will you? I want that packet.'

Grundt stood like a statue, the rugged face set inflexibly. Only the eyes seemed to live, sparkling with a certain ironical contempt as Robin went forward. Without the flicker of an eyelash he watched the contents of his pockets spilled out upon the writing-table — keys, wallet, a pistol, which Dallas promptly appropriated, some loose change and, buttoned into a flapped pocket contrived in the lining of the waistcoat, a large, blue linen envelope, sealed at the back with three red seals which had been broken.

'Is this what you're looking for?' said Robin. He passed the envelope back to Fane and, raising the pistol to cover Grundt, added, 'All right! I'll take care of him now.'

Fane pounced on the packet. A second envelope, the seals of which had also been broken, was contained in the first. From it the young man drew a set of blueprints on transparent paper. He unfolded one of them and glanced over it eagerly.

'Okay!' he said and, restoring the prints to their envelopes, thrust the packet in his pocket. 'Come on!' he cried. 'Let's get out of here. — Oh!' He broke off. 'What do we do with him?'

Dallas was staring at Grundt. 'Take your sister outside,' he said to Fane over his shoulder.

Patricia stepped forward. 'Robin, what are you going to do?'

Dallas said again, 'Fane, please take your sister outside.'

She spoke tremulously. 'You can't shoot a man in cold blood!'

Grundt confronted them in a stony silence, his arms above his head. He betrayed no emotion save that he moistened his fleshy lips with his tongue from time to time.

Gazing at him steadfastly, Dallas said, 'Four of us had scores to settle with you, Grundt, but it looks as though I

should have to be spokesman for all.' He paused. 'Do you
remember an American secret service man called Ross?'

The cripple nodded indifferently.

'He was sent on a mission to Holland during the war.
They found him hanging in a wood.'

Still Grundt did not flinch, but merely shrugged. 'He
was a spy,' he retorted gruffly. 'He only got what he de-
served.'

'Major Hartigan was his friend,' said Dallas, 'Major
Hartigan, whom you or one of your people shot down at
the door of this house this afternoon. In Hartigan's
absence you'll answer to me for George Ross's life — if
Ned Hartigan is dead, for his life as well. The third of us
is a Frenchman, Captain de Cantigny.'

A shadow seemed to fall across the brutish face.

'You recognize the name, I see,' Dallas proceeded.
'Alain de Cantigny was his brother.'

The dark eyes flashed. 'The Armistice had been signed,
but we were still at war. With the French, at least.
They were trying to disrupt our German Fatherland.
Lieutenant de Cantigny was corrupting our citizens with
French gold.'

'He was no spy, at any rate, but an intelligence
officer operating openly. Yet he was ambushed and
foully murdered by your orders. His brother will hold
you to account. The fourth of our number is a German,
Colonel von König.'

Grundt frowned. 'Colonel von König? I never heard
of him. A German colonel?'

'His rank is Mexican; but thirty years ago Wolf von
König was an officer of the Prussian Footguards. You
cost him his commission' — he made a deliberate pause
— 'as you cost me mine.'

The cripple's expression changed. His manner was
suddenly cringing.

'As for that, *lieber* Herr Dallas, or should I say, Merrall?' he broke in deferentially; 'I was about to say, with regard to that unfortunate experience of yours, that I might be in the position, through certain papers that are in my possession, to help you to regain your...'

'Listen!' said Fane suddenly.

There was no doubt about the sound that penetrated the stillness — it was the racket of an aeroplane engine being warmed up, faint but unmistakable.

'That's my ship!' cried Patricia.

Dallas looked at Grundt and laughed. 'They got the engine started at last,' he remarked dryly. 'Too bad they couldn't wait for you!'

Grundt said nothing, but for the first time he showed signs of uneasiness.

'I asked you about Wolf von König,' Dallas reminded him. 'Do you remember him? Answer me.'

Dourly, the other inclined his head. 'Oh, *ja!*'

'And what have you to say?'

His face was unyielding. 'There was a woman in the case — this young jackanapes of a Guardsman had the presumption to take her away from me. Between them, they laughed at me, taunted me with my infirmity. I broke him, *gewiss*, smashed his career, drove him into exile, as I've done with others, before and since, who flouted me. And why not?' The deep voice swelled exultantly. 'Is not the race to the swift and the power to the strong? They had social rank, riches, good looks, while I, I was of humble birth, miserably paid, a cripple. They thought it a good joke to make a mock of me, never realizing, the fools, that I held them and all their caste in the hollow of my hand, I, the lowly official, whom His Majesty, my august master, had graciously deigned to choose as the secret instrument of his authority, I, Grundt whom they laughed at behind my back as old Clubfoot, for nearly thirty years the power behind one of the greatest thrones on earth!'

An impressive silence followed this harangue. The distant drone of the plane had ceased.

Inexorably, Dallas returned to the charge. 'Then you admit that you destroyed this man's career out of spite,' he observed coldly. 'If my good friend Wolf were here to answer you ...'

A voice behind him said, 'Wolf is dead!'

From the doorway the major regarded the scene. Patricia screamed, 'Major Ned!' and sped to him. With an abstracted air, he brushed her aside and came in. His face was set and white, his eyes merciless as, ranging past Dallas and Fane, standing with pistols levelled, they rested on the burly form erect behind the desk with arms uplifted.

Robin said tensely, 'So it was Wolf and not you?'

Hartigan nodded, his gaze rivetted on Grundt. 'He thought I was hit and came out to rescue me. I stayed with him until he died — he's still there in the wood.'

The blue eyes clouded. 'And Cant?'

'He took the car back to the Goldene Rose. He came back just now with Maier, men, ladders. We climbed the wall near the landing-ground. Three men ran away as we appeared — Cant and the others went to investigate; I came on ahead.' He paused, while his eye bleakly contemplated Grundt. 'We shall have to do without old Wolf, but Cant will be along in a minute. You haven't forgotten our oath, Robin?'

Impassively, Dallas shook his head.

Patricia laid her hand on the major's sleeve. 'Major Ned ...' she began pleadingly.

'Your car's outside,' he told her briskly. 'You run along.'

She stood her ground. 'I've told Robin — you can't kill a man in cold blood.'

The major flushed angrily. 'And what about those two poor things yesterday? And George Ross, and Cant's brother, and now Wolf? Let him have a gun and defend himself, if you like, but, by the living God, one of us is going to die!'

She said quietly: 'You don't understand. You've got to spare his life and I'll tell you why. He can clear Robin and help him to get his commission back.'

An odd sound broke the tension. Grundt was softly chuckling.

'Spoken like a practical *Amerikanerin*, Fräulein!' he purred.

She turned to him. 'You said you had papers?'

'*Jawohl*. The whole dossier is in my safe.'

She glanced round the room. 'There's no safe here?'

He laughed. 'No?'

'Where is it?'

He eyed her cunningly. 'We'll go into that when I know that your proposal has been accepted.'

She appealed to the major. 'It's for Robin's sake,' she said.

Ned shrugged. 'If he can really clear him...'

'I don't give a damn one way or the other,' Dallas declared. 'But Patricia's right, Ned. We can't do it.'

'We can spare his life,' said Ned. 'But we're not responsible for what Maier and his friends will do with him.'

Patricia looked at Grundt. 'You hear what they say. Are you content?'

He smiled at her engagingly. 'I fancy it is the best I can hope for. Am I permitted to take down my hands?'

'Stay as you are!' the major barked. 'You tell us where the safe is — we'll find it.'

The German shrugged his shoulders. 'The bookshelf behind me — the third book from the right of the second row is a dummy. Pull it out and you'll see a knob which you must press...'

Ned went behind the desk and a moment later, as though a hidden spring had been released, a whole section of the bookshelf swung outward, revealing an iron door. The major rattled it.

'It's locked. You have the key?'

'The flat bronze key on the bunch,' said Grundt, nodding in the direction of the blotter.

Patricia brought the bunch and Ned opened the door. A small strong-room was disclosed, a safe built into one of the side walls.

Grundt craned his head round. 'You'll have to let me work the combination,' he remarked, turning back to Robin.

'Go ahead,' said the latter. 'But no tricks! I'm behind you with a gun, remember!'

With a grunt of relief the big German dropped his arms and, retrieving his stick, which had fallen on the floor, hobbled into the strong-room. He bent over the safe and in a moment had it open. For an instant, he burrowed within, then brought out a file of papers which he flung on the desk.

'There you are,' he remarked with his most roguish air, 'and if the documents you find there don't get you reinstated, then come back to me and I'll give you a job myself.' He laughed his rumbling laugh as he stood in the doorway of the strong-room, his huge bulk almost completely filling the entrance, leaning on his stick.

The major pounced on the file, turning over its dusty pages.

'Gosh, Robin,' he exclaimed presently, 'he's right. Look at these letters and wires from Liselotte...'

Patricia and her brother had joined the major at the desk and were leaning over him as he examined the file.

On Ned's eager cry Robin glanced towards the group. For an instant he took his eye off the massive figure towering in the entrance of the vault and in that instant it happened. Without warning the light went out and the library, the windows screened by heavy curtains, was plunged in darkness. They heard the clang of iron.

'Head him off!' the major shouted, and tore the curtains of the nearest window aside. In the dimness they saw that Fane was already guarding the library door. Now he fingered the switch beside it.

The light came on again. Grundt had vanished. The bookcase still gaped, but the strong-room door was shut and the key gone. Frantically the major tore at the door, but it was fast.

'After him!' he stormed. 'We'll catch him in the grounds if we're quick.' With Fane at his heels, he dashed out.

Robin would have followed him, but he found the girl in his path. She did not speak, but her eyes said, 'Let him go!'

Robin was frowning. 'I might have known it,' he muttered. 'Clubfoot would always have a line of retreat. A second light switch, a secret exit to a waiting car — once he could get to that strong-room, he knew he was safe. He had it all planned.'

'At least, he kept his part of the bargain,' said Patricia and showed the file in her hand.

Without speaking, he took it from her and sat down in Grundt's chair at the desk. For a moment his fingers idly turned the pages, then suddenly he began to laugh and went on laughing.

She ran to him and, putting her arms about him, held him close. 'Don't, Robin,' she murmured, 'don't, my dear!'

His laughter died and, putting up his hand blindly, he

drew her head towards him until her face lay against his unshaven, grimy cheek.

'You're so understanding,' he murmured, 'so lovely and so understanding. I never dreamed the world could still hold anyone quite like you. Oh, my dear, my dear' — and his arms clasped her more tightly — 'I've been frantic with anxiety about you.'

'And I about you,' she returned. 'When that horrible old woman came forward with the tongs ... You know. It was the real word I gave.'

He laughed. 'You bet. That was why I had to do something about it.' He sighed. 'Lord, how tired I am!'

Caressingly she passed her hand over his crisp hair. 'You drive yourself to a standstill,' she said reproachfully. 'I had a most terrible shock when you walked in on us upstairs. You can't have slept for days.'

'Or even washed,' he observed ruefully. 'I'm not fit to be touched.'

He would have drawn away, but she hugged him closer. 'You look like a tramp,' she declared gaily. 'Such a dear, dear tramp, though!'

'It's strange,' he told her musingly. 'All these years, in prison and after, during that ghastly time I was in Canada, I looked forward to the day when I should meet this man face to face. Yet a moment ago, when I had him at my mercy and you spoke up to save him, I suddenly realized that, in spite of this atrocious business with poor Liselotte and even though it was almost certainly he who'd shot dear old Wolf, I didn't care a damn whether he lived or died. It was the sound of your voice, I think, but I knew then that the only thing that mattered was you.'

She gave him a wistful smile. 'Your future was more important. You brushed his offer aside, but I saw what he was leading up to. He's nobody's fool, your Doctor

Grundt, let me tell you. He held the trump card — and
he knew it.'

He touched the dusty file. 'You've given me back my
life, Patricia. The trouble is,' he added with a sigh, 'that
I don't know what to do with it — without you.'

She echoed his sigh, her arms about him. 'That's my
trouble, too. But it gives me an idea, Robin.'

He flushed. 'Forget it!' he told her.

She sat up abruptly. 'You're not going to be stupid, I
hope — about my having the money, I mean?'

Despondently he shook his head. 'Much too much
money, my dear.'

'Nonsense,' she said with spirit. 'We're partners already in a manner of speaking. The firm owes you what?
— a third, it would be now, of a hundred thousand
dollars, the fee which you and the others were to receive
for finding Jimmy. Well, you needn't draw your share
out — you can leave it in the firm so that I shall still be
in your debt. How's that?'

'Sweet and kind like everything you've said to me.
But, honey, it won't do ...'

She jumped to her feet. 'Do you realize I'm asking
you to marry me?'

'Only too well,' he answered miserably.

'You can't have your own way in everything,' she declared. 'I've got to be humoured sometimes. Aren't you
going to kiss me — Captain Merrall?'

It was an iron curtain shutting down on his tragic past,
the way she spoke his old name and title, significantly,
her eyes shining, her face lifted expectantly towards him.
He caught her in his arms, stooped to her lips ...

A hurried step in the hall drove them apart. Fane
came in quickly.

'Vanished into thin air,' he announced. 'It's sheer
waste of time to look for him, and so I told the major —

for all we know that bolt-hole of his comes out on the far side of the Schloss wall. He didn't reach the plane, at any rate — it's still out there on the apron. There's room for us all in it — it's a six-seater, isn't it, Patricia? It'll be dark in half an hour. Come on, you two, let's collect the others and scram!'

The major now appeared, hot and disgruntled. 'Well, he's away!' he grumbled. 'I'm glad you got those papers out of him, Robin, old man, but I hate to think of that limping ruffian cocking a nose at us that way.'

'Major Ned,' said Patricia demurely, 'I'm trying to persuade Robin to marry me. But he doesn't seem keen about it. Will you have a word with him?'

The major gasped. 'Well, I'll be hornswoggled!' He grinned. 'But I warned him. On the boat coming over — do you remember, Robin?'

Before Dallas could answer, Cant, grim and breathless, thrust his face in at the door.

'The Feds!' he gasped.

CHAPTER XXXII

Sometimes Jupiter Nods

THE Frenchman was almost inarticulate with excitement. 'I see them from the turret window — Wilson, the friend of Brewer, and two others, who arrive in an auto. They got out at the foot of the avenue — they wait.'

The silence of panic had fallen on the quiet room.

'Ouch!' said Robin with a grimace, his eye on Fane. 'Any sign of Brewer?' he questioned.

'Not yet. But my opinion is, they wait for him.'

Ned laughed wryly. 'I must say I take off my hat to those babies. They certainly know how to stick along. They said they'd get him and no sooner is he in our hands than here they are, right on the dot to collect, like the rent-man.' He cocked his head at Fane. 'I guess the jig's up, Jimmy boy, unless you and your charming sister can persuade these bozos to listen to reason.'

'Like my foot it's up!' Robin declared wrathfully. 'And they won't listen to reason, either, because they have their orders and their orders are to pick you up, Jimmy, and dump you down, dead or alive, in Washington, D.C.'

'Gosh!' ejaculated the boy blankly.

'Don't let it worry you,' Dallas reassured him. 'I promised your sister I'd deliver you and that packet of yours to your Chief in London and, by the Lord Harry, I'll do it.' He swung to Cant. 'The plane's still there, is it?'

'Sure,' was the reply. 'But Maier and his boys aren't. I left them guarding it, but they're away. They don't want any trouble with the law, I guess.'

'Is the main gate locked?'

'Barred and bolted.'

'That should hold 'em for a bit,' Robin commented, his eyes on Patricia. 'If it don't, well, there are three of us here, all armed — we ought to be able to put up some sort of a scrap and let Miss Fane and her brother get clear in the plane.'

The major spoke up promptly. 'You can't start anything like that, old son — not as far as I'm concerned, anyway. I mayn't be so hot as a citizen, but I'm an American and these guys are on Uncle Sam's payroll — you can't expect me to shoot it out with them, like I was a gangster or something. And, believe me, if one of them gets knocked off, it won't do Jimmy any good, you must see that! On the other hand, I don't believe that Miss Patricia has a chance in a million of getting that plane off the ground in time, for they'll be here any minute now. And if she does, it'll be a darn close call. What if they start shooting and she crashes? Have you thought of that?' He shrugged despondently. 'I'm as sick about it as you are; but I guess young Jimmy has to take his medicine and like it.'

Robin was about to reply, but Patricia forestalled him. 'Ned's right, Robin,' she struck in crisply. 'We can't fight the Government. It's unthinkable!'

Dallas flushed. 'All the same, I'll see Brewer in hell before I hand Jimmy over!'

'And who said we're going to hand him over?' was the demure reply. She turned to Ned. 'You and Captain Cant run along and see what they're up to,' she told him. 'Let me know as soon as they reach the front door.'

Cant led the way to the turret window beside the gate. The last vestiges of the sunset glowed in the west — it was still light enough to see. A second car had joined the first at the end of the avenue and a figure, rather paunchy in light gray, was sedately descending from it.

The major groaned. 'Brewer, damn it!' he remarked bitterly. 'And that dead pan behind him with the brolly is Preuss, the dick who trailed Robin and me at Baden-Baden.'

The whole party proceeded to climb the gate.

'I think they find Wolf,' Cant whispered suddenly. A plain-clothes man had appeared on the drive, pointing behind him and gesticulating. The cluster of figures halted, bunched, then spread out and banished under the trees.

Ned sighed. 'It's the showdown, old hoss,' he confided mournfully to his companion. 'They'll pinch the kid and there's our hundred grand gone blooey, for, whatever story he puts up, his arrest is bound to make the dickens of a stink. We undertook to find him and stop a scandal, and we've failed. We're licked — it's a case of no tickee, no washee, I guess. Though, mind you,' he added sorrowfully, 'I'd gladly have passed up my share of the loot to bring old Wolf back to life.'

'So would we all,' said Cant, then touched the other's arm. 'See, they come back.'

The two Federal agents and the three detectives had emerged from the wood and were marching up the avenue, Brewer at the head. Ponderously the five pairs of feet crunched the gravel in unison.

'*Eh, bien, quoi?*' Cant demanded under his breath. He was trembling with excitement.

'Stay there, but don't let them see you,' Ned replied in the same tone. 'I'm going back for orders.'

That tramp of heavy boots, inexorable as the leaden feet of destiny, rang in his ears as he scurried back to the library. Only too well he knew what the orders would be — surrender. So this was the end of the chase! Over its many vicissitudes his mind went back in a wide arc, snatching at memories that crowded in at random upon him — Wolf, with his taxi-driver's cap cocked over one ear, drinking his beer at Schulte's, dinner with Patricia in the Bois, their flight together to Baden-Baden, Jimmy and Liselotte locked in one another's arms at the pension, the horror of the châlet at Wildsee. Robin was cleared, at any rate, and now, God bless us, Patricia spoke of marrying him. What a kick old Wolf would have got out of that! Wolf had been so fond of Robin — a born soldier, who had seen his own career cut short, he had grieved over Robin's misfortune as if it had been his own.

The pillared vestibule was empty. The great doors with their huge lock, tremendous bolts and chains, looked impregnably solid. Through the windows of the sun-porch in rear of the hall he had a glimpse of the park, isolated behind its lofty wall, tall trees massed blackly against a copper sky. He ran to the library, but got no farther than the threshold. The room was deserted.

He started violently as in the hall behind him, with groaning of wires, a bell jangled loudly.

At the same instant Cant came flying. 'They're at the door!' he cried. 'Where's Robin? What are we going to do?' The bell pealed again.

A voice above them said, 'Open the door!'

The major looked up. The great brass lantern which hung by a chain from the lobby ceiling had been switched on, and in its feeble rays he beheld young Fane. In his gray cap and sweater, a camel's-hair overcoat slung from his shoulders, the boy gazed down at them from the gilt railing that enclosed the first landing.

'Where's Robin? Where's your sister?' the major snapped.

The front door was now loudly hammered while the bell continued to send forth its clamour at intervals.

•

'Don't waste time!' said Fane, and came quickly down. 'If they ask for me, I'm in here.' He disappeared into the library.

The two friends exchanged a glance. No word was said, but by eyebrows, shoulders, hands the Frenchman disassociated himself from the consequences. Then Ned turned the key in the massive lock, while Cant stooped to the bolts.

The door swung wide. Brewer, plump, unruffled, stepped out from the group assembled there. He was quick to recognize the figure who, under the archway, stolidly awaited his approach.

'Well, Major,' he greeted Ned, 'I told you we'd be along. I guess you know what it's about. Do we have to rip the place up, or do you hand him over?' His eye ferreted shrewdly in the other's sullen countenance. 'It'll probably save trouble if I tell you we know he's here.'

'You win,' was the terse rejoinder. 'Come in!'

Brewer entered the dim hall, gazing with interest about him, the rest of the party following.

'That's one of your people back in the wood, isn't it?' he said, regarding Ned over the top of his glasses. 'Who laid him out?'

'Grundt — if you know who that is,' the major retorted bluntly. 'And by the way, you didn't run across him outside, by any chance — a clubfooted gentleman?'

The Federal agent shook his head. 'So he skipped, did he? The gendarmerie are after him — that business at Wildsee! They should have been here before us, only I guess our cars made better time. Where's Fane?'

'Listen, old man,' said Ned, 'you ought to give the kid a break. He'll tell you the story himself. He didn't sell those plans — they slugged him and grabbed them. He'd have reported himself weeks ago, but he lost his memory, see? He's wearing a bandage yet.'

'Tough luck,' was the impassive answer. 'But I've got to take him along. Where is he, old-timer?'

Fane stood at the desk in the library, rather pallid in the indifferent light. Brewer halted on the threshold of the room and beckoned Wilson forward.

'My colleague met him in London,' he explained, *sotto voce*, to Ned.

Burly and self-possessed, Wilson walked up to the desk. 'Department of Justice, Mr. Fane,' he introduced himself briskly. 'My name's Clarence Wilson. I called on you once in London — the Ambassador turned me over to you in connection with that counterfeit job I was working on. Remember me?'

'Sure,' was the rather nervous reply.

Brewer stepped to the front. 'The State Department has been looking for you, Mr. Fane. My instructions are...'

A sudden noise, a dull, droning sound that rapidly swelled to a roar, drowned his voice — an aeroplane was in the air somewhere close at hand. The roar seemed to swoop down on them as the plane swept over the house. Cant rushed out into the hall, the whole party at his heels. Except Brewer.

At the sound of the plane the figure at the desk had recoiled. Something fell with a tinkle into a brass ash-tray beside the blotter. Brewer reached for it, held it in the light. The major saw it in his hand — a bronze hairpin. Then the secret service man leaned forward and with a brusque movement pulled the woollen cap away. A mop of reddish-gold hair was released.

For a long moment Brewer did not speak. He looked at Ned and then at the girl.

'His sister, is it?' he said sharply.

Patricia laughed nervously. 'If that darned hairpin hadn't given me away...'

The secret service man fingered a long upper lip: his air was unchangeably calm.

'Twins, aren't you?' he remarked stolidly. 'I knew it, and yet I forgot it. But then, of course, I didn't expect to find you here.' He jerked his head in the general direction of the sky. 'That was the brother, eh?'

She nodded, her eyes dancing.

'Whose plane?'

'Mine.'

Brewer scratched his chin. 'And I know who was at the controls,' he remarked. 'Well,' he went on to Ned, 'even the old gent with the whiskers is caught napping sometimes.'

The other grinned. 'Boy, you're telling me?'

Impassive to the end, the secret service man lifted his hat gravely and went quickly out.

The major threw his arms about Patricia.

'Honey,' he cried ecstatically, 'that was the swellest trick I ever saw.'

'I knew I wouldn't get away with it altogether,' she said, 'but Jimmy and I are really alike and in this rotten light —— I only wanted to give Robin time to get clear. If you knew the fuss he made about leaving me behind!' She sighed. 'Major Ned, darling, I'm so worried about him. Robin's flown a Lockheed in Canada and he swears he used to know every inch of the air route between Vienna and London. All the same . . .'

She broke off, gazing tearfully at the nubbly face. 'I care for him so terribly, Ned. He's a stubborn devil and it'll mean a fearful battle, but I'm going to marry him. Will you help me?'

'Sure — if I have to take him to the altar at the point of a gun!'

Her face lit up and she clasped her hands together 'Oh, Ned, what a good idea! A shotgun wedding!'

He laughed uproariously. 'Okay, honey! But the preliminaries are up to you.'

She nodded gaily, the light of battle in her eyes.

'Find my car while I'm changing out of these things,' she told him. 'We're leaving for London right away!'

THE END